tHE HOLLOW HEARt

THE HOLLOW HEART

MARIE RUTKOSKI

FARRAR STRAUS GIROUX
New York

Farrar Straus Giroux Books for Young Readers
An imprint of Macmillan Publishing Group, LLC
120 Broadway, New York, NY 10271

fiercereads.com

Our books may be purchased in bulk for promotional, educational, or business use.
Please contact your local bookseller or the Macmillan Corporate and Premium Sales
Department at (800) 221-7945 ext. 5442 or by email at
MacmillanSpecialMarkets@macmillan.com.

Library of Congress Cataloging-in-Publication Data is available.
ISBN 978-0-374-31384-5 (hardcover)

10 9 8 7 6 5 4 3 2 1

Printed in the United States of America
First edition, 2021
Book design by Elizabeth Clark

for Trisha de Guzman and Joy Peskin

tHE HOLLOW HEARt

THE GOD

YOU HAVE MY HEART. *You know you do.*

I have heard this said, from one of you to another. Mortals say it as though they can feel the hand of the beloved inside their ribs, palm supporting the heart, fingers curled lightly around the trembling muscle. Pain could come so easily. All it would take is a good, hard squeeze.

Once there was a girl who traded her heart to a god for knowledge. It seemed, at the time, a fair bargain. One should never bargain with a god, let alone this god, yet Nirrim had been raised to think more of others than of herself, and as such people often do—the orphans, the underlings, the lesser-thans—she soon tired of being trod upon. She sought power. Eventually, she would seize it with a vengeance. A heart seemed a small price to pay. Anyway, it was broken.

Yet she hesitated. I can't live without a heart, she told the god, who said, Not that lump of muscle beating in your chest. I mean what makes you *you*.

If you take my heart, what will I become?

Who can say? said the god.

Nirrim made her bargain. She plotted to make a palace fit for the new person she was, and looked out at the sea, which glinted like beaten tin. She placed a palm against her breast, and her heart knocked back. I am here, it said. But was it truly? *Something* was gone. Nirrim, self-crowned ruler of Ethin, our lost city, Queen of the Hollow Heart, discovered that her bargain had not taken away her longing as she had hoped. No, she was not done with wanting. Now she wanted all the world.

And me?

I warn you now: do not think well of me. I have murdered your kind before. Nirrim's black-eyed lover, Sid of the Herrani, will know this when she meets my gaze. Fear will shiver through her.

How does a story end? For you mortals, it always ends with your life.

NIRRIM

$\diamond$

MY PEOPLE COME TO SEE me in my triumph. The words I have just spoken ring in my mind: I am a god, and I am your queen. Half Kith fill the agora, curious, their souls surely sweetened with the knowledge that I have given them: that they, who for generations were scorned by the rest of Ethin, are the children of gods.

At least, some of them are.

"Bring all the Half Kith to me." I pitch my voice so that it rings against the white walls of the agora. "Even the smallest child."

"Why? What will you do, Nirrim?"

I can't see who calls, but I would know that voice anywhere: Annin, whom I once considered my little sister, despite any lack of blood between us. A new tone of suspicion infects her voice.

I lift a hand to my shoulder for the Elysium bird, as soft and red as a rose, to shift its perch onto my fist. It obeys, trilling, and rubs its head against my cheek. It loves me, just as I deserve. I remember feeling grateful, like a beggar, for any scrap of love tossed my way. I yearned so badly for a mother that when Raven, the woman who took me in, hurt me I invented reasons to explain her behavior. My only other choice was to face the truth that she cared nothing for me. I was weak. Desperate. Never again. I look into the crowd of Half Kith. They will love me, too, just like my bird, and I will reward them by returning to us the power that was stolen long ago. I will raise the Half Kith on high. We have been ignored for too long. Treated cruelly. My people surely believe this as I do.

If they don't, they must be *made* to believe it, for their own good. I will need their loyalty, and for that I need their trust. "I am here to protect you," I say gently. "This is the gods' bird, whose ancestor, hundreds of years ago, drank the blood of the god of discovery. My Elysium will know which of you has magic running in your veins. Don't you wonder what you could do?" I smile at the crowd. For the first time in my life, I am aware of my beauty and relish it. The crowd's mesmerized faces relax as they regard me. My black hair must be wild, windtorn: a dark crown. My eyes: green as jade. Skin pure, sun-warmed. A sweet, quiet face. For now, let them think I am as sweet as I look. "The bird is harmless. All it will do is sing—if, that is, you are gifted. Aden, step forward. Show them."

Aden knows full well that he is god-touched. He glows. A golden smirk curls his lips. He looks as though he has lifted the goblet of the sky to his mouth and swallowed the sun. Once he was my lover, and believes he knows me well, yet when our eyes meet he hesitates, appraising me. He must wonder who I am now, and can't help but see how I have changed. I am no longer the shy, easily controlled girl he knew. "Aden, surely you are not afraid. It is but a bird."

With a squint to his eyes that says he thinks my challenge to his courage is a cheap trick, yet that he will indulge me for his own reasons,

Aden steps close. His light runs over my skin. It feels nice enough. I remember how he was with me when all the Ward knew I was his sweetheart, how his love, like this honeyed light, felt like a too-warm blanket, like something that wouldn't let me breathe and made me long for cool water.

For a moment, I remember Sid's skin on mine. Her weight. Need pours into my belly, dizzying me, dazzling my flesh. A sharp breath escapes my lips. I thought I was past this desire, that whatever I gave to the god when he demanded my heart would make it impossible for me to feel anything for Sid. What *did* he take, exactly, from me?

There is no time to wonder. Sid is gone. She will never return. I am here, and nowhere else. This is my city. My moment.

Mine, the bird sings, staring into Aden's face, stirring its crimson-and-pink wings.

"Why don't you show them," I whisper to Aden, "what you can do?"

"I am not your toy."

"No." My voice is still low enough for this to be a conversation only between us. "You are a child of the gods, yet your entire life you have been trapped within this Ward, walled off from the rest of the world, told by the Council that you were not worthy. You didn't even know what power you had until I returned the memory of Ethin's past to everyone in this city. Don't you want everyone to recognize your skill, your strength? Won't that feel good?"

His eyes still narrowed, he lifts one hand for the crowd to see. Flame erupts from his palm, and an excited murmur rises like the sound of cicadas. Surprise at what he has done leaps across Aden's face, but he hides it quickly. I imagine that before today, he had probably noticed that he could see into the twilight a little longer than other people after the sunset, or that he stayed warmer than everyone else during the chilling spell of an ice wind. But he would not have thought this was anything different than being taller than most people, or having keener eyesight. And now, to create flame? How incredible that such a change could come simply from knowledge, from knowing something today that he did not know yesterday. Yet is that so strange? Once I saw, in the center of a High-Kith agora, an acrobat flip and spin her body as though it were a toy. I could not conceive of even trying to do what she did. Yet how it would be if I were filled with the knowledge that I *could* tumble through space, that the gods were my ancestors, that the skill lurked in my limbs? If I knew this truth, knew it in my bones, how could I not try? How could I not succeed? When I think about all that the High Kith took from us, what angers me most is that they tricked us into not seeing our own skills. They dulled us. They stole our knowledge of our own selves. This, I will never forgive.

My people push their way toward me. But others, like Annin and our friend Morah, slip away. Sirah, an old woman I once cared for, though it is now hard to conceive why, disappears into an alleyway. A few people trickle away from the crowd and vanish. Let them. I do not need these weaklings.

"May I try?" It is a little boy of perhaps eight years, lifted by his father above the crowd. I invite the brave boy forward. I try to look benevolent, my lovely face as calm and gentle as a statue's, because the crowd will appreciate that. I touch his cheek. The bird sings again.

It sings for another Half Kith. And another, and another, its call jangling in the agora as the sky darkens.

Later, when the sun fades and the crowd has divided into the disappointed and the lucky, Aden turns to me. "What game are you playing?" he murmurs. "What do you want?" I look straight into his blue eyes and then over his shoulder, letting my gaze trail to the wall that for centuries imprisoned our people. He knows, as I know, how we once feared being tithed for committing small sins. We were made to give our blood to the High Kith. Our hair, our limbs. Our hopes. Even children were taken. We will not return to who we were: cowardly, pathetic animals penned in a cage. We will never be the same, any more than I will return to the person I once was—kind, considerate Nirrim, so ready to put others' needs before her own. That girl is gone.

What do I want?

Revenge.

SID

USUALLY, I LOVE THE SEA.

Yes, even during a storm, Nirrim would add, teasing yet serious, too. *Especially* during a storm.

But that's not true. Storms can kill. They grind ships against unseen rocks, shred sails, tip the world upside down, wash sailors overboard. Frustration fills me, as if Nirrim has actually said this to me, and I must defend myself, to say I am no fool, that I don't seek danger (not *always*). So I am good on the water. Is it wrong to take pleasure in my skills? I have but three. And this skill is one any true-born Herrani should have. The sea is in my blood, and if I like the roll of a ship's deck beneath my feet and can taste a storm in the air long before it arrives, well, that is my birthright.

Nirrim, you say I love a storm only because you have never set foot on a ship. You have never seen the sea as more than a twinkling blue expanse meeting the horizon. You think me braver than I am.

A gull tilts low over the too-still water. I push the imagined conversation from my mind. Nirrim refused me. I gave her my heart and she gave it right back. There is no conversation one can have after that. Why am I imagining she thinks me brave? Why do this to myself? I don't know what she thinks. I know only that she decided I was not enough.

"Itching for a storm, are you?" says a smooth voice over my shoulder.

"Oh, shut up, Roshar."

He leans against the taffrail and gazes at the becalmed water. His mutilations are stark in the sunlight: the missing nose, the wrinkles of flesh where his ears once were. People flinch when they first meet him. I can't see him as anything but familiar. He held me when I was a baby. He taught me how to stroke his tiger's broad head so that it would not bite. He has a warrior's body, not broad like my father's, but lean like mine, his gestures firm yet with a lazy kind of elegance my father has said, amusedly, that I imitated for years until Roshar's sly way of speaking and moving had become my own. Roshar's black eyes, narrowed against the sun, are rimmed with the green paint that marks his royal status, a color echoed in the flag of his ship, a narrow Dacran sloop, which lies not far off from this one, barely dipping in the too-peaceful water. He insisted on staying aboard my ship. "Little runaway princess," he said, smirking when he saw how much I resented that last word, "do you think I will let you out of my sight?" Then he ousted me from my captain's quarters. "I outrank you," he said, and when I spluttered, he added, "There was a beauty contest. The crew said I won."

I keep my gaze on his sloop, which I have seen cut through choppy water like a blade. It is narrowly designed and beautifully made, the captain's quarters a jewel box of tiny windowpanes.

"I don't like the look in your eyes." He stuffs tobacco into his pipe and lights it easily, not even having to shield the bowl from the wind, which is nonexistent. "That is *my* ship. Don't look at it like she's some girl you want to bed."

"If you were a good godfather, you would give her to me."

"Ha!"

"I stole my father's ship. Who is to say yours isn't next on my list?"

He smiles. "I, too, like to threaten people when I'm worried." He smokes, a cloud curling around him. "A stiff wind would be nice, if it doesn't blow us off course."

Fine, maybe I do like a storm every now and then. Roshar knows me all too well. Nirrim doesn't, not quite, but she *saw* me well. She understood me, which apparently was enough to make her stay behind in a city that treated her terribly, even when I offered her my heart and my home.

Tiny, scalloped waves lap the side of Roshar's sloop. My hands feel heavy, although they are empty. They hold a memory. I do not have Nirrim's preternatural gift for memory, her ability to see every moment in her past as clearly as though it were the present. What I have instead is a memory of a memory, the moment so old that what I remember is my frequent return to it. It haunts me.

My mother placed an apple in one hand and a small stone in the other. We stood on the royal pier, hoping to glimpse the ship of my father, who was due to return from a visit to Dacra, our eastern ally. Which object is heaviest? she asked.

They weigh the same, I said.

Drop them, she said. The water gulped down the stone. The apple bobbed, a friendly red and yellow.

If they weigh the same, my mother said, why does the apple float?

"What I wonder," Roshar says, interrupting the memory, "is what you want more: for a wind to push us to Herran so that you may see your mother, or for it to carry us away as swiftly as possible from Herrath and that forlorn girl of yours."

Despite myself, I cast a glance southwest toward Herrath, to where it lies hidden beyond the Empty Islands. Herrath can't be seen, of course. We left its shores several days ago. I practically begged for Nirrim to come with me.

Roshar grins, which makes him look like the sign of my father's god. A skull for King Arin, touched by the god of death. Since it is my father's sign, it has become my family's, too. Death loves you, people say. When, impatient, I have demanded what exactly that means, they say, Death grants you mercy.

But sometimes people mutter, Death follows at your parents' heels.

There it is again, my old annoyance. My father's god is not *my* god. I was born in the year of the god of games, and although I have my religious doubts and light a candle in the temple mostly to please my faithful father, I take comfort that my patron god is no serious member of the pantheon. She is a rascal. Of the three skills I possess, winning a gamble is one.

It is my mother's, too.

"You're lying," I tell Roshar. "My mother is not sick. This is a trick to make me come home. Some game of hers."

The humor leaves Roshar.

"She probably put you up to it," I accuse him.

"No."

"It would be just like her." A lump of worry and anger hurts my throat. I, too, don't know why I most want the wind: to carry me away from Nirrim, or to bring me to my mother. Part of me dreads a swift voyage. I am afraid that as soon as I reach Herran I won't be able to pretend anymore that my mother is all right, that the news of her illness is a hoax to call me back as if *I* were the kestrel, wheeling toward the bait in her uplifted fist.

"Little godchild," Roshar says, "I have never lied to you." He rests a hand on mine where it grips the taffrail, his dark brown skin covering my pale fingers. All gold, Herrani say when they see me. They don't say it nicely. I look very Valorian. I look like the people who conquered my country thirty-some years ago. Like my mother. I slip my hand out from beneath Roshar's and the weight of his heavy ring, set with a dull black stone. He says, "I wish I didn't worry that Kestrel might die, but I do."

Think, tadpole, my mother said as I stared at the floating apple.

Because the apple is bigger? I said. Like a boat?

She smiled in encouragement—which is against her rules. She disdains giving hints, and if you go up against her you can be sure that nothing in her expression or gesture will reveal what she does not wish to show. But I was small, and she *did* want me to see a truth: her love. She gently tugged one of my braids. My hair was long then. When I cut it a few years ago, on my fifteenth nameday, her expression radiated hurt, because she believed I had done it so that I would look less like her.

She was right. She always is.

But the apple and the stone weighed the same, she said. You felt that when you held them. Why would one sink and the other float? Why would the apple's bigness make it buoyant?

I had no answer. I studied apples and stones for days. I dropped pebbles into the atrium's fountain. I cut open apples. I pried out seeds— brown teardrops, as though each apple, cheerful on the outside, wept at its core, or had several tiny, hard, bitter hearts.

Tell her, my father said to my mother.

No, she answered.

Finally, I announced, It is because an apple is filled with air. It doesn't look that way, but it is. The air makes an apple go crunch between your teeth.

She looked so proud. I felt proud, for making her proud. My darling, I knew you could do it.

She promised a ride on her stallion as a reward. Javelin was strong, enormous. He was in his prime then. I always begged to ride him. She would say no, not because she worried that he'd throw me, but that I'd lose my seat and fall.

This time, I didn't even have to ask. Javelin was a gift freely given. Up you go. She boosted me into his saddle. I was a sudden giant. I looked down at the crown of her head, her braided hair the color of lamplight. She fussed with a stirrup. She was going to walk beside me, I could tell, and I became instantly frustrated. I had done what she had asked. I had worked hard for my answer to her question. And now, to be babied? Rebellion lit my blood. My heels kicked into Javelin's sides. We flew. I did not fall.

I think I was five years old.

Many years later, when I yelled at her, when I said I would never do what she wanted, that she could go to hell, when I shouted with all the fury she might have shown me that time I took off recklessly on her horse, she said, You are an apple, Sidarine.

What? I wanted to tear my hair out. I had no idea what she was talking about. I didn't, then, remember that day by the pier, her test. I said, For once, say what you mean! I am sick of your riddles. I am sick of you. How dare you expect me to marry I do not want him, I do not want any man. Do you hear me? I never will.

I think, she said coldly, you know exactly what I mean.

I remembered, then, the apple and the stone, and saw instantly her insult. This was how she saw me: filled with sweet air. I had given myself over to pleasure. All the girls I had taken to bed. She knew about them. Of course she did. She was the queen of spies. Clearly, she thought I liked a fresh dessert so much that I had become one. What did I know, her expression said, of duty?

Well, she was right. I knew nothing of duty. I refused to know it. I slammed the door to her suite behind me. I gathered my things and stole a few others. I cast off from the city that very night.

Roshar has left me alone at the ship's rail. I wipe my wet face. My old hurt pushes against my new one. Was this why Nirrim said no? I love you, I said, but she didn't feel the same way. Maybe she saw in me what my mother saw: someone unworthy.

My mother might die.

I say this to myself, over and over. Though I only half believe in gods, I pray for wind.

She cannot die. Impossible. She is strong. Hard. A weapon if need be. You'd have to break her open to see what's inside. My mother: dropped down deep, secret and invisible below the waves.

My mother is stone.

NIRRIM

⬥

THE TAVERN IS DARK AND cool when I open the door, the iron handle hot from the lowering sun. I have no time for this. No time to see, with new eyes, the place I used to call home. No time to hunt my victim. A war is brewing, one of my own making, and my enemies will know the cost of what they did to me and every one of my kind. But one enemy must come first. My blood demands it.

I was so innocent, so easily ruled.

Where is she?

Slipping into the tavern's interior is like sliding into a fresh pool. I close the door against the dusty heat of the street.

"Raven," I call, making my voice sweet, timid. The name echoes over the empty tables. It sits in empty chairs. "Ama," I try again, using the word small children call their mothers, "are you here? I am sorry we argued. I am here to make things right."

I lift the Elysium bird from my shoulder and set it on a rough-hewn table. The bird trills at me, tipping its crimson head left and right—trying, I think, to win me over, or ask for something. It scratches the table with a green talon. I remember everything from my past perfectly, from the grain of the orphanage floorboards that I mopped by hand when I was four years old to the number of petals on the first flower I saw. But sometimes I don't pay attention to memories I hold inside me, and it takes a moment as I stare, irritated at the bird for distracting me from my purpose, to connect its behavior to the act of begging. It nudges its head under my hand.

Feed it, says a quiet voice inside me.

I frown, unsettled. The instruction came not as a thought formed by me, but as an intrusion, as though someone had whispered in my ear. Surely I have imagined it. I fetch a hunk of stale bread from the larder in the corner. Of course I will feed the bird. It is useful to me. Anyway, it is loud and unpredictable. Let it be occupied by satisfying its hunger while I pursue my prey. I tear the bread into pieces and drop them onto the table in front of the Elysium bird, whose inky beak jabs into the dry morsels, wings fluttering excitedly.

The slight grit of my dirty sandals scuffs the stone floor as I leave the bird behind. My feet drift down the stairs to the kitchen, where I once worked hard to please my mistress. At the orphanage, when she personally selected me, Raven touched my cheek and said, I know a good girl when I see one.

The kitchen is empty. Her bedroom? The steps leading upstairs creak beneath my feet. Did Raven see me in the agora? Does she fear me now, and hide? Then I must tempt her forth. "I have a gift for you, Ama. You will love it!"

No answer. Her room, into which I was admitted only to brush her hair or rub her soft hands with cream before bed (I work so hard for my girls, she used to sigh, and I would believe her), has the familiar smell I associate with her: indi soap made from the perfume of tenacious purple flowers that grow wild in the Ward. The clothes in her wardrobe are nicer than anything I wore during my childhood, when I never thought it wrong that her dresses were made of cotton, not wincey, like mine. I never thought it wrong that her sandals were more comfortable and didn't leave blisters. She was Middling, after all, so the law allowed her things it didn't allow me. Even if the law didn't, I would have wanted her to have the comforts that I did not. Wasn't that what a daughter should want? Maybe I wasn't Raven's daughter, not really, but I loved her like one.

I go through her things, snorting when I see a tear in a dress, neatly mended by Annin. How Raven must have laughed inside as she played her charade of selflessness! Oh, I scrimp and save, she said to me once, so that I can put more money aside for you girls. And of course—she leaned in to whisper—for our cause.

Meanwhile, she extracted every coin she could from Half Kith desperate to flee the Ward, even this city. She gave them passports that faked their kith—passports forged by me, the idiot, who believed we helped people for nothing.

I am grateful to the god of thieves. Joy thrills down to my toes, to know that I am no longer who I was. What use was my soft heart? It convinced me to excuse the bad behavior of others, to let myself be used, to forgive Raven when she hurt me. The loss of my heart is no bad thing. It left room for something else.

Freedom.

Anger.

My heart was full of guilt and love and tender forgiveness. Let the god of thieves keep it forever. Now nothing will stop me from doing what I want—for myself and everyone loyal to me.

I riffle through the drawer of Raven's wobbly bedside table. Next: the desk where she once sat me down and exclaimed over how perfectly

I could imitate a signature. My little artist! she said, and I glowed from her praise, not understanding then that there was little art to what I did, only the power of a perfect memory.

She is not here. She left nothing of value behind. She must have squirreled it all away in that house she built for herself in the Middling quarter, lining it with the nicest things the law allowed her. She must be there. Well, I will find her, and we will see who is the fool *now*. I fling open a roughly carved wooden jewelry box and snarl at the trinkets inside. Tin earrings. A tarnished silver chain I gave her when I was fourteen, having bartered work in a neighbor's scraggly little garden. How beautiful! she said, adding, I will put it with my treasures.

When I noticed she never wore it, she said, It is too good to wear, my lamb. People will get jealous.

I see it now for what it is: trash. I toss it to the floor.

Where is the crescent moon necklace that once belonged to my mother, which Raven stole? Still around Raven's weathered neck, most likely. My hands twitch as though I could wring that neck like a rag. Yet I pause, surprised by the force of my longing for a sentimental object, my irrational hope. What *did* the god of thieves steal from me, if I can still hope, still seek comfort in a symbol that doesn't even prove its original owner loved me?

A hand lightly slips into mine. Instinctively, I crush it between my fingers. Someone cries out. I turn and see Annin, her blue eyes wide as she begs me to let her go. "You're hurting me!"

"Nirrim," comes a new voice, low and calm. Morah stands at the threshold of Raven's bedroom. "You are not yourself."

Aren't I? Aren't I the most perfect version of myself, who can look at these two young women and care nothing for the opinion of Morah, who used to lord her supposed wisdom over me, and care nothing for Annin, sweet little Annin, so easily biddable? She is a pretty doll with a porcelain head filled with pins. She would rattle if you shook her. She reminds me of *me*: who I once was. I double my grip. She screams, face contorting. Good. She no longer looks so pretty.

Morah slowly crosses the room toward me. "You will break her fingers. She won't be able to sew. She loves to sew."

Morah expects these words to move me and make me loosen my grip, but Annin needs to learn not to be so trusting. She scrabbles at me, like a kitten might twist against a grip at the nape of its neck, and I am momentarily amused. Neither she nor Morah seem to consider I possess a power more formidable than a mere grip. I am so distracted by their ignorance that I don't notice—until Morah sets the sharp blade against my throat—the kitchen knife she must have held at her thigh, hidden in the folds of her skirt, as she crossed the room to me.

"Let her go," Morah says.

The threat is ridiculous. Morah does not understand my god-gift. I could force a false memory into her mind. You dropped the knife, I could say, and re-create the past so that it becomes her present and she sends the knife clattering to the floor. I could make her freshly feel her most painful memory. Years ago—how many? Ten?—Raven stole Morah's baby. Morah never knew what happened to the newborn boy. Yes, *that* might be a good thing to make her remember.

Don't, says that quiet, internal voice, the same one that told me to feed the Elysium.

Startled, I loosen my grip. It's enough for Annin to tug her sweaty fingers free.

My scalp crawls. Earlier, my impulse to feed the Elysium was easily dismissed as a stray thought . . . and a practical one that suited my goals. Now, however, I pay attention to that eerily familiar voice that seems at once inside me and outside me. The voice is low and steady. Like a candle flame, Sid once told me.

That voice is mine.

Morah presses the knife harder to my throat, so close it bites the skin.

A knot hardens in my belly. Once, I loved Morah and Annin like sisters. They should be my allies and strive to achieve my goals. I dislike having my will checked by some whispery ghost in my head: a shadow of the girl I used to be.

Annin wipes tears from her cheeks, her skin lighter than mine—always ready to blush or pale, quick to show her emotions. Her face might as well be a painted sign announcing her thoughts to the world. She reddens in distress.

Very well, I tell that needling little voice, which I sense waiting for some response. I won't hurt them. That would look bad to the Half Kith, whose loyalty I need to consolidate. I bat the knife from Morah's hand. It clatters to the floor. She never would have used it anyway. She is too fond of me.

The old me.

Morah's expression betrays no fear, even though her weapon lies out of easy reach. Once she was the toughest of us three, as resilient as the sturdy kitchen worktable downstairs. "Nirrim, you can't simply walk into the agora and proclaim yourself queen of Herrath."

"I already did. Have you come to try to reason with me? Fair fortune to fools."

"I am not *here* for anything. This is my home. Annin's, too. And yours."

I glance around Raven's shabby room, remembering how mysteriously grand it seemed when I was little and knew no better. "I don't want this home. You may keep it. My people will know me as a generous queen."

Annin, cradling her hand, casts Morah a skittish look. Annin says, "You claimed you are a god. But there are no gods."

I wave away her stupid words. "You think I'm mad, I suppose. Well, you shall see." They clearly have not a drop of god-blood in them, nor much ambition. Having decided not to punish them, and certain they can do little to advance my cause, I return to my task, tearing apart Raven's room to find whatever secrets she might have hidden. You will never know anything more about your mother, she warned me. How you were born. Who you are! I ran from her, horrified at how she had used me—and wanted to continue using me. You will be nothing to me, she promised—she, who revealed herself as my mother's sister, and might know from which god I came. The kind of power I possess is no certain clue. The god of thieves's history book revealed that the gifts of the half-gods were not mere copies of those of their immortal parents. When the gods abandoned Ethin long ago, retreating to their realm, the powers they left in their half-god children diminished and changed through generations. Probably Aden is a descendent of the sun god. Everything about Aden has always been so *obvious*. His boring, handsome face. The foregone conclusion the entire Ward shared that of *course* I should love him. His jealousy. His insecurity. No doubt his glowing god-gift could be traced to the most obvious source.

The same is not true of my gift. There is no god of memory.

Perhaps my long-ago ancestor was the god of some aspect of the mind, such as dreams.

Or the god of stars, the one that rules fate.

Or vengeance. What is memory, if not an account of all the wrongs done?

Maybe I can trace my kin back to the god of wealth, who demands a balancing of the scales, for surely I was born to demand payment for each wound inflicted on me and my own.

I retrieve Morah's knife from the floor and cut into the mattress, pulling out handfuls of straw-and-rag padding. I probably *do* look mad. There must still be streaks of color in my hair, put there by Madame

Mere, a High-Kith dressmaker, who also painted cosmetics on my face—smeared now, I'm sure. I attack the bedding, cutting more deeply, looking for that necklace, or for anything that might give me a clue to my parentage. Nothing is hidden there, but I keep stabbing. It feels good.

Morah says, "We think something happened to you, *damaged* you. You are no longer the person you were."

"Because I am angry? Because I am strong? Why aren't *you* angry? You have been treated just as badly."

Annin says, "We are worried about you."

"Don't be. I feel wonderful," I say, and it is true.

I abandon the gutted mattress and lift Raven's handheld mirror from her dressing table, though not to look into its glass. When I shake the mirror, the glass rattles in its frame. Believing there might be something hidden between the mirror and its frame, I crack it against the vanity. Silver shards clink to my feet. There is nothing but a lead handle and a simple wooden backing to the frame.

"Nirrim—"

"You bore me. You are stupid chickens, clucking away. I am tired of people who know nothing, who lie to themselves that one day things will be better if they only have patience. A tale for children and idiots. Brave people take matters into their own hands. Learn this now, or learn later and be left behind." I snap my fingers rapidly, as though to wake them up or hurry them along. "Will you help me or not?"

Annin says, "Help you destroy Raven's room?"

"Help me with the *war*."

"War?"

"Yes, *war*. Do you believe the High Kith will simply give us what we want? We must take it." They look at me as though I am a bee that has unwittingly flown into someone's home, and thuds itself against a window to get out. Their expressions show me more than the mirror I broke: how erratic I appear. Erratic is how I *feel*: seeking one thing and then the next, desiring something and then changing my mind. It is true that a void lurks beneath the giddiness of my new freedom and power, as though the god of thieves stole not my heart but the center of my being. That void is a hollow chamber that echoes with only one command: those who made me suffer will pay.

Uncertainty marks Morah's and Annin's faces.

They never hurt you, says the voice inside me. They loved you.

They are useless, I tell Other Nirrim. Just like *you* were useless.

I reach for a metal hairbrush. In the past, I would gently draw it through Raven's silver hair and untangle each knot with careful fingers. Like the mirror, the brush has a backing—hard and painful, as I know well, from every time Raven struck me with it. I pry at the backing and feel again like that bee I imagined, banging softly at windows. A buzzing rises within me, blocking my ears against Morah's and Annin's questions, their silly concerned tones. The backing comes off in my hands. Two whitely bright lights tumble out of the revealed space and onto the dressing table.

Earrings. Jewels unlike anything I have ever seen. Each earring is a tiny star, its light pure. Annin gasps. I don't recognize the earrings, but instantly know they form a set with the crescent moon necklace my mother once wore. Like the necklace, they are otherworldly.

They are mine now.

I have no piercings for earrings, since Half Kith were never allowed even the most modest jewelry. No matter. I push my hair aside, set the sharp tip of an earring against my earlobe, and press until the stud pops through the flesh. Blood dribbles down my neck. Happily, I fasten the earring and do the same with the other. A broken shard of mirror lying on the dresser catches my reflection. Yes, I do look crazed: cosmetics streaked across my face, my mouth open in delight, lines of blood down my throat, twin stars glowing at my ears.

I didn't find what I was looking for, neither my revenge upon Raven nor her secrets about my parents nor the necklace, but perhaps these jewels are an even better discovery. I grew up so starved of beauty, so used to the starvation that I couldn't even recognize, then, what I was missing.

I deserve beauty, and I shall have it.

What Morah and Annin see in my face, or think of me, I neither know nor care. I push past them, out of the bedroom and down the stairs, whistling to my bird, which swoops from the rafters to my shoulder. The jewels make my ears throb. The bird's talons grip my shoulders as I dive into the warm dusk of the street in search of Aden and the rest of my god-blooded soldiers.

The High Kith come at nightfall. Weapons bristling, they enter the Ward through the wall's gate.

Aden sets their skin aflame, roasting them inside their armor. Rinah, whose garden I once tended, its abundance surprising, the sun melons always unusually large and honeyed, steps forward. She teases indi vines, those pretty weeds that lattice the entire city, into snaking ropes that bind the invaders.

The wall the High Kith built to contain us also *protects* us. The High Kith and their Middling militia pour through the gate as thickly as they can, but it is a narrow entrance. They cannot enter the Ward in great enough force to overwhelm the god-blooded Half Kith. Not Aden, lighting their bodies into torches, nor Rinah, nor that little boy whose father had brought him to me, Sithin, who is gifted with making holes.

Black space appears in living flesh. He makes skin pop with empty buttons, riddling the skin like a disease.

When most of our enemies have been captured, killed, or subdued, I step through the wall's gate into the Middling quarter to face the rest of the horde. "You were so tired." The power of my gift curls into my lovely voice. "You wanted to fall asleep." The trick to controlling people with my god-power is to present them with my version of the past. A memory might not kill a man, but I can push false memories into a weak brain. The High Kith are used to nothing standing between them and their pleasure. The Middlings, who serve the High Kith, are used to obedience. What resistance can they possibly raise against me? I make them remember a sleepiness they do not feel. One by one, they drop unconscious at my feet.

All my life, the people of Ethin lived as instructed, the Half Kith behind the wall built to contain them and the gifts they didn't even know they had. The High Kith lived diamond lives, clear and glittering, as they threw wild parties in their lavish homes and consumed whatever they wanted: wriggling rainbow fish, clouds of pink cream on airy cake, and our god-blood, watered down and served as a tasteless elixir in teacups so fine you could see lamplight through their creamy porcelain. Our blood was their delight: a little burst of magic on the tongue so that the High Kith, at least for a few hours, reveled in borrowed glory. They floated inches off the ground. Their faces shifted into more beautiful lines. Rainwater trailed from their shoulders in a veil. Lightning traced crowns above their brows.

How many of the High Kith understood what they did? How many knew that they drank the blood of the people they most despised, and how many believed the elixir was an innocent delight offered to them by the Council, a drink made from fruit or a flower, perhaps? Maybe some suspected the pink elixir had an unpleasant origin, yet did not seek its source, because to know and drink would then be wrong, and they wanted the taste of magic without the bitterness of guilt.

Their life was sweetly blessed. They had everything they wanted. Days of endless luxury. I, who had a taste of sweetness with Sid, understand why the High Kith never sought to learn whether they deserved what they had. I once feared that if I considered too closely why Sid wanted me, I might discover that her attention would never truly be mine, that I didn't deserve it, or that it would be wrong to keep it.

Do you not love me like I love you? she asked. My perfect memory, a gift and a curse, makes me hear again the fear in her voice, and feel again my devastation to hear her ask that question at the moment of abandoning me.

The god of thieves has done me a favor. I desire Sid still, but I cannot feel my love for her. I feel love for no one, not even my people.

This is a good thing. Love is a problem. It blurs your sight, and stands in the way of what needs to be done. If I listened now to the love I once had for Morah and Annin, their kindhearted worries might trouble me. Instead, I tell my Half Kith to bind our sleeping enemies and carry them to prison. Morah and Annin might stay my hand as I reach for Rinah's shoulder. "Tear down the wall," I order her. "Use the indi vines."

Rinah hesitates. The wall is too familiar, the most important element of our lives from birth. It stood the whole of our parents' lives, and their parents' lives, encircling the Half Kith for centuries. When I lived with Sid in the High quarter I sometimes missed the wall for its reliable, calm strength. The wall corrals us, but it also creates our home.

"Do it, Rinah, for your children. Remember how you feared they would be snatched away in the night. Remember how as they grew old enough to play in the streets, you dreaded that they might break one of the High Kith's many rules, and be taken to prison, and come home with a missing limb, or weak from blood loss. Think of the world you want for them instead."

Rinah's face contorts. Indi vines thicken to the width of a burly man's arm. Their green darkens to near black. They knot together and wedge into tiny pockmarks in the wall's granite. Vegetal fingers dig into rock, then disappear, driving into stone like worms into earth. Rinah watches vines split the granite. The wall begins to crumble, dust sifting down. Rubble spills loudly from the cracks, hissing and thumping to the ground. With a thunderous crack, the wall breaks, pieces heaving down in chunks.

From the scattered debris, dust rises like smoke.

"Good," I tell Rinah, who looks stricken and angry and glad.

"I suppose our days of forging and selling passports are over," Aden says, "now that the wall is gone."

I do not like his poor attempt at jovial familiarity, and at leaning on our history together so that he might share—or perhaps eventually control—the authority I now possess over this city. I do not like his smug expression, as if this is his victory, when he simply obeyed my command. It was I who foresaw how this clash would go, I who knew how to use my god-soldiers to strike. Aden is convenient to me for his power and popularity, but he is sorely mistaken if he thinks I have forgotten how he wished to control me with his so-called love, how he blamed me when I wanted someone else. He shamed me for wanting Sid. What a tiny-minded man, to construe my choice as shameful, simply because I did not choose him.

Let him watch his step. He lives only because I allow it.

"I never sold passports," I tell him. "I made them to give away. To help." How naïve I was! How easy it was for Raven, whom I loved like a mother, to manipulate me, feeding me sugary stories about the good we were doing for others. With the passports I forged, people trapped behind the wall could pretend to be Middling and escape. And they did . . . at a cost I never suspected. Raven made them give her all they had. She enriched herself, padding a home in the Middling quarter with luxuries. I—meek, trusting—had never guessed. I needed her love so much that I made myself believe she was the good person she pretended to be.

I am finished with love.

Aden must see some of my thoughts in my face. "You have changed."

"Good."

"You used to be kind, Nirrim. Gentle. I liked you better before."

"Of course. I was easier for you to use."

Aden's expression twitches with genuine hurt. "All I wanted was to make you happy. Tell me how, and I will do it."

"Make plans for public trials of the High Kith," I say, "and mass executions. We shall tithe them as they once tithed us. Ten percent of all High-Kith adults shall be culled from the prison to pay the price for their people's sins. Sharpen an ax, Aden. That will me very happy indeed."

SID

WHEN WE REACH HERRAN'S BAY, a feeling as resonant as song fills my chest. I have not once felt homesick since I ran away, but now that I am back, homesickness floods me, belated. It is strange to feel longing for something just when I am about to get it, and when I had decided I didn't want it. Longing thickens inside me, as though deriving its sudden strength from coming so late, so far after the fact.

Herran's mountainous coast is lush with trees. Once the jewel in the Valorian Empire's crown, the city grows out of the rocky cliffs that hug the bay. The newest homes, built after the war my parents won, are painted in soft pastels with bright blue shutters that must be shut when autumn comes and green storms riot up the coast. Nirrim's island was summery, with odd bursts of icy wind that would last for a few days only, but my country has its seasons, and although the laran trees now hold their leaves like thick, green shawls, and all I smell is the sea's brine, I know autumn is not far off. Soon, it will be Ninarrith, when my people light a hundred candles in honor of the last day the gods walked among us. I always thought the holiday a pleasant fantasy, an excuse for giving gifts, but after what I saw on Nirrim's island, I wonder. I went searching for magic, and magic I found, but what was its source? Whatever her people could conjure was fleeting, thin, like rivulets from a nearly dry creek bed that cannot quench anyone's thirst.

Nirrim, though, had something more. Deeper.

I try not to think about her. I think about the weather, as a true sailor would, for her life depends on it. I think about how the coming of autumn smells like honey and a lit match.

It smells like Nirrim's hair, when I buried my face in it. My throat closes. For a moment I cannot see, my vision blurred. Then it clears.

A tall, broad figure waits at the pier. The shape of my father is instantly familiar.

I shouldn't have hoped that the arrival of our two ships—Roshar's an obvious Dacran vessel, skinny and long and flying his green flag, and mine one of the finest in my father's fleet, which I commandeered the night I left Herran—would go unnoticed. A fool's hope.

Perhaps I should be glad that my father hasn't appeared with his entire guard. A small mercy. At least my prodigal return home isn't public gossip. Yet.

Roshar rests a hand on my shoulder. "Best to face him sooner rather than later, princess."

"Best you kiss my ass, prince."

His hand tightens. "Don't apologize to him for running away." Surprised, I turn to him. He adds, "Never apologize for who you are or what you needed to do to be yourself."

I *almost* believe my godfather. My eyes *almost* prickle with relieved gratitude. Even when I was small, I longed to have his self-possession, his easy-seeming way of flouting expectation. Of demanding people meet him on his terms, not theirs. I wanted this even though—or because—I knew nothing was easy for him. He shares his true feelings with few people. His mutilations keep them at bay. He has done things for which he will never forgive himself. So yes, the words sound like something he would mean. But as we disembark, I decide Roshar's advice is a pretty-sounding lie. Be myself? Don't apologize? I am supposed to marry Roshar's sister's son and inherit the realms of Herran and Dacra. He knows this. He helped *arrange* it. He might say understanding things— and he, who likes men just as I like women, understands me better than most—but he would never break my betrothal.

When we meet my father, the king, on the pier, he places his palm on Roshar's cheek, and Roshar does the same: the traditional Herrani greeting between men who are friends or family. I cannot look away from this gesture, this closeness between them. I am filled with envy.

My father's hair turned silver, they say, at my birth, so frightened was he to lose my mother, who had bled too much and was close to death. He lowers his gray eyes to meet mine. I have some of his height, but not nearly enough. He towers above people, his arms stony with muscle. His skin, a few shades darker than mine, the same light brown as Nirrim's, is weathered by sun and wind and age, save for the shine of a long scar that cuts down from his brow and into the hollow of his left cheek. He does not wait to let me speak. He pulls me to him.

"God of life," he says. "I thought I would lose you, too." He holds me as if I were a child. Despite what Roshar advised, I instantly apologize, my face pressed against my father's chest. Water seeps from my eyes into his linen tunic. "Etta," I say, "forgive me."

He tells me there is nothing to forgive, that I am here now. "My girl. I was so worried. Why did you leave us?"

I cannot answer. I don't want to blame my mother, whom he loves so fiercely. I don't want to blame him for not protecting me from her schemes, and ignoring them. I want, for once, to be a good daughter. So I give him my silence. It is the best I can offer. He accepts it, as I knew he would. He, who was enslaved from the time he was a child until he was a young man, never likes to force an answer.

What could I say? You expected too much from me. I chose to put my pleasure first. *You are an apple, Sidarine.*

What I'm truly sorry for, what makes the tears still come, is that choosing myself meant hurting him, and I did it anyway. I cannot promise I won't do it again. I am sorry for my guilt—and my anger. When I saw my father greet Roshar, anger rushed into me like a wind-fed flame, because my father will never place his hand on my cheek like that. He will never greet me the way Herrani men do. I am his only child, his beloved daughter—a girl, not his equal. I am not a man.

My father doesn't like the trappings of his stature. Arin the Plain King, people call him with pride. They love him and his simple clothes, his quiet manner. My mother, with her hive of spies, is fully aware that the way he presents himself to Herran only encourages the other name people call him: Death's Child. Death, after all, needs no velvet or silk to remind you of his strength. He announces his presence with a mere tap on the shoulder.

My mother told me, People believe that your father survived the war because he was born in the year of the god of death. He is god-touched, they say. The god of death loves him.

What do you believe? I asked. My father worships the gods. He lights candles in their temple. My mother, whose features are practically a song for the fallen Valorian Empire and its many crimes, her skin honey-colored, her hair woven gold, has no religion. The Valorians believed in no god but their own strength. Infidels, the Herrani call them. Murderers. The Valorians deserved their destruction, they say.

I, for one, agree.

My mother said carefully, I believe it is important for the people to believe Arin is Death's Child.

Because it makes it easier for you to rule them, I said, my tone rude.

My mother's light brown eyes narrowed. No, she said. Because it makes them hopeful, and fear the future less.

As I follow my father and Roshar on horseback through the city, which still bears the scars of the last war before my birth, when Herran overthrew the Valorians and my mother murdered her emperor, I remember how I had wanted to point out that the Herrani's love for my father exempted my mother from their long-held hate against anything Valorian. How could they even stand to look at her, when her people had enslaved this country, when three decades before my birth, Kestrel's own father had brutally crushed the Herrani? How convenient for you, I wanted to say, that they adore Etta.

How convenient for *you*, she might have replied, leveling me with one of her perfectly aimed comments that I have seen strike home in other people.

There is no hiding that I look like her. I used to hope my blond hair would darken with age. I searched my face for traces of my father, but nothing will change my Valorian features. Still, I don't like to be reminded, and I definitely did not need to be reminded by my mother. She is too keenly aware of the vulnerabilities of others, and on that day we discussed my father, chosen by Death, I feared saying something that would make her be cruel to me. While not a cruel person, she has a gift for knowing what hurts most. She used to show her love by never turning that gift against me.

◆

My home is no palace, despite our royal titles, but rather an elegant villa, smaller than many of the enormous, marble-columned Valorian mansions from the decade-long colonial era. Sunlight splashes through trees that canopy horse paths leading out of the city's center. The three of us, my father and Roshar side by side, and I behind, ride into the green tunnels created by trees and bushes, cicadas whirring in the branches, to the house that was his as a child, before it was stolen by the Empire. He reclaimed it during the Firstwinter Rebellion, when Herrani slaves rose up against their masters. He once even kept my Valorian mother prisoner within the villa's east wing.

I ran to my mother on small, bare feet when I learned this, the marble tiles slick and cool against my soles. Even then, I hated pinching lady slippers. In a shocked voice, I announced, Etta captured you.

She frowned. Where did you hear that? she asked.

He locked you up.

Who told you?

Worried I'd get my nurse in trouble, but more worried I'd get *myself* in trouble, I confessed: Emmah.

Emmah cannot know the whole story, my mother said.

What is the whole story?

Emmah has no right to chatter gossip to my child. It is not her tale to tell.

Tell me.

When you are older. It is not a tale for little ones.

I am old enough for Needles, I said, referring to the set of deadly knives she was training me to wield. Though she had no natural gift for weapons, she had worked for years to be skilled at Needles.

She smoothed flyaway hair off my brow. Yes, he imprisoned me, but

I imprisoned him first. Do not worry, tadpole. He is mine, and I am his. Always.

The grounds surrounding my home are still green with summer's end, pomegranates heavy and dark fists on their low trees. My father's orange grove has been harvested.

"Did you eat them all?" Roshar asks my father, nodding at the grove. My father's love for the fruit is legendary. Really, everything about my parents is.

My father allows Roshar a small smile. "Almost."

"And left none for your dearest, most charming friend, I bet. Well, Arin. You know what this means. Not a drop of my finest Dacran liquor for you later when we listen to young Sid regale us with all the fun she has had breaking foreign hearts."

My father shifts uncomfortably in his saddle.

"She *did* run through all the ladies here," Roshar says.

And there we have it: my third skill.

Roshar smiles at me over his shoulder. "A rake after my own heart."

I tip my head to him, every bit the arrogant wastrel my father has cautioned me not to be. It is bad behavior in one so recently and easily forgiven, but I simultaneously do not like my father's silence, and want to prove that it does not bother me.

The villa glows under the rising sun, the windows winking. Its set of peaked roofs rise and fall, sloping down to the west. The glass atrium is a pointed jewel. As my boots crunch gravel covering the walk, the front door opens, and a tall, gray-and-black-haired woman stands on the threshold. Sarsine, my father's cousin and chief counselor, looks much like him. Same steely hair, same gray eyes. Bold brow and large hands. Her craggy face hardens with disapproval as she appraises me.

I brush imaginary dust from the shoulders of my jacket, a man's garment I had made for me in Ethin. I tug at the cuffs. My boots are less than shiny. Still, I can play my part. Ne'er-do-well, Sarsine silently calls me. Bad apple.

Fine. I am.

I grin at her behind my father's back as he and Roshar enter the villa. "Better late than never," I whisper sideways.

"Better *never*, or so some have said in your absence." Sarsine holds my gaze as I hear the men's footfalls diminish into the villa's interior. "You wasted countless resources in our search for you. Your parents grieved each day you were gone. Yet here you stand, smiling cheerfully, without a care in the world. Arin let you off easy, I see."

"No one can hold anything against me for long. I am too adorable. It is my handsome face. My winning charm. All the ladies say so."

Sarsine looks as though she would like to slap me. "May the heart you break one day be your own."

I do not give Sarsine the satisfaction of knowing her curse has already come to pass.

I linger in the salon where my mother's piano hulks, its shining black shape as big as the boulder of guilt that rests on my chest. I touch the keys lightly, soundlessly, remembering my awe as a child to see my mother play, the simple harmonies I initially produced, how I grew in skill only to realize that I would never be more than merely good. For a few moments, I do not know how long, I believe the disquiet in my belly is shame, but then I realize it is more than that. It is fear of seeing her. Frustrated with myself, annoyed with the salon's stillness, how it now seems like a smug, knowing witness to my cowardice, I bound up the stairs to the east wing, boots loud on polished oak.

On the outermost door to my mother's suite, the kestrel carved into its wood peers down at me with narrow-eyed reproach, its expression dangerous though its body is small, its wingspan dainty, its tailfeathers spread in a dark-patterned fan. The door is not locked. My heart raps against my ribs. The indigo flowered rug of the empty greeting room deadens the sound of my boots. The quiet reminds me that my mother might be sleeping. I must not wake her. I walk softly but swiftly through her suite, hoping I can make everything right, that the queen's forgiveness will be as easy to receive as the king's. Nothing has been done that cannot be undone, surely. My mother will be well again. She will recover from this sickness. It is a matter of time. She is Queen Kestrel, master of spies. She survived so much. She is daunted by no one. Nothing.

I lift a vow to the god of souls, in whom I half believe. The god, who rules love, brokers deals for what mortals want most. Save her, I plead, and I will marry to please my parents.

As I move through each gray-and-pearl-colored room of the suite, I imagine telling my mother my vow. She will smile, and love me like she once did.

I pause before her bedchamber. The door is ajar. Beyond it, the tiny form of my mother rests under mounds of blankets though it is not so cold; autumn is not here yet. She has the body of a child. I shot up past her years ago. Towering over her used to give me some satisfaction, but now she looks too small, like she will dwindle away. Her loose hair, undulled by age, is a fire against the bedsheets. Her dagger, normally worn at her hip as I do mine, hangs from its hook on the bedpost. My father kneels next to the bed, his back to me, his hand on hers, his shoulders bowed. My mother doesn't see me standing at the door. She sees only him. Her whisper reaches me: "I don't want to die."

"Little Fists." My father's voice is rough. "You won't die."

"I don't want you to grieve. I don't want to leave you alone in this world."

My father is silent. I know without seeing his face what is there: his devastation. His large fingers trace the thin gold ring on her smallest finger. He made it for me, my mother told me, her face luminous with memory.

My mother says, "Who will protect you when I'm gone?"

My father, all muscle and strength, gently presses his face into her palm.

"I worry," she says.

His shoulders lift and fall. Hurt burns my throat. I am like my father and mother: full of grief. And I am *me*, too: so jealous. I know it is wrong. Selfish. But I wish my mother worried about *me*, that it was me she wanted to protect, for me that she wished to live.

I know I am second best. I cannot measure up to their love for each other. Yet I want to be at least enough.

"Sid has returned," my father says.

"She has?"

"You must not worry. You will live. And I have her."

My mother sighs. "No," she whispers, "you don't."

When I enter my rooms, which were my father's rooms when he was a child, before the invasion, when Valorian soldiers forced their way into this house and murdered his family, I find Emmah going through my wardrobe, unwrapping my clothes from their tissue paper shrouds. The paper rustles as she catches sight of me and grips the clothes. Her deeply wrinkled face splits into a smile. "Sid! You sneak. How dare you skulk away for months on end!" She offers her cheek. "Come and give your nurse a kiss."

I do, grateful that if she sees anything wrong in my expression, if she can sense how my mother's words stamped down into my chest, heavy as a war horse's hoof, she makes no mention of it. She still wears the little gold earrings I made for her when I was a child. My father refused to teach me how to blacksmith, saying he did not like to remember how he'd been forced to learn the skill, and no child of his would be made to work. I argued that this was not smithing, it was jewelry making, and if he had made my mother's ring, surely he could help me. I want to make something Emmah loves, I said, and he smiled, and said, All right. Emmah cried when she unfolded the velvet I had wrapped around her Ninarrith gift.

She holds my face between her palms, green eyes shining. They are pretty, and make me wonder, as I often have, how she looked before the war. Her wrinkles were not caused by age—she is no older than my parents—but by fire or acid. Once, when I was little, I asked my parents what happened to Emmah. You must never ask her, my mother ordered, appalled. More gently, my father explained that we could not expect to know all that the Herrani had suffered during the invasion, when General Trajan, my Valorian grandfather, conquered this country and enslaved its people, or during the decade of colonization that followed.

You love Emmah, don't you? my father said.

I nodded.

Then don't pry.

But Roshar has scars on his face, I said. And I love him, and I asked him, and *he* told me.

What did he say?

That Arin did it, I answered. When I saw my parents' startled expressions, I hastily added, I mean, Arin the tiger. Not *you*, Etta. Roshar said his tiger did it, that bad boy.

Dear one, my mother said, Roshar lied.

My father touched my cheek. He explained, Some truths are too hard to say.

"What a fright you gave me," Emmah says. "You could have gone down in a shipwreck! You could have fallen in love with some girl and never returned!"

"Never." I ignore the twitch of pain in my chest. I ignore the heat in my belly, my chest, my throat, as I remember peeling away Nirrim's dress to kiss her skin. The feel of her body beneath mine, the way her eyes slid shut with pleasure. Nirrim's eyes resemble Emmah's, though Nirrim's are larger, more luminous. Greener: a leaf lit by the sun. Look at me, I told Nirrim as I touched her. Open your eyes. She did, and I was lost.

No more. The memory is punishing. I must forget Nirrim. At least, I must do my best. Trying on a sly smile that feels fake but is familiar, because I am performing an old version of myself, I tell Emmah, "I am too canny a sailor to be sunk, and the god of souls knows I am too delicious to be given to one woman. I must be shared."

Emmah turns serious, hands falling to her sides. "Have you seen your mother?"

I toy with a bit of downy tissue paper. It is tishin paper, made from pounding the stems of mulberry trees and soaking the pulp in a vat of water and hibiscus sap. Incredibly thin and sheer, tishin is barely paper. It feels the way clouds look. Made a little thicker than what I hold between my fingers, it can be used for paper lanterns. A little thinner, and my mother can use it for her own purposes. Watch, she once told me, laying an airy sheet of tishin over a page filled with writing. The writing vanished, and appeared to be a blank page that could easily be stitched into the final pages of an innocent-seeming book shipped along with its secret message to the recipient, who would scrape away the tishin to reveal the words beneath. Even paper, my mother said, has its secrets.

I think about the paper, and not the way my eyes burned to hear my mother dismiss me to my father as though *I* were tissue-thin. Next to nothing.

"Well?" Emmah presses. "Did you see the queen?"

"Yes."

"Don't lie to me."

"I *did* see her. She simply didn't see me."

"Let's choose something suitable for you to wear, then, to visit her again."

My gaze flicks warily to the dresses gathered together like flowers.

"Something you like," Emmah corrects herself, and reaches for a Herrani men's jacket: deep blue, with a high collar. My lungs loosen. It means something, that Emmah knows who I am and has never tried to change me. It gives me the courage I need.

My mother's eyes are closed when I enter her bedchamber. I am clean from a bath, sea salt scrubbed from my skin. My boots are glossy black leather, my jacket tight across my chest, a Valorian dagger heavy on my hip. I refuse to kneel by her bedside the way my father did. She and I are alone in her bedchamber, and as she sleeps I take this moment to study her. I am glad my features are not so delicate. Even now, with the pallor of an invalid, she is beautiful. Beside her, on the dove-gray wood of the nightstand, rests a speckled yellow feather that I have sometimes seen in my father's suite, sometimes seen in hers. It is a kind of code between them. What it means, I will likely never know. My parents might as well have their own language.

Her eyes flick open, startling me. I can't tell whether she was faking sleep, or if her intelligence is such that even her dreams can't keep her from sensing that for one moment, I had the advantage and was able to study her without her studying me.

"Sidarine." Her voice is weak.

"Sid," I correct.

She nods slightly, golden hair brushing the pillow. "Sid," she says, and I feel petty for forcing her, in her illness, to use my little name. But she knows my preference. It is not new, and she is too smart to pretend she forgets. "I need to tell you something," she says.

"Yes?" I try to keep the eagerness from my voice. Is it that she missed me? That she is glad I'm home?

"You cannot tell your father."

Gods in their heaven. Never, to my knowledge, has my mother shared a secret with me that she kept from him. I bend closer. I find that I *am* ready to kneel, to hear her better, and stop myself just in time.

She must notice; she smiles. "I need my spy."

"I quit being your spy."

"I can't tell Arin," she continues, as if I hadn't spoken. "He will raze Herran looking for the culprit."

I crush my disappointment into a ball inside my chest and make my voice sound bored. "You are stringing me along, trying to stir my curiosity so that I become desperate for your secret, when really you're assigning another job for me to do. Might as well say what it is."

"I am not sick," my mother says. "I have been poisoned."

NIRRIM

A FULL MOON POURS ITS silver over the city, whitening the pavement as I leave the Ward. I pass through the ruins of the wall, stepping carefully through the rocky debris. Cheers erupt behind me, the sound large yet softened by distance. A few minutes later, as I enter the Middling quarter, with its modest yet pretty houses, lit by blue-paned lanterns, the cheers echo again from the agora. Aden selected the prisoners to be executed, beginning with several councilmembers. They had once ruled over all of Ethin, acting in the name of the Lord Protector, whom we believed was elected by the Council whenever the former Lord Protector died. Instead, he had been the god of thieves, punished by the pantheon of gods to watch over this island. Every generation, the god of thieves pretended to be a new Lord Protector, risen from the ranks of the Council, and stole everyone's knowledge of the truth.

The Council is complicit, Aden said, and I agreed. Only High Kith could become councilmembers, and they saw to it that their laws were ruthlessly enacted. If a Half Kith wore sandals that were too nice, the leather too smooth, by the Council's orders she could be arrested, her toes lopped off one by one. If a Half Kith dared to leave the Ward, and was caught, as Aden's mother had been long ago, the sentence was death. Their blood will spill in the agora, Aden said, as red as the Council robes they once wore.

Kill all the councilmen, I told him.

And all the High Kith.

I felt a prickle of annoyance. No. I said ten percent.

That is too little.

Don't do this, said that voice inside, that other, old version of myself.

Silence, I tell her. I do not listen to you. My resistance to Aden was not out of guilt, or some ghost of my former self. It was because I had given Aden a clear command, and he had decided to act as if he knew better. "Ten percent only," I told him. "Do as I say, or I will add you to the tithe." He smirked as though I had been joking, his smile edged with resentment, but he agreed.

Another burst of cheering comes from the agora, even fainter now.

In the Middling quarter, the streets are empty, the houses' shutters closed, though one shutter creaks open, revealing a child in the window, his head just above the sill. His eyes widen when I meet his gaze. A hand from behind snatches his shoulder and drags him back into the room's darkness—to protect him, I suppose, from me. My people, free now, are roaming the street, dragging High Kith from their homes.

And what of the Middlings? Aden said.

I have not yet decided.

They carried out High-Kith orders. The Middlings are just as guilty. They must be punished, too.

I lightly touched his cheek and let my power shudder into his skin, giving him a memory as fresh as though it were present, not past. I made him remember when I rejected him, and said I would never marry him. He flinched away. Do not make me repeat myself, I said.

Fatigue drifts up my body. I do not know when last I slept. I remember how Sid, when I first met her, and I huddled in the prison cell opposite hers, had fought sleep. She held it off as though it were no burden to do so, as though it were an entertaining game, and she enjoyed wakefulness. She claimed her people had trained to get by on little sleep. That could very well have been true, yet Sid was skilled at using the truth to hide the truth. Now I know that she stayed awake to protect me. She kept a watchful eye while I slept.

My breath is shallow, my ribs tight. I am not inexhaustible, it seems. The power I have used comes at a price, though I was able to affect greater numbers in the attacking army with my power than Aden could with his. Rinah tore down the wall with her magic, but she collapsed soon afterward, and is still sleeping. Aden looked terrible after the battle, his skin dull, eyes stamped with dark circles, and it is possible he didn't resist my orders because he lacked the energy to do so. I am not exhausted, yet my feet feel as though they are made of stone, and I lug them up the hill toward the High quarter, toward the house I shared with Sid.

The keys rest in the pocket of my frayed and dirty dress, which I have worn since the night Sid left me. The silk is the color of the sky just before it deepens to true night. The keys tap against my thigh, light as Sid's fingers.

The High quarter screams. Terrified cries ring out into the streets as my soldiers haul High-Kith lords and ladies from their homes. It is as if the buildings themselves are shrieking. I survey the scene with pride, catching the eyes of my loyal people, their expressions aglow. The god of vengeance must smile down upon us, to see what I see.

Flames blaze against the horizon. Half Kith have set a palatial home on fire, and while I make a note to forbid this sort of thing—it is a waste of resources, of luxuries we now claim as ours—I decide to allow my people's entertainment for now. They had nothing for so long. What could be wrong with a little fun for them, this one night? Their loyalty to me will only grow with it, for it was I who gave them this pleasure.

And yet—a feeling like panic pinches my lungs—Sid's house must not be touched. I hasten to it, worried about both the house and my need to preserve it, but I decide the need is because the house belongs to me, not to Sid, at least not any longer. I beckon one of the Half-Kith men I recognize from the Ward and order him to spread the word that the narrow house on the steep hill with the view of the sea, which Sid chose because she cared more for the extravagance of the view than the extravagance of the accommodations, is to be spared. "There is no one there," I tell him. "Not anymore."

And yet there is. When I enter the home, I smell her perfume. It lingers, smoky and sweet, in her favorite chair. Sid's ghost walks beside me, her hand staying my course, light on my hip, sliding up my ribs. She presses me down into the chair, the brocade unusually dark, as black as her eyes, the wood slippery and scented with orange oil. She presses her mouth against my neck, and my head tips back.

Do you miss me? she asks.

You know I do.

Show me how you miss me.

I sit up straight in the chair, shaking away my vision of her. The chaos in the streets echoes through the windows. I light a lantern, and the oily flame gives a wavering dimension to the room. On the table beside the chair rests a glass with a remainder of green liquor at its bottom—what she was drinking when the monstrous-looking man, the one with no nose and no ears, came, and she chose her old life over the one she was making with me.

I no longer pretend she is there, but I cannot will away the perfect memory of her, and although I feel a blankness when I think of love, a feeling as thin and empty as a glass bubble in my chest, I resent her for leaving.

And I still want her. I want the feel of her mouth on me.

What is this? How can she affect me still?

It is your memory, Other Nirrim whispers. Your memory of her haunts you. Your memory of *me* haunts you.

I bat away her voice as though it is a fly. I am tired. That is all. I ignore the twinge of worry that maybe my mind is shivering into pieces.

Nirrim, Other Nirrim says.

Go away.

I cannot go away. I am you.

You are who I used to be.

Tell me, Other Nirrim says, what will you do with the Middlings? Outside, the sound of shattering glass cracks the night. What will you do with the High-Kith children?

THE GOD

---◆---

ONCE THERE WAS A GOD who wearied of the pantheon. One hundred gods. That was all, for eternity? Little wonder we connived against one another, fell in and out of love, and nursed resentments that could last a human century or more. Yes, there were gods who somehow did not fall prey to inevitable boredom, who cherished certain fellow gods. The Seamstress and Death remained true to each other, and rose above the pettiness of others. This only intensified the restlessness of the rest of the pantheon. We are gods, they said. We are eternal. It is tiresome. We crave newness. An escape from ourselves.

When we walked in Herrath, our island of jungle and pink sand, with its stone city of Ethin reared by mortals in our honor, what we sought was easy to find. Mortals touched us with their dragonfly lives, with their courage in the face of inevitable death. By living alongside us they changed us. They gave us children. They surprised us with their own gifts. Their rage, their hope.

But you know as well as I that it did not last. Our demigod children, with the aid of the god of thieves, murdered Thievery's brother Discovery. The pantheon erupted in fear and fury. One of the hundred was dead. An immortal could die. The rest of us—save the spurned god of thieves—fled to our realm. We pulled our opaque cloak of divinity around us. Mortals forgot us, almost, and we were left with one another.

What was there to do but quarrel? I taunted another god. Had it been any other god, I might have emerged unscathed, but this was the red-haired god of games, as bright as the edge of a knife. You seem very sure of yourself, she said. Would you care to make a wager?

Though reckless, I am no fool. I knew that she had tempted me to taunt her, so that she could offer her challenge and make it seem as though I alone had provoked it. It is her nature not only to game, but also to make a game of games. Mortal, never play against a god, let alone *this* god. Yet she had pricked my honor, and I was bored. What are the stakes? I demanded.

She ignored my question. She said, You have been talking with the god of foresight.

No, I lied.

Yes. You have been meddling in human affairs. You have been watching the lands beyond Herrath, and the great war that consumes them. You have a mortal favorite: Arin of the Herrani.

I denied it. Death loves him, I said. One did not stray into Death's territory—at least, no one wise.

Wisdom, however, has never been my strength.

Lucky mortal—the red-haired god smiled—to have been blessed with the love of not one, but *two* gods. Arin seeks his revenge, and he will face General Trajan in the field.

So the god of foresight had told me, but I kept silent about that.

The god of games continued, One of them will fall. Trajan, how-ever, will escape Arin's sword. Trajan will live.

That is not true.

Who are you to tell me about truth? Wager me, and we shall see. I wager you: Arin of the Herrani shall not have his revenge.

She set the stakes: the winner would seize the power of the loser, who would be cast down from heaven and into whichever form the winner chose. You will not be free, the god of games warned me, until a human pities you.

She won our wager, of course. She always wins. When Arin met Trajan in battle, one of them *did* fall: Trajan, his army vanquished, his hopes and honor ruined. Yet he did not die. Arin stopped his sword from delivering a death blow, and the god of games laughed.

You might think I was lucky she did not turn me into a dirty goat, or a toad, but the god of games is clever. Instead, after she stole my power (I am *borrowing* it, she said. Do not sulk! You may have it back when you have earned it), she changed me into something beautiful: a rose.

What human would pity a rose? Better that I had become a goat.

I grew in mortal soil. My thorny stem thrust up from the earth. My flower was a tight, hard bud. Even before I bloomed, I despaired. I knew humans. Flowers, to them, were a simple pleasure. A flower could not feel or think. Cut the stem and take it home. Place it in water. Enjoy its scent and color. What was there to pity?

It always amazed the pantheon, to see what might inspire a human's compassion. Who would have thought that Arin, having lost everything at the hands of General Trajan, would find compassion enough to spare the man's life? Kestrel of Valoria, the general's daughter, had made Arin swear not to spare her father in battle, yet when the moment came, Arin could not murder the man. Compassion demanded he stop his sword. How could he kill the father of the woman he loved? She would never cease to grieve, no matter what she had made him promise. Her grief would grieve him.

Nirrim, Queen of Herrath, wondered what the god of thieves had truly taken from her. Regret, maybe, she thought. Or love.

But it was not regret. It was not love. It was what makes love and regret possible.

Then what?

Nirrim could have wondered about the truth of what she had lost for every moment of her little life, but she could not have named it, for it was compassion, and it remains the fate of all humans who lack compassion never to understand that they lack it.

SID

---◆---

I LOAD THE GUN, STUFFING the wad of blackpowder and the bullet down the short barrel; curl my blackened fingers around the grip; and take aim. The grip fits snugly in my hand. My father made it for me, just as he made my dagger. The barrel doesn't waver. I pride myself on a steady aim, and when I miss it's usually because I'm bored of impressing people on the sidelines. No one's watching now, but I feel jumpy anyway, remembering my mother's words. The painted tin target, set on the lawn near the tall white bones of birches, is fifty paces off—challenge enough, since that distance is where the gun begins to lose accuracy. I cock the firing mechanism.

"You'll be late for dinner," someone drawls in my ear.

The gun cracks, a plume of smoke rises in the air, and my shot goes wide. "Gods, Roshar! I could have killed you! I am *going* to kill you."

"You love me." Roshar takes the hot gun from my hand, turning it over in his, making an impressed grimace as he inspects the ivory handle.

"Is this one of your father's newer versions? You know, I gave him the idea for the gun, years ago, when he was but a poor, lost Herrani in my nation's capital."

"You did not."

"Well, not *directly*." As if confessing a secret, Roshar adds, in a lowered voice, "It was the mere presence of my genius that gave him the idea. I'm like one of your Herrani gods. I blessed him with divine inspiration." He peers inside the flashpan. "I really like this new, small, handheld model. I think I'll keep it."

I take the gun from him and slide it into the holster at my right hip. It is my nicest holster, made from embossed black leather, and it shows boldly against my tan breeches and white tunic with its high, masculine collar and intricate black embroidery. Given that the state dinner is in my honor and I will be greatly stared at, I feel obliged to give the attendees a good show. I always draw the eye, not just for my good looks but also for what I do with them: my men's clothes and boy-short hair and dramatic flair. I have decided to play to expectations tonight. No one, save my father, knows that I worked as my mother's spy, or that I am useful for anything beyond spending my country's gold and bedding its women. Let everyone believe I am the good-for-nothing princess. It is close enough to the truth, and if that makes the court let down their guard around me, it will be all the easier to investigate my mother's claims. "Get your own gun," I tell Roshar.

"No one takes me seriously," he complains. "I miss Arin the tiger. I shouldn't have left him in Dacra. Everyone takes me more seriously when he's around."

I examine my black-dusted hands, wondering whether to clean them before dinner. I like the disreputable look they no doubt give me, which would play well to the image I want to cultivate tonight, but my father won't like it. He used to dream of being clean. A bar of soap was a miracle. He is too proud to remind me of this, but he *would* mention that my showing up dirty makes our guests think I don't respect them.

Well, I *don't*.

Pretend you do, my mother would reply.

"Your father wants a report on your time in Ethin," Roshar says. "Before dinner. If you are quite finished with target practice. Not a single hole in the target, I see. That shot of yours was quite bad, little god-child."

I ignore him, snapping the strap of the holster in place. It feels good to have my gun back. I like having my gun on one hip and my dagger on the other, my Herrani and Valorian birthrights in plain sight. I didn't wear the gun in Ethin. Once I realized the island had no knowledge of this kind of weapon—indeed, no knowledge of blackpowder at all, and no cannons—I kept the gun hidden. No need to let a foreign nation know about a military advantage. Keep your strengths and weaknesses hidden, and reveal them only to your gain. "Etta sent you to find me?"

"I came purely for the delight of your presence."

I remember staring down at my mother's pale face. Poisoned? I said. Who would poison you?

That—she smiled—is a foolish question.

Oh, right. I forgot how many people hate you.

She looked up at me as though *she* were *my* child. In a small voice, she said, Is it so many?

I felt cruel. Well, I said evenly, as though the problem at hand were some boring mathematical equation we would solve together, it only takes one disgruntled person.

Yes, she said, her voice stronger. Exactly.

I know when your mother tells you she has been poisoned, it isn't very daughterly to feel good—but I did, because I always liked working on a problem together, instead of *being* her problem, and when my mother respects you and takes you into her confidence, it is no small thing.

How do you know you've been poisoned? I asked.

I don't, my mother said. I suspect it. Her lids half lowered. In that light, her brown eyes looked golden. Tired. She was at the end of her strength. Quietly, she said, Do you believe me?

When are you ever wrong?

All the time.

You?

I need to correct my mistake, she murmured, and this was like her: to be cupped in Death's palm yet still hunt for something she had missed, to examine a puzzle for a better way to solve it. The gods alone knew what mistake she meant. It could be anything. There was always something she needed to perfect. Amma, I said suddenly, desperately, as though ready to beg, I will help you.

I know, she said, and was asleep.

Hope stirred within me. I brushed a lock of loose hair from her face, careful not to touch her skin. Maybe, if I could find who did this, I could also find a way to save her.

"To tell the truth," Roshar says, still staring at the blank target, "I thought there might be something you'd want to tell me that, for personal reasons, you do not wish to tell your father."

He has my full attention now. "Like what?"

"Oh, something to do with that girl, maybe."

"I have nothing to say about Nirrim." She did not love me. I was good enough for a time. It didn't matter, in the end, how I kissed her. It didn't matter how her body arched at my touch. It didn't matter that she was tender. What mattered was her honesty when she admitted that she didn't feel what I felt.

Do you not love me like I love you? I asked. Won't you come with me?

No.

"Are you home for good?" Roshar asks carefully.

"Yes."

"Then shall we?" He nods in the direction of the house. As I walk beside my godfather, I sneak a glance at him. He is not very tall for a man, and I am tall for a woman, so we are of a height. I see clearly the tension along his jaw—the way he avoids my gaze, yet feels it. My father's truest friend. My mother loves him, too. Yet Roshar is no Herrani, and we have always known that his political loyalties are due first to his queen, not my country.

People don't like to imagine the worst possibility, my mother often warns. And so they are caught unprepared when the worst comes.

Roshar quickens his pace. The smell of grass is raw and strong.

Could it be you? I wonder as he strides just ahead of me, as though to escape my glance, which I know has turned into an examination.

Did you pour poison into my mother's cup?

My father smiles when I enter the library and touches my cheek—a light, fond double tap, as though he is settling something into place, and that thing is his idea of me. I bristle, though I know he means to be kind, and say, "What is so amusing?"

"Not amusing. I'm happy you're home."

I cannot say, I heard your silence in my mother's suite. I have Sid, you said. No, she answered, You don't. I cannot say, Why didn't you defend me? I cannot say, I spied on you in your moment of fear, when you exposed what every single person in Herran, down to the smallest child, already knows, knows as intimately as they know the signs of a coming green storm: how utterly lost you would be if anything happened to your wife.

I say, "You find *something* funny."

"People say you look like Kestrel, but no one looks like you. You would stand out anywhere."

I look down at my freshly cleaned hands. "This is about how I am dressed."

"It is more than that. But yes, a little."

"Why must what I wear be such a favored topic of conversation?"

He considers this, rubbing the scar on his face. The open window lets in a warm breeze that lifts the edge of the curtain and lets it fall. Gently, he asks, "Do you not mean it to be?"

I fling myself down into an elegant reading chair, slinging my trousered legs over one arm and lounging against the other. "Yes, sometimes I want to be noticed. It also annoys me, how everyone finds my appearance so interesting. I can't explain it. You want to have a state dinner to show everyone that your heir has returned and Herran is safe, the hereditary line unbroken. So here I am, your prize pony." I hear my voice shrink. "I want to look good. But not your way. Mine."

"Sid, you do."

I look up at him. He does not tell me to sit up straight or remember my manners. He does not remind me of my duty as a princess. I say, the resentment clear in my voice, "You found me funny."

He takes the chair across from me. He is too large for it, like a wolf in a birdbath. "If I found anything funny it was how we are different."

A cold stone sits in my throat. I wish I had his height, his strength, the way he commands respect without uttering a word.

"What I mean is," he says, "in a crowd, I would rather be invisible."

"You are saying I'm a show-off."

"Can we not have every word between us go wrong? I am saying that I like how you're dressed, and if you enjoy holding the center of attention, that is no bad thing."

"Right. Important for a princess and future queen."

"Sid, why did you leave Herran?"

"I was bored."

"That is not the real reason."

"The parties here are always attended by the same people and I've slept with all the interesting ones. I require more variety in my entertainment."

Nirrim calls this sort of thing a midnight lie: where I tell a truth that functions like a lie because I've said it in order to disguise a greater truth I don't want known. The thought of Nirrim makes me wince. My father notices. He says, "If you sought pleasure, that doesn't seem to be what you found."

"You underestimate my ability to take pleasure in almost any circumstance, save this conversation."

"Please," he says, "answer a direct question. Don't make a game of it."

I shrug. "The god of games loves me."

"You stole one of my ships."

"Borrowed."

"Sailed in the middle of the night."

"The tide was right."

"Left no note or word."

"My actions spoke for themselves."

"Why can't you trust me? Why can't you tell me what's wrong?"

I shouldn't have to. It should be obvious. No one has forgotten I am engaged to Prince Ishar, son of Queen Inishanaway, ruler of Dacra from its northern grasslands to its watery capital to its islands sprinkled in the sea. If my father cannot guess that I don't want to marry any man, it is because he does not want to. My mother, who knows full well my refusal, since I screamed it at her the night I left, probably has said nothing of it to him. He would have mentioned it by now if she had. But he should *know*, and the fact that he does not proves that he does not know me.

The window brims with dark green lawn. An irrielle bird sings, ending with a percussive chirping as dry as the sound of snapping fingers. My father's gray eyes search mine, worried, and I fill with anger, my pulse sharp in my throat. Yet I know how this feeling will end, because I have felt this way before, and the outcome is always the same. I will not show my anger because I am afraid of wounding him with it—especially now, when the person he loves most lies sick and he prays daily to his god, saying, I have served you. I am yours. Show mercy, and take me instead.

Do I know he does this for a fact? No. Yet he is Arin the Plain King. Death's Child. My father. It is easy enough to imagine.

I want my father to imagine *me*.

My anger dissolves into sadness. I run a hand along the chair's old brocade silk, which shines in places, lies flatly dull in others. My hand is not my mother's hand, with her narrow fingers, strong yet soft. My hand resembles my father's—rough from the sea and marked with scars, though mine are not from battle, merely training for it. Herran has been at peace the whole of my life.

My father's eyes grow stern. Their gray is a typical Herrani color, but sometimes they look uncommon, even unnerving. He says, "I want an answer."

"Maybe—" My voice cracks and sounds too high, truly like a girl's. I clear my throat. "Maybe I wanted to make a name for myself. Arin and Kestrel, Kestrel and Arin. Everyone knows your story. What about mine?"

"Our story," he says slowly, "is about how we suffered."

"And found each other."

"It is about how we never want what happened to us to happen to anyone else."

"Yes, your love for the Herrani is well-known."

"It is *you* of whom we think first."

"Sometimes it is cold in your shadow." I see him accept this, and his easy acceptance wrenches at my gut. My midnight lie has been too quickly swallowed. What I have said is true, and embarrassing, but I have offered up this woebegone tale of seeking fame and glory because it is believable. It keeps the rest of my reasons private. I continue, doggedly, "Do you remember how Amma suspected the southern isles of planning an attack on Valoria?" The southern isles—or the Cayn Saratu, as they are called in the tongue of their people—were once part of the vast Valorian empire, but were liberated when Verex, my mother's old friend, was elected Magister in the days following the last war. As head of the Valorian senate, Verex ended rule over its stolen territories. This did not, however, make everyone happy. The southern isles are a well-known hotbed of Valorian malcontents who seek to restore the Empire's former glory. They have plotted blackpowder attacks on the Valorian capital and its Magister, many of which my mother uncovered and foiled. "She asked me to examine all the known maps of the islands. She sent me hither and thither even to dilapidated country manors, to search their libraries. Every crumbling scrap of a map wasn't enough. Valorians possess better maps, she said, then packed me off to Valoria."

"This was last spring," he said, recalling. "You went as our emissary for the introduction of Verex and Risha's new baby to society. *Six* children, all healthy, thank the god of life."

"The god of lust had more to do with it." This makes him uncomfortable. I cannot resist needling him. "Nothing wrong with that. I am the god of games's own child, but I light a candle in lust's temple, too. It is because I am so pious." I get cozier in the chair, wagging my polished boots.

He coughs. "So you went to Valoria."

I roll my eyes at his discomfort. "I went to Valoria. Amma was right. They have better map collections."

"Yes. It helped them win the first war."

"And on one map—ancient, so delicate I had to glue a layer of transparent tishin paper to its back in order to handle it—I found a speck that shouldn't have been there, that was on no map I had seen, a lost dot near the southern Herrani coast, amid the empty islands. Amma thought maybe the imperialist plotters were hiding blackpowder on this secret island, but when I sailed to the Cayn Saratu, practically no one had heard of the island. They said that region of the sea was known for shipwrecks. They warned me away. I believed they were lying, of course, and that Amma was right. Rumors of dangerous seas would be a good way to keep nosy spies like me away from secret stashes of blackpowder." The Caynish had no guns or cannons or easy access to blackpowder, but Valorian imperialists imported it from the northern tundra and hid it in caves on uninhabited islands, or buried it in strongboxes in sandy beaches. "But the Caynish warned me of more than shipwrecks: local legend had it that travelers had come from that region of the sea, bearing magic trinkets."

"Magic?" he says slowly.

"They showed me a couple of artifacts—a bracelet, a tooth-shaped box—but they were inert. Nothing special, beyond their ancient appearance. But, people insisted, the items *used* to be able to work magic. The bracelet *used* to be able to charm the wearer into shrinking to the size of a cat. The box *used* to be able to bite an enemy."

"Sounds like a Caynish story."

"So I thought. But I returned to Herran to consult our naval history collection, and speak with our older sailors, who knew the sea before the first war. It was true enough that that region of the sea was known for shipwrecks. Ships went missing in those straits. I decided to sail there, and see what was what."

"You endangered yourself."

"Just a little."

"You could have died."

"Yet here I am, safe and sound, your favorite child."

"My *only* child."

"Mad at me, Etta?"

"The least you could have done was to tell us this, and warned us where you were going, if you needed a vainglorious adventure," he says, frustrated. "You are irresponsible, reckless—"

"Don't you want to hear the best part?"

"I worry we sheltered you too much. You are afraid of nothing."

"The magic is real."

"Everything is a joke to you."

"I mean it. I swear by the gods. What I saw on the island of Herrath has no logical explanation. I saw magic. I tasted it." I remember the drop of blood, dark as a pomegranate seed, falling from the tip of Nirrim's finger into my mouth. Later, Nirrim described what she had seen happen to me. Her magic immobilized me. My body lay rigid, my mind driven deep into a memory I hadn't even known I'd forgotten.

My father's silence grows heavy, wary, and while I know from my aunt Sarsine that the king has a temper, he has never shown it to me, not directly. Instead, he gets like this: warlike, his gaze acute, his expression showing that he does not know his enemy's moves but he does not like what he suspects. Instead of looking angry he simply looks *ready*. "Etta, I am not lying. I am playing no game. Not this time, at any rate. I doubted the rumors, too, when I anchored in the harbor of the island's city. The Caynish were not wrong: it *was* a tricky bit of sailing. The currents are nasty, the rocks sharp. Pretty place, though. Along the coast, I saw pink-sand beaches and fields of sugarcane, much like what the Caynish grow. The climate is hot enough to make clothes stick to your skin, the coastal waters a sheer teal. Lush vegetation, vines with purple flowers climbing over everything. And while I might have dashed the ship against the rocks several times, and split the belly of my hull along this kind of extremely hard, lavender coral that gave shallower waters a purplish tinge, I don't think it was shipwrecks, really, that made sailors disappear in that region. Once I anchored in the island's only city, and mingled with the people there, I realized an odd forgetfulness clung to everybody. The people *seemed* normal, and although the island's climate and terrain share more in common with the Cayn Saratu, its people look like us." I correct myself. "Like *you*. Like regular Herrani. Same skin, similar features. Your gray eyes. They are all light-eyed, with a little more range than we commonly see in Herran. More green." I swallow, thinking of Nirrim's earnest, jade-eyed gaze, then hurriedly add, "Even blue. They call themselves Herrath, and their language resembles ours so much that I picked it up even more quickly than I usually do a new tongue. I suppose because it felt familiar, not like a new language but like a faded memory of my own." Most people would stare at me right about now, confused, but my father nods. My parents have a gift for languages—my mother especially, her speech flawlessly free of any accent. People do not often consider that my father's thick accent in Valorian comes from how much he hates using that tongue. "The Herrath language's habits, the grammatical turns . . . it all felt like that godsawful ancient Herrani poetry you have made me read. The city welcomed me. They were fascinated. I'm quite easy to adore, especially when I make clear that my family is wealthy nobility—don't worry, Etta, I didn't make it *that* clear. I told no one—ah, almost no one—that I was your child. But the people liked me; they liked my gold. They invited me to endless parties with beautiful people in sparkling attire, who ate dust that made the world seem joyful."

"I am surprised you ever returned," my father says dryly.

"The longer I stayed, the more eerie everything seemed. No one had any knowledge of the country's history. If I said, *Why* do you have a Lord Protector who rules over the city and country? they looked at me blankly." I describe how the people I encountered in those first few weeks thought I was an appealing novelty, a rich, fair-haired traveler from afar, which suggested that travelers had arrived on that island before. Yet no one could tell me when, and there was no evidence of any immigrant population. "*Any* question about the past made a Herrath sleepy-eyed. It is as it is, they would answer, which makes me suspect that it was not that sailors in those waters *all* went down in wrecks but that the cobwebby forgetfulness that clung to Herrath began to cling to them, too, and they never returned home. Or maybe the Herrath vaguely knew that travelers existed but they had come so long ago, maybe generations ago, that the memory of them was lost in a murky past. In that country, there was no such thing as a history book. The *concept* of history seemed foreign to them. Things felt strange—even the constant pleasure-seeking of the people I first met there struck me as odd. How did the wealthy fund their parties, pay for their elaborate clothes? Then I explored the city further, and saw the wall." I explain the strata of Herrath society, how it was ordered into three strict classes—High Kith, Middling, and Half Kith, the word *kith* meaning something like "kind" or "sort." The Half Kith were imprisoned behind a wall, their labor exploited by the noble class. The whole of society depended on making the Half Kith as drab as possible, as though forcing them to live in the very center of town, behind an enormous wall they could never pass, eating food without salt or spice, dressing in grays and browns every day, would make them forget they were human. The Middling class served the interests of the High Kith, acting as their servants and militia, helping to suppress the lowest class, who would pay with their lives if they ever tried to go beyond their wall—or would pay with blood, drained in vials, or hair sewn into wigs for High-Kith ladies, or organs for surgeries to improve the health of High Kith. The Half Kith, depending on the crime, could even find themselves Un-Kith: cast out of the city and forced to work in the sugar fields.

My father's tight, jaw-hardened expression has nothing to do with me anymore. I say, "It was a . . . quieter kind of exploitation than the imperial conquest of Herran. It was not like what happened to you."

"You can never really understand what happened to me."

I will always sit outside my parents' experience of the two Valorian-Herrani wars. "I am no judge of it. How can I be, when you are so loath to discuss it?"

Softly, he says, "I do not want you to understand it."

"I am not complaining."

"Sid, you are."

"I like my soft life."

"It was an ugly time. I have no words for it."

"Good thing, then, that you have Amma, who understands you perfectly, with no words at all."

The line of his mouth erodes, his expression going inward with sudden sorrow, and I feel like a sullen ass. Then a sharp sorrow of my own slits its edge along my belly. I remember my mother's frail face, her gray cheeks, her blue-tinged fingers. My mother's illness feels impossible. In my mind, she is immortal. "Etta," I say, wanting to push past this horrible moment I have created, "the Herrath share our gods."

He leans back in his chair. Surprise wipes his face clean. "They believe in the hundred?"

"Believe? Not quite. But they know the full pantheon. Sometimes their gods are called by other names—our god of souls is their god of love. The Herrath are not religious, though. To them, the gods are a quaint tale for children." He takes a breath, as though to speak, but in the end says nothing, studying my face. He knows I am not a believer. I do my duty to the gods because he would harass me otherwise, with his gentle yet insistent disapproval, and because it makes me feel more Herrani, despite my looks. "Etta, I did not imagine that my report would be *quite* this uninspiring. I encountered a people who share our gods. And can work *magic*. I did good work as Herran's spy. Amma—"

"Don't trouble your mother with this. Let her rest."

"How can you act as if I just described how the Herrath sift their flour and sweep their streets? Is it not useful to us, that we know of a land where magic exists?"

He cups his hands and spreads them wide, as though scattering seeds, or letting fall a thousand useless, invisible things. It is the Herrani gesture of skepticism.

I say, "How can you doubt me?"

"Sweet child, you are not known for your honesty." When I protest, he says, "It is not that you are a liar, only that you are devious with your words and sometimes you prize your own amusement above all else and can say things you do not mean, for the fun of it."

Fair enough. But I press on. "At first I didn't believe it, either. I thought it was science, or sleight of hand. Then I met someone, a Half Kith. She had an eerily perfect memory." I envision how Nirrim glanced at a letter in my hand, in my language, even though she could not understand it, and then recited my letter to me by heart, her accent heavy, the mispronunciations many, but each word correct, a sharp nail that drove into me. I had never meant for her to read the letter. *Nirrim, I must leave you. It is too hard to want you, and know that you do not see me.*

My father makes a noncommittal noise. "Some are born with such a gift. They can recite a poem they glanced at once, years ago. This is not magic."

"She made me remember something I had forgotten. Her blood did it to me."

"Her blood."

"I drank it."

His eyes widen.

"Just a drop," I say.

"Describe this woman."

She was Half Kith, I explain. An orphan who worked against the rules of her society to provide her people with forged passports that lied about their kith, gave them a chance to escape. "She reminded me of you, Etta." I describe her serious manner, her goodness, how starved she was for love, so much so that she could not, at first, question her devotion to Raven, the woman who raised her—and used her. How resilient Nirrim was, and brave, to risk punishment—even death—for her actions, with no expectation of reward.

My father's expression becomes knowing. "I see. One of your conquests, was she?"

"No."

"I can tell that you liked her."

Heat rises in my cheeks.

"Sid, it is always the same with you. Such feelings are precious, yet you treat women as though they are interchangeable, and one will do as easily as the other."

"That is not true. Not with her."

"As soon as a new one catches your eye, she is all you can think about, until you get what you want."

He is not wrong, usually, but . . . "I am good to them." How many of them said so, their lips parted beneath mine?

"You break their hearts."

Would Etta chastise me if I were a man? Resentfully, I say, "I will do what I will."

His expression closes. "I am not interested in your seductions, or this story of magic. I wish you would stop playing with people, Sidarine. You certainly will not play with *me*. You will describe the country you saw, their military assets, their customs and trade, and then we will attend the state dinner, where you will stand in your mother's place and greet our guests."

When I was little, he would sing a lullaby to me every night before bed. How did I get so far away from that moment, when I was cherished? How is it that right now, all I can see before me is the intimidating man who drove his sword into the chests of countless Valorians, who even once threw them off a cliff? Who orchestrated the poisoning of an entire gathering of Valorian lords and ladies, dancing and sipping iced apple wine until the first one began to choke?

My thoughts, hurtling ahead of me, stop hard.

Earlier, I had contemplated Roshar, wondering whether he could have poisoned my mother. Aloofly, even smugly, I told myself it was important to consider the worst, even if it meant thinking my beloved godfather had poisoned my mother. But that was not the very worst possibility.

It cannot be my father. I refuse to believe it. If it is true that my father harmed my mother, then my life is a lie, the world I understand does not exist, I know nothing, and I am no one.

THE GOD

---◆---

WHEN I WAS A ROSE, blooming on a bush outside the city walls of Ethin, the rain fell on my soft, silent head. The sun forced me open. An ice wind came and went, chilling me, casting a thin glaze of ice over my petals and down my stem, so that I looked made of glass. I did not die and I did not fade, for I remained a god, no matter my form. When the sun came again, the ice melted and dripped away. I bloomed again.

Mute, I watched the human world. The hummingbird that delved inside me. The velvet nights. The snake that hid from the sun in the cool of my thorny branches, my serrated leaves. My presence in Ethin violated the promise the pantheon made, each to the other, never to return to the mortal realm. Yet one does not wager with the god of games and neglect to pay her due.

As I watched the sugarcane grow in the distance, and yearned for a human, any human, to take the path that led to me, I watched the rest of the world, too.

In Herran, Kestrel lay on her back in the grass, head pillowed on Arin's lap as he sat, the scent of summery earth carried by the breeze. Two horses wandered nearby in the meadow with its haze of blue and violet wildflowers. Arin, looking down at his wife, traced the curve of Kestrel's cheek with a speckled yellow feather.

Are you asleep? he asked.

Yes, she answered.

Do you think you might ever tell a simple truth when asked a simple question?

She opened her golden eyes and smiled. I love you, she said. Is that a simple truth?

It will do.

I had a dream like this once, she said. Long ago, when I was in the Valorian capital, and you were far from me, and I missed you. Am I dreaming? If I am, I don't want to wake up.

Don't wake up.

Kestrel closed her eyes again. He felt her grow heavier. As she slipped into sleep, he counted her freckles. Ninety-eight. They would fade, come autumn. He was beginning to feel hazy with the heat, with the soft pleasure of her head in his lap, when she startled awake.

Bad dream? he said.

She shook her head, her braids rustling against his trousers. She reached for his hand and placed it flat against her belly. I felt something, she said. I felt something move inside me.

He didn't dare hope. Her face was alive with wonder.

It felt like a tadpole, she said.

Still he could not speak.

Arin, I think I felt a baby.

He saw her brush away a drop of water that had fallen like rain onto her cheek. She sat up and kissed his wet eyes, kissed the scar that sliced down from his brow into his left cheek.

Are you happy? Kestrel asked.

Yes. He held her to him. The yellow feather fell to the grass.

Yes.

NIRRIM

I WAKE UP SANDY-EYED, a fresh breeze silky on my skin. It tastes like salt. Before sleep, I left the balcony doors open so the sea air could come in, just as Sid liked it. The memory of her stretches out next to me in bed and finds me. She is a slow riser, the way people with soft lives are, but I never resented it in her, not when she would nuzzle her face against my back and wake up wanting me.

Enough.

I am starting to think that my gift might be a curse, the way my memory conjures ghosts to stalk and distract me. I must be careful. The quiet floating in from the windows in this house as I move through it, searching, tells me that the chaos and destruction of last night has died down. I need to renew it, yet focus it in my name, according to my goals, my rule. I will re-create Ethin. The purge of High Kith has already begun. The agora is wet with their blood. But the Middlings need to know they answer to me.

I open drawers and find little. The wardrobes hold clothes she could not be bothered to take. Shirts fitted perfectly. Jackets with neat, sharp lines. Floating dresses that have no reason to look so smug in their beauty. Sid never liked them.

Downstairs, I scan the slick tiles of the kitchen. I find a muslin sack filled with what seems like fragrant earth—the brown, granular substance that, mixed with boiled water, made the bitter eastern drink Sid liked so much. The brown grit pours like sugar, but more slowly, densely. I drag a finger through the sack's contents and lick it clean. The bitter taste shocks my tongue, but I like it. I can't help but like it. It tastes like her deep morning kiss. I close the bag and shove it back on its shelf hurriedly, as though it is dangerous.

In the sitting room, there are books, some open and facedown—Sid, like a true noble, had little reverence for valuable objects. A worn deck of Pantheon cards rests on a spindly table.

My Elysium bird chitters in the sitting room's corner, iridescent talons clinging to the back of a chair, and launches through the air to alight upon my shoulder. Annoyed, I brush it off. It squawks, fixes me with a green, reproachful eye, and flits back to its chair, watching me with a cagey, almost feline look as I continue my search.

I do not need things the way a human does, as vessels for lost moments, yet greed courses through me. I don't even know what I want until I find it: a vial of her perfume. It smells of citrus and wood roasted to the point of crumbling into the fire. I inhale it. I can practically taste it. I bring the scent of her inside me and make it mine. Then I stopper the vial and go out into the city, so that I can make the city mine, too.

The old paved stones of the agora are slippery in places, sticky in others. My sandals stain red. The executions have not stopped. A crowd still fills the agora, the morning light delicate on their sleepless, entranced faces. As smoke from last night's fires lingers in the air, Aden's friends, who have no magic of their own and so must be good for something, bring the next High Kith to the gory chopping block. She is a woman my age. She wails, bare heels scrubbing the marble pavement as she resists being brought forward by two men who clamp a grip on her arms and drag her when she sags, silk dress ripping along a seam, hem drinking the spilled blood. Headless bodies lie stacked around the broad, flat wooden block. Aden, who glances up and sees me, says something to his friends that I am too far away to hear, and they pause, too, which must give the woman some hope. She follows their gaze to me. As I approach, I hear the begging tone of her voice long before the words become clear. "Please," she says when I am close. She must intuit that these men will do what I demand. "I have done nothing to deserve this."

Did she not live her life at the expense of mine? Did she not drink elixirs made from my people's blood, and delight in the magic it gave her? She knew hundreds of Half Kith were locked behind the wall, where artisans made goods for which they were paid the smallest of coins. Those mirrors, those beautifully carved cedar boxes that smelled like the trees they came from, once decorated her home. A tortoiseshell earring dangles like congealed honey from one ear.

She pleads again. The crowd watches me.

No, says my old self. You can't do this.

But Other Nirrim was always too kind. She should understand that the god of thieves did her a service by stealing her heart. I must show her that. I want to pass the crowd's test, to impress them and make them loyal to me, but most of all I want to let myself feel how good it is not to forgive. Other Nirrim always explained away the harm that people caused. I will never make that mistake.

A watchful quiet grows over the crowd like a sheet of ice. The woman's cries echo against the stone walls of the buildings that surround the agora. The Half Kith watch me. They know what I am, but not what I am capable of. What will be the limits of what I will do for them? they wonder. If I am to be their leader, what work will I do on their behalf?

I motion for the men to press the woman's neck against the wooden block. They hold her down. A rusty stain has made the rings in the wood sharply clear. The tree rings circle the woman's flattened face. The ax handle is slippery. Her eyes squeeze shut.

It takes me a few tries for the ax blade to bite deep enough, but my arm is strong from a life of hard work, and eventually I cut through.

I am not sure how much time passes, but the sun has shifted in the sky, so bright it eats a hole into my vision, when the Elysium bird trills, swooping over the agora. I had shut the door of Sid's home behind me, locking it in. It must have gotten out through the open balcony doors. Pestering thing. But I enjoy its loyalty to me, and lift my bloody fist for a perch.

A leader must have icons. A queen cannot be everywhere at once. Symbols of power must take her place sometimes. We will make a new flag for Herrath, I decide, one that shows my bird in pink and red and green. The bird's talons bite into my knuckles and it hops discontentedly to my shoulder, clucking at me like a glamorous chicken. It did not like being left alone. It takes my earlobe gently in its beak, just above my starlike earring, and gives me a scolding nibble.

The sharpness shakes me out of a daze. The executions, taken over by others in the crowd, the ax handed from one to another, have grown monotonous, and then they end. The High-Kith tithe of ten percent of its people has been paid. I worry that the crowd might grow bored, but a murmur runs through it, and I notice that something different is happening.

The person brought wriggling to the block is not High Kith. He wears Middling clothes. He is the first Middling to be brought out for death. I lift a staying hand. "No." Other Nirrim agrees silently inside me, though our reasons are different. She would excuse everyone from a just punishment. I, on the other hand, have a vision based on strategy, not syrupy emotion. A queen, after all, must show mercy sometimes. The satisfaction of punishment can grow tedious, and everyone likes the thought that someone's sins might be forgiven, that a person could be born anew, their crimes forgotten. It makes for a good story. Stories, too, will help me rule. "The Middlings will be spared."

"They lorded over us!" someone shouts.

"They served the High Kith!"

"Yes," I say, "but they know what it was like to be forced to do the High Kith's bidding. We must open our hands to them. The old gods left this city long ago. We are the new gods, and must show our divinity. Let us offer the Middlings the chance to prove themselves, and join us."

The crowd does not like this. I wonder if my power is strong enough to push a false memory into everyone's mind, and make them do what I want. I was able to make the entire city remember its past, but it was a true memory, not a false one. It takes more of an effort to bend a memory out of shape and turn it into a lie. Anyway, I find that I do not want to force them to do what I will. I want them to choose what I want because *they* want it. They should admire me, and count themselves lucky that I rule. An idea occurs to me, one that I enjoy. "The Middlings shall live . . . all but one."

The dullness of the crowd, how easily they adapted to the repeated executions and even grew bored, sharpens with interest.

"You know who I mean," I say. "The one who lived among us. Who pretended to be our friend. Did you trust her, like I once trusted her?

She stole from you. She milked you like a goat. It is high time that you show her your teeth."

Someone calls her name. Then another person. It grows into a chant, and follows us as we abandon the agora, and the Middling man who wavers on his feet with relief.

Chanting fills the air.

Raven. Raven. Raven.

My people break through her freshly painted green door, tearing the splintered wood off its hinges. They wiggle loose stones from her sweet garden wall. They survey her Middling home, decorated with the finest touches a Middling was allowed—nice but not *too* elegant, not *too* luxurious. Raven, though, made sure to have the best she could. All the time I forged passports for Half Kith to appear Middling and escape beyond the wall, I risked my life believing that it was for something pure and good. Raven led me to believe she was helping people, that we gave our work freely to them.

She took their money, and enriched herself, and made me a fool. Rage flickers in my throat. It burns in my belly.

Half Kith funnel into the house as I wait outside. Muffled screams split the darkening sky.

Raven is dragged from the house. Her dress, made from good, dark green cloth with a grosgrain belt and touches of embroidery, tangles about her legs as she stumbles forward, her gray hair spilling wildly out of what was once an elegant hairstyle. I catch the glint of a familiar necklace around her neck, its pendant tucked beneath the bodice of her dress. Her eyes dart everywhere. Only when someone shoves her to her knees before me does she glance into my face. Shocked recognition flashes.

"Nirrim!" she says. "Darling girl! Help me, please. Everyone has gone mad!"

"Have they?" I say coolly. "Or have they finally come to their senses?"

"The entire Ward knows what I did for them. You and I, Nirrim. We *helped* them. Explain it."

"They already know exactly how you helped them."

Understanding wriggles across her expression. It looks just like fear. I see her realize that she must look guilty. I see her hide the guilt behind her fear, which she decides to perform for all she is worth. Her fingers tremble. I am impressed. I truly cannot tell, now, how much of her fear is real and how much is layered on, like icing on a cake. "Nirrim, they said—in my house, my very own home, which I have worked so hard to have, saved every bit of gold to make a nice home for you and me to share—they said that I must beg their queen for mercy."

"Correct."

"You—*you*—are their queen?" She gives a breathy, disbelieving laugh.

"All true." I nod at the people holding her. They release their grips. She gets to her feet, wobbles a little, then regains her balance, brushing at her skirts.

"Well, you *have* come up in the world." Her tone is approving, yet laced with something snide. More certain of herself, she settles calmly into her bones. "I always knew you would." She examines my torn, bloodied clothes. "Not quite the outfit *I* would wear, were I queen. Never worry, my lamb. I will help you choose all the right ensembles."

I feel the habit of listening to her. I remember excusing her cruelties. Every time she showed me affection again, I believed that the real Raven had returned. She had a temper, true, but she was a good person, one who gave me a home when I had none, and caressed my forehead when I worried. If I were her true daughter, wouldn't I forgive the sting of her slap? The unkind words?

Other Nirrim always forgave her. Other Nirrim always believed Raven's lies—worse, Other Nirrim believed her *own* lies.

Raven's gaze, traveling over my face, suddenly stops. "Those are *mine.*"

She means the earrings, shining like stars. "They are mine now."

She bites her lip in displeasure. The crowd notices. Someone hefts a garden wall stone, a threat that makes her school her expression into a smile. She touches the glinting silvery chain around her neck. "Of course, Nirrim, if you want them. After all, they were your mother's. A gift. Don't you want to know from whom? Let's go inside, into our home, darling, and I will tell you how I came by them."

"That is not my home."

"What a thing to say! We are family. My home is your home. I am your ama."

"You are not."

"I am as good as your mother. I am your mother's sister, after all, and I raised you."

"After you abandoned me in the orphanage, and let me grow up, ignorant of any knowledge of my parents, believing I was alone in the world."

"But then I took you in! Really, I don't think it's necessary to go over this personal history in front of so many unruly people. Come inside."

"You took me in, and then pretended I was nothing to you. For years, you kept it secret that I was kin to you."

"But then I *explained.* Honestly, Nirrim. I am sorry I didn't tell you earlier." Her lip quivers. "It was too painful. My beautiful sister died so young. Let's go inside. I will tell you all about her. She looked much like you."

Other Nirrim used to long for family. I have no use for it. My mother is dead. My father, whoever he was, vanished at my birth. One of my parents, perhaps both, was descended from a god. I am alone in the world. That is all I need to know.

"Nirrim, I don't think you understand how an angry crowd gets. I believe"—her voice drops to a whisper, her words just for me—"they mean to damage my home."

"It is not your home. It is theirs."

"I don't understand."

"It belongs to them."

"What nonsense. I bought it with my own money."

"That you took from them."

"For services rendered! No one forced people to buy our passports. Anyway, *those* people are long gone. They left Ethin. Who knows where they are now. This rabble has nothing to do with them, you, or me. Now be sensible."

I smile. My smile must be as bright as the blade of a knife, because she shrinks away. However, she does not believe, not yet, that she has lost her power over me.

Otherwise, she would run.

"My people," I call, "you have no reason to damage this house."

"That's right," Raven says, satisfied.

"Instead, consider what she *truly* took from the Half Kith. Your pride. How often did you set aside coins you could have used to clothe your children, in the hopes that one day you could have enough to pay Raven for a way out of the Ward? Remember," I say, and my magic enters my voice. The word delves down deep inside them. "Did you swallow your bitterness?" I call the name of the Ward's mirror maker. "Terrin, you gave her a handheld mirror once. Was it a heartfelt gift?"

The crowd stirs. The woman pushes through the crowd to make herself seen. "She asked for it," Terrin says, "and offered to pay, but I knew what that meant. If I didn't give it to her for free, I would never have a chance to buy the documents. She would make my life a misery by turning the Ward against me. People would listen to her, because if they didn't, she could do the same thing to them."

"Take your payment now," I say.

"Now, what is *that* supposed to mean?" Raven says. "What kind of foolishness is this? Pay for a gift?"

Terrin comes close. She eyes Raven.

"Go on," I say. Still, Terrin does nothing, so I reach for the thin chain around Raven's neck and yank. Raven cries out. The necklace snaps and comes free in my hand. The pendant—the crescent moon I remember my mother wearing when I was a baby at her breast—glows on my palm.

"Nirrim, how dare you!"

Then Terrin's hand strikes out and snatches the grosgrain belt from Raven's waist.

"Thief! Give that back!"

I curl the moon necklace into my fist. "Everyone," I call, "should receive fair pay."

Someone in the crowd reaches out and rips a fistful of hair from Raven's head. She screams. "Nirrim, stop them!"

A man holding a garden wall stone throws, and strikes Raven's shoulder.

"Please! They listen to you. Help me, you ungrateful girl!"

Hands dive in. They tear at her. More rocks thunk into the center of the circle the crowd has formed around her. I step away. My people swarm her. I cannot see her anymore, but I hear screams as I walk away.

She curses me. She begs.

She claims she loves me, but I now know better than that.

Later, in the calm, when the crowd has dispersed to sleep, I wander back to the High quarter. The night is cool, its blue translucent. Debris litters the street, but the chaos of last night has dissolved into peace.

Other Nirrim is quiet within me—horrified, maybe, at Raven's death. Spineless girl. Or maybe Other Nirrim doesn't want to challenge me, since I gave orders that all the High-Kith children will be spared from execution.

I am too noble to punish the innocent, I tell her. Even if she is silent, Other Nirrim is still *there*, waiting and judging. Let the guilty fear me, I add.

Other Nirrim says nothing.

I laugh, the sound ringing against the colored glass pavements, the wrought-iron balconies that look like piping on a cake. I tease Other Nirrim, my disdain mixed with patience: Be glad, I tell her. I could do so much worse.

There is a park in the High quarter Sid brought me to once. I follow the path to it, remembering how I slept in a tree that told my fortune. *You will lose her*, the fortune read. It had come true. Sid was gone, and would never return.

Yet I had always known I would lose her. Even as I loved her, as she kissed me, as she made me hers, I knew it was only for a time, a moment she would give me. She would leave. She told me she would, and she did. My liar had told at least one truth. I had not needed a tree to make me know it.

Lush grass tickles my ankles. The earth exhales the heat of the day into the night. A breeze carries the scent of green things.

I wonder what Sid is doing now. I wonder if she thinks of me sometimes.

My feet carry me to the tree. It has no magic of its own, I understand now: only what it borrowed from an elixir made by councilmen of some Half Kith's blood.

I must find the Council's supply, I decide. I must go through the library in the Keepers Hall and search for records of arrests and tithes. Who knows how old the elixir that watered the tree was. Perhaps the blood came from an imprisoned Half Kith long dead. Our power was stolen from us for generations.

Still, it is not the tree's fault. Pink glass lanterns light the park well enough for me to see how its branches spread wide above me, its leaves a dark, hissing blur. The trunk shows patches of gold, from where people tore strips of bark to read their fortunes, and gardeners painted the scars prettily to ward off infection. I lay a palm flat against the cool, rough trunk. The tree is like me, like any Half Kith. Yet I do not feel sorry for it. Why should I feel sorry for anything with power?

I remember what it was to feel pity. I try to feel it, to see if it is possible. I try, even, to feel pity for myself, for how I was used and left behind.

I feel nothing but the bark of the tree.

I wonder how long the tree will tell fortunes, now that no one will water it with my people's blood. I dig my nails into the papery bark. As I tear it away, I think of Sid. Tell me, I ask the tree, about her.

Even though the sky has deepened in color, and the light from the lanterns flickers, I still can read the spidery writing that appears on the bark's pale underside.

If you wish to rule alone, you must destroy her.

THE GOD

⬥

FINALLY, SOMEONE CAME DOWN THE path. I leaned toward the sound of footsteps the way a normal flower would toward the sun. How many human years had I been trapped inside this form? Time means little to the gods, but loneliness affects each member of the pantheon, and the god of games had deprived me of companionship, of speech, of being *seen* for what I truly was. Anyone would pity me, surely, if they knew my lot, but of course a rose cannot speak.

The young woman's black hair shone in the sun. She wore what the people of Ethin had come to call Middling clothes: a simple sleeveless dress, dyed green as many Middling dresses were, with light decorative touches—in this case, embroidered pockets and several hot-pressed pleats. I heard her sandals scuff the dirt path. She hummed, the sound mingling with the birdlike chirrup of frogs hidden in the jungle. Over her shoulder, the sea sparkled. She consulted a badly drawn map made by the hand of her High-Kith mistress. She was to meet with the Middling farmer who oversaw the mistress's cane fields and bring a report of the harvest to come. Thick greenery framed the path, and flowering vines threaded through the trees. Were this woman to step off the path and wander into the thick vegetation, she would find a strangely vacant plain, a blank space made as if cut from the trees and vines. No mortal hand had created this emptiness, this square where blue sky could be seen above instead of leafy canopies, climbing pink frogs, and the dart of slender birds with frilly crests upon their heads.

Fortunately for me, she did not stray from the path. I nodded in the light breeze, exhaling a lovely perfume. Roses do not normally grow in Ethin. I enticed her, and it was enough.

She stopped, tracing a finger over my petals. I shivered. Take me, I willed . . . though, of course, possession is not compassion. To be plucked by her was not to attain the pity I needed to be free.

She reached for me. Roses, however, were unknown to her, and as her fingers gripped my stem to break me, one of my thorns pricked her.

She cried out in surprise and pain, a drop of blood beading on her thumb.

SID

AFTER THE STATE DINNER, its many courses perfectly calibrated to show a delicious frugality—the dishes all Herrani, no imported delicacies slipping in to undermine such patriotic fare as pulped erasti dusted with savory spices, small hens stuffed with dried apricots, and tender beef flavored with paper-thin slices of my father's oranges— Arin the Plain King gives me a somber look that reminds me I must play my mother's part, and mingle with visiting dignitaries in the atrium as they sip a rosy dessert wine served in delicate glasses. I refuse a glass. It is too girlishly pretty, and I prefer to keep my hands free. My mother, were she here, would have arranged beforehand to be served a glass that looked like it held wine when it really held tinted water, so that people might think alcohol dulled her perception. One of her favorite tricks. But also pointless. I could have told her that she might as well not bother. Everyone knows how dangerous she is. An ambassador or discontented lord from a country manor would never forget *that*, no matter how many glasses of wine she pretended to drink.

Music floats over the room: a flute and three violins, the cool river of the flute flowing over the honeyed string trio. Music is always arranged for state functions to please my mother, and tonight is no exception even if she cannot attend. Piano performances, however, are rare. They make her impatient, even when she pretends they do not. At my last piano recital, when I was thirteen, I flubbed a tricky melody. I was so afraid of getting it wrong that I attacked it too quickly, and it spun out of my control, the notes tangled by my tripping fingers.

Sidarine, it does not matter, my mother said, kissing my hot eyes. Anyone can make a mistake.

You wouldn't. Those words, which I did not speak, burned in my chest. I refused to perform again.

I weave among the crowd, artfully sliding past a group of young Herrani women who would probably like a few words with me. One of them, Ceciliah, gives me a look so sharp it could draw blood. It takes me a moment to figure out why, since I thought we were on good terms before I left. Then I remember that although we were on very good terms indeed, after she asked me to teach her how to shoot a gun, and "target practice" became our private term for a different kind of activity, I *might* have ignored her in the weeks before I fled Herran.

I didn't ignore her on purpose. I simply got busy doing my mother's bidding. It was for the good of Herran! I cannot be blamed for that.

I see from her expression that oh, yes, I *can*.

Sorry, I mouth at Ceciliah, but she turns back to her friends, who notice everything, of course, and try to flay me with their eyes. One of them has just a tinge of disgust in her sneer, which she tries to disguise as loyal anger alone, but I have too much experience with that kind of disgust, and no patience for it.

No longer sorry at all, I shrug and saunter off.

Roshar catches my eye from across the room, where he is deep in conversation with delegates from his country. He smirks to see the circle of ladies tighten around Ceciliah as I leave them, as though cattle around a calf threatened by a wolf.

"You did well." It is Sarsine, having snuck up behind me.

She cannot possibly approve of my dalliances, so she must not have seen that special little moment with Ceciliah. I have no idea what Sarsine means. "I did?"

"You spoke well during dinner." My father's cousin looks stiff in her blue poplin dress. Like Arin, she prefers simple clothes and says that eschewing luxury means people are less likely to try to bribe her, the monarchy's most trusted counselor. "You were poised. Serious. Regal."

"I had no idea I could fake it so well. I should run away again and join a theater troupe."

She ignores this. "You reminded Herran that the country's future is stable again."

Because the heir has returned. I inhale to speak, but everything I would say I have already said: There are other ways to govern a country. It does not have to be a hereditary line of succession. Look at Valoria, where they now hold elections. True, the populace *did* elect the murdered emperor's son, but at least they went through the effort of entertaining other choices.

Herran, however, loves my parents, and so they love me. The people want *me*.

Really, what they want is for the beloved story of my beloved parents to continue after they are gone. I am a convenient plot point.

Already exhausted by an argument I cannot bear to have again, I say, "We have had twenty years of peace. Herran is stable enough."

"You don't know how easily it can all be lost."

She—indeed, everyone of my parents' generation—cannot help that I have inherited their trauma. Even if I did not live through it, I live in its wake, knocked back by the passing of a heavy ghost ship that carries all their memories. "Yes," I sigh, "you are right."

Her stern features soften. "I missed you, little one."

"You did not. I cause nothing but trouble. I am a disappointment to the crown." Not that my parents wear one.

"I was angry because I worried." She sees my expression and says, "Not about the line of succession. About you."

I have my doubts but play nice. "If you say so."

"Let's not quarrel. I am the only family you have, save your parents." There is an awkward silence as we both remember that this is not, technically, true.

I have a grandfather: General Trajan, who led the Valorian imperial forces in the first Herrani war, conquered this peninsula, enslaved the population, and colonized it. Who condemned Kestrel, his only child, to a labor camp in the northern tundra when he discovered she was working against the Empire on Herran's behalf. Trajan, whom my father could not bear to kill, for love of my mother, when he bested the Valorian army in the second Herran war.

My grandfather lives still: imprisoned, an old man an entire country hates. Herran's nightmare. Its monster.

Sarsine believes that he and I have never met.

I regard my father across the room. Roshar has made his way through the crowd to him, curtly dismisses anyone standing nearby, and says something to my father, his face unusually serious. My father glances up, sees me looking, half smiles distractedly, and returns his attention to Roshar, whose words seem to grow in vehemence.

"Sarsine?"

"Yes, Sidarine."

I am, in a way, named after her, the ending of our names similar in an old-fashioned, soberly feminine way, like fusty, perfumed lace.

"Are people still angry at Amma and Etta for letting my grandfather live?"

"That decision was made long ago."

"It is made again every day that he lives."

She gives me a dry smile. "And people say you don't have a mind for politics."

"He eats. He sleeps in comfort. Taxes pay for it."

"It was and remains an unpopular choice," she says stiffly. "I do not like it myself. Why are you asking about this?"

I am thinking of my mother, weakened by poison. The only way to find the person who did this to her is imagining who could bear her so deep a grudge as to attempt murder. "Oh, I am studying the philosophy of statecraft."

She snorts.

"For when I am queen," I say in exaggerated earnestness, "and make careful, considered decisions with great moral impact. What, I wonder, will the legacy of my reign be?"

She starts to say something, then stops herself, smiles, and pats my cheek with a dry hand. "You will do just fine," she says, and leaves me.

I survey the crowd. The atrium is usually one of my favorite rooms in the house, for its cool tiles mazed with streaks of gray over cloudy white, and the fountain that spills into itself. I like the room's quiet. Its clarity. It holds none of that now. It is simply a space filled with people who either do not know me, or do not know me as well as they believe. A room of noise and gossip and heat. A crowd that it is my duty to entertain.

As Sarsine engages the Valorian ambassador, an older woman named Lyannis, whose fox-colored hair—"warrior red," the Valorians call it—is braided into a heavy crown, I consider whether the Valorians plotting against Magister Verex could have learned of my mother's investigations through me and her other spies. Perhaps a band of Valorians who seek a return to imperial glory have slipped an agent into our midst, and seek to remove the obstacle my mother represents. It would not even need to be the malcontents holed up in the Cayn Saratu, stashing black-powder in the grottos of the tinier islands, the ones inhabited by only a few dozen people and some goats. Watching the red-haired ambassador sip from her glass, I make a mental note to speak with her when there is no risk of being overheard. It makes me impatient, to do nothing but wonder, and prowl around the edges of an idea, considering motives and suspects, yet this is my training.

Do not draw attention to yourself, Sidarine, my mother would always warn in the days when I was newly her spy and eager to please her, flashy in my efforts to ferret out information. Conceal how much you want a piece of information. Be the spider, sitting on the web, feeling the trem-ors of what touches it. Do not let your prey see you until it is too late.

Sarsine brushes a wrinkle from her blue dress. The violins cease, and the lone flute plays a slippery melody.

Her, too.

Consider your father's cousin.

Sarsine's friendship with my mother is well-known, as is how Sar-sine nursed her through an illness after Arin rescued Kestrel from the northern tundra's work camp. Sarsine loves my mother. Yet she loves my father more, and although there has never been even the faintest hint of attraction between them, I must consider that cousins sometimes marry, and that Sarsine and my father hold a history more complete than they do with anyone else, steeped with their shared childhood. My father trusts Sarsine. Aside from my parents—and me, I suppose—she holds the most power in Herran. Could Sarsine harbor an invisible feeling for my father, and view my mother as her rival? Could she have grown ambitious, and seek to remove my mother from power, and rule at my father's side? She hates Valorians as much as most Herrani. Look at her now, how she hides her dislike of the Valorian ambassador, glancing down to brush again at the fabric of her blue dress. She gives a strained, polite smile.

Perhaps my mother ceased being an exception—the one good Valorian—and Sarsine, who can never forget what was done to her people, felt her affection for my mother slowly erode.

Fear swells inside me. Too many people could resent my mother.

I leave the party abruptly, not caring how my absence will be perceived, and descend to the kitchen, which rattles and bangs with chores and the sound of plates from the dinner slung into steaming copper sinks.

I give an order that my hands alone will prepare my mother's meals, and pour what she drinks. I alone will serve her.

"Was it horrible?" Emmah says. She heard the tread of my boots down the hall, she said ("How you stomp!"), and came from her room to help me ready for bed. I said that was not necessary. I do not enjoy fussy clothes that need extra hands for removal, and my weapons are my responsibility. A Valorian hones her own blade. Emmah asked, then, that we light a candle together.

"The dinner was no worse than usual," I say, selecting two long, pale tapers and setting them into holders clotted with old wax. I strike a match and Emmah does the same, the dusky smell of sulfur rising into the air. Emmah still wears a thimble—she loves to embroider, and must have been working on one of her many projects as I thudded past her room—and the silver catches the candle's flame. The windows of my dressing room hold the black night.

We set our candles in a window. In its glass, the reflections of the twin flames glow like a god's eyes. I ask, "What will you pray for?"

"You," she says simply. She never married. She has no children. She cared for me from the moment I was born, and my mother was too weak from the birth to nurse me. "May the gods love you."

"And you."

"That is not all you pray for."

My mother, that she may live.

Nirrim.

Prayers are private. I make them less because I believe the gods listen than because praying helps me feel more like a true Herrani. And it is no bad thing, to concentrate a wish in your heart.

I wish I could see Nirrim again. I wish for her skin against mine. I wish for her bravery, her compassion.

I wish she had chosen me, as I chose her.

"May the gods love us all." I wonder which god I have offended. Which one watched me to set sail to Herrath, and placed Nirrim in my path?

"May they love us all," Emmah echoes. She kisses my forehead and bids me to sleep well.

I cannot. After she leaves, the wax drips, the flames sputter and lower. The oil in my table lamp burns out, leaving a heavy, slick scent in the air. There is no light but the candle flames and their reflections. One hisses, and then the other, and I am left alone in the dark.

Of all the people in Herran, one might resent my mother most.

I push open a window. The night is dense. Warm and sticky. Sweet, too, with the scent of white, night-blooming flowers that have opened their faces to the moon. The night holds summer's end: the honey left at the bottom of an almost-empty jar.

I pass into my dressing room, where I leave my gun and dagger on the table and shuck my tunic and trousers. Because I believe he will be more likely to speak with me in a dress, I select the first my gaze falls upon. If I must wear a dress, I don't want to agonize over which one will feel less terrible.

The moment I am in it, I no longer feel like myself. I feel like a ribbon marking a page in a book about someone else. The dress—a lilac, lutestring silk affair that makes me sweat—swishes as I hunt for slippers. Practically a living thing, crawling all over me, the dress keeps getting in my way. It gathers awkwardly between my legs and slips under my bare feet so that I stumble. Its hem is too long without heeled shoes.

Yet all such shoes in my wardrobe are stiff, new, never worn. I swear that even *more* have been added in my absence. That will have been the doing of either Sarsine, who likes me to look "proper," or Emmah, who sometimes commissions new garments and accessories fit for a lady, so that Sarsine will not pester me. Then Emmah stuffs them away to be forgotten. As soon as I see these slippers, I know they will cut my feet, even with stockings.

Stockings!

No. I have my limits.

I reach again for my favorite boots. After all, the dress is long. Maybe he will not notice the boots.

I lace them. I belt my dagger around my narrow hips. In the mirror, I could be a colonial Valorian girl: my eyes large and dark, my short hair the perfect golden color, even if it should be twined in braids as long as snakes. It is the right look—or close enough—to encourage him to want to speak with me. He does not always.

I take gold, to bribe the guards, and slip out of my quiet home to visit the prison that holds Herran's most reviled criminal.

The god of the moon is not mine, but sometimes I think that mercurial god loves me. The moon's fullness casts a pure light, and it is no trouble to make my way across the lawn to the stables and saddle a horse.

Javelin whickers at me hopefully, but I would never risk riding him. The warhorse has bony withers and is prone to saddle sores. His face, gone gray, looms over the stall gate. He likes winter apples, and every season my mother stores some for him, her expression more anxious with each year. Javelin has already lived longer than any horse should. I stroke his nose and the hollows above his eyes. He whuffs, disappointed in my lack of apples, disappointed in me. Whenever he sees me, he looks for my mother.

I saddle a roan mare. Doesn't matter what her name is. She will answer to whatever I call her.

I never put my heart into a horse like my mother did. Javelin was the best, and he was hers. When I was little, all I wanted was for him to be mine, too. By the time I grew old enough to understand that that was impossible, I was also too demanding to settle for second best, and too afraid of my mother's vulnerable expression when she looked at him. So I chose whichever horse struck my fancy on a given day. My father said that made me a better rider. In a way, Javelin was *too* good, he said. Too careful of his rider. Better, my father said, for me to learn to a range of different equine tempers, or one day I would find myself on a horse I did not know how to control.

I think he was trying to make me feel better. He must have at least guessed that I was jealous of my mother, that she had such a special horse, and jealous of Javelin, that my mother adored him.

Reluctantly, yet gently, my father said, Javelin was a gift from your mother's father. It is the last thing she has of him.

I ride out into the whitened night to see him.

My gold slips into the guards' pockets as they step away from the locked iron gate. They will give me privacy, but they are not about to leave me fully alone to my devices. Although they do not *think* Kestrel and Arin's child would free the country's most notorious prisoner, they will not take any risks.

Lamps glow within the prison, which bears no likeness to the dank cell that imprisoned me in Ethin, where I first encountered Nirrim, locked into the cell opposite mine. Trajan's prison is a small house with no upper or lower floors, and a series of rooms that might allow him the illusion of privacy if it were not for the fact that every room has a large, barred window outside of which a guard typically stands. There is a dining room where, I know, no cutlery is used, for fear of them becoming weapons, and no porcelain plates are served. My mother warned they could be smashed into deadly shards. The corners of all furniture have been sanded down into smooth bumps. Oil lamps designed of wrought iron hang high out of reach.

The small library holds many Valorian volumes. Each book is examined before it enters the cell. Years prior, when I was still small, a book bound with toxic glue was somehow slipped into Trajan's prison. When the guards noticed my grandfather slumped on the carpeted floor, surrounded by torn pages, his mouth full of glue, they found that a page ripped from the book had a message in Herrani script, written in a woman's hand: *A true Valorian is bound by honor. Once lost, it can never be regained. May you devour this book and know its worth.*

Doctors poured a tonic down Trajan's throat that made him vomit the poison. No one knew who had delivered the book. If Trajan knew, he refused to say.

In winter, his bed is covered with furs. In summer, his sheets are made of thick tishin paper. He is not allowed sheets, which could be torn into strips for hanging. That would be difficult, given that he is missing one arm below the elbow, but his guards have learned not to underestimate him.

The prison designed to contain him also protects him—from himself as well as others. Well-lit at all times, it reminds me of an eerie dollhouse, for how easily one can look inside. He never knows a moment's privacy, save when he sleeps.

I see him writing or drawing at a desk, the shoulder of his amputated right arm hidden beneath a light cloak too warm for this weather but just right for his pride. He is not trusted with a pen, not even a quill, ever since the time he drove a goose quill into the eye of a guard in a bid to escape. He paints. His paintbrushes are specially designed, the horsehairs bound to fresh, thin willow wands too supple to do harm. When they begin to age and harden, they are taken away.

I step toward the bars, and he must hear the scuff of my boot against stone, for he looks up. Though as gray-haired and hollow-eyed as Javelin, Trajan is still a large man, his reflexes alert. "Kestrel?" he says.

His rooms must be too bright to see me well in the shadows. "No."

"Sidarine," he says softly. "It has been a long time."

A few years.

He comes closer. His expression is such a mixture of timidity and tenderness that I could almost forget he is responsible for the most horrific crimes ever visited upon my country and my parents. I remind myself that he is cunning. His expression, which seems to be that of a lonely old man, has likely been crafted to make me believe, even if only for a moment, that he is harmless.

"Your hair was longer then," he says. "You still look so much like her."

I am encouraged. The first time I came to his prison, a weeping child, he would not speak with me, not even when I begged him to explain how he could betray his own daughter. I was ten years old, and had just learned that he was alive, and what he had done. Emmah told me. Your parents wish to protect you, she said, but no one can protect you from your history.

Tell me, Trajan, I demanded, my fists at my sides as I stood outside his prison. How you could do that to her?

He simply looked at me. It was not until I heard his silence that I understood the reason I needed to know was because I was afraid. If a father could do what he did to his daughter, what might my parents do to me? How would I know the limit of their love, until I had violated it?

The next time I visited him, a year later, I had a more considered plan. I asked no questions. I demanded nothing. I greeted him in respectful Valorian, not the howling Herrani I had hurled at him the previous time, and introduced myself as though we were at a formal gathering. Almost like a normal grandfather, he asked what I was studying. He inquired after my weapons training, and seemed satisfied that I was doing well. After that, I visited him once a year or so, never being anything other than calm and polite, biding my time until I might make him— either through trickery, the passing of time, or ensnaring his affection— answer the question that haunts me still. Sometimes, such as now, I think he likes me.

"You resemble her greatly," he says. Amusement has crept into his tone. "Though she would never wear boots with that dress."

He cannot see them. He must have heard them, and guessed from the depth of the sound of their scuffing stone, a slower drag than slippers would have.

"Kestrel is very ill," I say.

His expression does something my mother's does occasionally when she plays me at Bite and Sting. It is her only tell. Her face empties of emotion and looks simply . . . concentrated. His does that now. As soon as I figured out, a few years ago, that my mother's expression did that only when she cared very much about what she held in her hand, I won with greater frequency.

"She might die," I tell my grandfather.

With his one hand, Trajan brings a soft chair, made entirely from stiff cushions, to the prison door. He settles into it and looks up at me, waiting, his light brown eyes—the same color as my mother's—bland. Politely, he says, "I am sorry to hear that."

"Are you?"

"She is my only regular visitor. I wondered at her absence lately."

Annoyed at his calm, I do exactly what he intends—even as I *know* he intends it—and recklessly say, "What if I told you that her sickness is not natural? Someone has tried—*is trying*—to kill her."

His silver brows snap together into a stern line. "Do you know who?"

"No."

"And yet you tell me   *me*   this?"

"Perhaps you orchestrated it from prison."

"Yes, perhaps I did. And so you come to confront a potential assassin with your suspicion, and no proof?" He shakes his head. "Kestrel has not taught you well."

"I don't believe you did it," I say, certain, though I had not been certain until this moment.

"Then you are a fool. You know as well as anyone that I once consigned her to her death. What would keep me from doing it again? I have no time for fools." Yet he does not stir from his soft chair. He does not dismiss me, as he has done before, and retreat into his prison.

"You love her too much." I know it from his desperate attempts to punish himself. I know it from the way his face contracted into an unreadable expression the moment he learned she was sick. I know it from how desperate he is to see her in me.

"I hate her," he whispers, his eyes too bright in the lamplight.

"If she taught me poorly, then *you* teach me better. Who could do this to her? Was it Valoria? Do you know of her enemies, hidden in this country? She was in good health when I left Herran. By the time I returned, after a mere few months, she was almost gone. She looks like the quiet god will kiss her and make her his. Who could want to eliminate her from power? Who could despise her so much?"

"You ask the wrong question."

"Tell me the right one."

For a moment I think he will demand a fair exchange, and insist on his release, or that I slip him a weapon he could finally use. He shakes his head. "You cannot answer *who* until you answer *why*, and you cannot answer *why* until you consider *when*."

"When what?"

"Consider your own words, Sidarine."

"What words?" My fists are clenched so hard my knuckles ache.

"The words you just said, a moment ago."

"*Help* me, damn the gods." My anger feels murderous, and I want to weep for how tired I am of always wrangling it under control. When my elders accuse me of being too merry, of shrugging away anything serious, I think: you would not like me better if I showed what I truly feel. You do not know how hard it is to pretend to be unbothered.

To be, at every turn, confronted with an order—spoken or silent—to be different, *more*.

Be better, Sidarine.

Smarter.

Grow up.

Not *this* way. *That* way.

Do your duty.

Figure it out on your own.

I turn to leave, but he says, "Kestrel has always had enemies." The strain in his voice makes me realize that his efforts at self-destruction over the years might have stemmed not only from pride and grief and self-blame, but also from an awareness that his very existence posed a risk to his daughter's life and well-being. For who in this country could tolerate well his comfortable prison, his continued safety? "There have been attempts before to assassinate her."

"That is not true."

He makes an impatient noise. The flickering lamplight falls in orange ripples over his weathered face. "You do not know of it because she does not *want* you to know. The attempts were made long ago, when Herran was newly independent. They stopped soon after your birth." He sees my growing understanding. "The question you must answer first does not concern motives but rather timing. You said the words yourself: you left Herran. The poisoner chose to strike while you were away. Why? What spurred this person to attempt Kestrel's murder *then*?"

Oil sputters in a lamp. Above me, bats sing in high, thin voices.

"The reason," my grandfather says, "begins with *you*."

NIRRIM

IN THE DEPTHS OF SID'S house, on the hill with its view of the sea, I touch the bodice of my tattered dress. I feel the crackle of the letter Sid once wrote in a language I cannot read, will never read. There is no one to teach it to me. Before I met the god of thieves, I imagined the letter offered me promises. That it laid bare her heart. Now, I imagine it as advice, the counsel of a princess born to inherit a kingdom. I should have guessed Sid's true, regal status, however much she hid it from me. She walked through the world as though she owned it.

I touch the snarls in my hair. My unchanged, filthy dress.

My people follow me because I placed power in their hands. Yet some are squeamish. Not everyone enjoyed the executions. Many Half Kith are useless, empty of god-blood, but they could still interfere with my plans, should their silly moral qualms grow.

They fear me, which is good, but I need more.

I need them to love me.

If Sid wrote counsel to me, she might remind me of how carefully she chose her clothes to shape how others saw her. *Nirrim*, her letter might say, *You need to* look *like a god.*

I write an order and hold it out, rolled to the width of a twig, to the chittering Elysium. The bird clutches it and seems to understand when I instruct it to find Aden. As the god of discovery's bird, the Elysium senses immortal blood. This is an experiment to see if the bird can obey my command, and distinguish between one god-blooded person and another. It is also an experiment to see how readily Aden responds to an order from me. A queen should not seek out her servants. They must come to her.

It takes some time, but Aden comes to Sid's house, the Elysium trilling above him. He brings me a woman whose face I almost do not recognize, since she wears no cosmetics and has not the benefit of the beautifying elixir she once drank. Still, she has the traits we called Old Herrath—gray eyes and hair that would be black were it not aged with streaks of white. Madame Mere: dressmaker for the High Kith, the only one of her kith I knew who worked, simply for the reason that she enjoyed it. She still carries herself with elegance, though she reeks of the prison. Her eyes widen as she recognizes me, yet she wisely says nothing. Her silence, perhaps, saved her from being one of the High Kith selected for execution.

Aden pushes her to kneel in front of me on the woven rug.

I cast a glance around Sid's home—its comfortable, worn luxury. I will need a grander setting. Cold marble floors. The trappings of luxury. Regret flickers in my chest. I am fond of this home. My future, however, cannot be determined by such a mortal feeling as fondness.

I look down upon the dressmaker's bowed head. Her bound hands tremble until she clasps them together, hard. If her knees hurt, she does not betray it. I once liked her. Although she knew my true kith when

I lived with Sid here in the High quarter, she did not betray me, but rather helped me hide. She was kind to me.

"Mere," I say, deliberate in my choice not to use a title that never belonged to her, that should not have belonged to any High Kith. "Tell me: Would you like to live?"

Quietly, she says, "I would like that very much."

Mere pins scarlet fabric close to my clean skin, which exhales the dusky scent of Sid's perfume. We are alone in Sid's house. Luckily for Mere, her dress shop was left untouched during the nights when Half Kith raged through the High quarter streets, probably because the shop was unassuming and tucked away from the more attractive targets of gilded mansions. When I instructed Aden to have all the contents of the store brought to me, his face showed his displeasure. "I am not your errand boy," he said.

"After you finish that task, remove the bodies from the agora. Scrub it clean of blood." Delight bubbled within me. How delicious it was to make him do what *I* wanted, to subject him to demeaning obedience. It was fair recompense for all the times he ignored my reluctance and persuaded me into his bed.

His blue eyes burned with resentment, but he made no reply, only spun on his heel and left. I almost wished he had objected. His sly silence was suspicious, and I would gladly punish him for any sign of disobedience. How could I ever have agreed to marry him? Why did I heed his promise that I would enjoy being with him, and then when I didn't, why did I return to his side, simply because I felt guilty for not sharing what he felt?

Let Aden do what *I* want now. Let him obey *me*. Let him dread my displeasure.

Mere chose to alter an already-made dress. She works in wary silence, save when she asks if I would like a pink petticoat that will reveal itself when I walk, with a slashed red silk overlay that will drift behind me. I give permission for her to touch my divine person, and she weaves green ribbon into my shoulder-length black hair and binds it into a braided crown. She gasps when she sees the beauty of my starry earrings, but asks no questions. She tuts over the broken chain of the crescent moon necklace, but makes no comment other than that an added link can easily mend it. She does not say she is designing me to look like the Elysium bird, nor observe how the red silk falls around me like liquid. She need not say what we both know: that in the suggestion of the bird and of blood, she has chosen to figure me as a thing of immortal beauty and mortal danger both.

I grow bored with her silence and say, "Well? Do you not find me greatly changed?"

"You look regal beyond measure," she says after a slight pause. "But you were always beautiful."

"I do not mean how I *look*. Was I not a weak simpleton when you knew me before? Now the city is mine, its people mine. I saved them. They will adore me for it, for that and my manifest power."

"As you say."

"As you say, *my queen*."

She repeats the honorific, but my annoyance grows. I do not like her meek obedience. I do not like her closed box of a brain, with secret thoughts of me that she will not share. She obeys me not because she loves me, or even believes in my right to rule, but because I will kill her if she does not. Dissatisfied, I close my hand around her wrist. "Remember," I command, and feel my magic pulse into her skin. As she stares into my face, she looks suddenly dizzy, perhaps because she sees me now, in my glory, and also as I was when we first met. "Tell me how I am different."

She starts to speak, then chokes on her words, gray eyes wide with fear. "I can't," she says finally.

I shake her wrist. The prickly pincushion she holds falls to the floor. "Why not? Go on, tell me. You protected me once. You liked me. Was it because you pitied me?"

"Yes, a little."

"You *dared* to pity me?"

"Nirrim, you are trapping me. There is nothing I can say to please you. Not the truth, and not a lie."

I release her. Loneliness slides into my chest: hard and thin and fragile, like a glass blade. "I have decided to honor you. In addition to being my handmaiden, you may be my friend."

"What," she says carefully, "would it mean to be your friend?"

"Do as I command, and I will protect you."

"What an interesting definition of friendship."

"And you must tell me the truth. Friends do not lie to each other. How was I then, and how am I now?"

With sudden, exhausted surrender, Mere says, "You are more powerful. But you are not stronger, or braver, or better."

Her loyalty to Other Nirrim maddens me. It is not even so much that I resent when people prefer Other Nirrim to me—although I *do*. What troubles me most is that I do not understand the preference. They say Nirrim was so brave, kind, sweet. What good did it do her? No one put her first. No one chose her above their own interests. Even Sid did not. She left. She always planned to leave. In the mirror before me, I see a young woman who radiates beauty, from the dark glow of her hair to the firm set of her full mouth, her figure framed in shining red. Even the scar on my cheek, from when Raven smashed a lantern against my face, entrances. A streaky burn left by the lantern's oil, the shiny pink scar looks almost deliberate, glamorous. *This* woman could never be abandoned. She need not even insist that someone stay. Sid would never leave me, not as I am now.

"Come," I tell Mere, and step off the dressmaker's block, ignoring the pins pricking my skin. Alterations can wait. I will have rivers of gorgeous dresses to display my worth. They will make people grateful to have a god for their queen. I call to my Elysium, which swoops into the house through an open window and bites its talons into my shoulder. "There is something we need to see."

The Keepers Hall's stained-glass windows are smashed, the shards a broken rainbow at my feet. My handmaiden hangs back warily, unwillingly, staring at the hall's open double doors, which hang, splintered, on their hinges. This hall once housed the councilmen, the people closest to the ruling Lord Protector. They decided our laws and instructed the militia to enforce them. They possessed the city's largest library when Half Kith like me were forbidden from reading. Not so long ago, when I entered this hall for the first time, councilmen in the library sat calmly drinking my watered-down blood, served to them in glass teapots, as they read their books and enjoyed their improved memory. I know how they had obtained my blood—it was drained from me every day during my imprisonment. But where did they get the blood that watered the fortune-telling tree? Who in this city had the ability to read the future? What other powers lay hidden in my people?

"You drank an elixir," I say to Mere, who shrinks from me, clearly worried she has provoked my wrath. "You served it to me, and it made us more beautiful."

She is frightened again, and scrambles for refuge in an empty compliment. "You do not need an elixir to look more beautiful. You are beauty incarnate."

"I *know* that. Do you believe I would knowingly drink the blood of my people, the children of gods? I want to know where you obtained it. The Council provided many different elixirs to High Kith for a price. Where did they keep their supplies? Where did they keep the blood?"

"I don't know." She backs away, stained glass cracking beneath her feet. "I didn't know the elixir contained blood. I didn't think—"

"Indeed, you did not think. You simply drank it, and enjoyed it, and never questioned its origin."

"Nirrim, what can I say? I would never drink it now that I know."

"Oh, would you not? You enjoyed how the elixir smoothed your skin. Do not tell me you would have sacrificed beauty for the sake of your scruples. You would have drunk the elixir . . . so long as no one would punish you for it. You would drink, provided you could keep your sin secret."

Mere's expression slackens in fear, yet her chin lifts. "Think what you like. I know that I would not. I am sorry I ever did."

"If you are sorry, then be of use!" I storm ahead into the Keepers Hall, and hear her follow alongside me, her sandals scraping against more broken glass. "Who sold you the elixir?"

"A councilman."

"Who?"

"His name was Jasen. He was born into a well-respected family with many sugar fields two hours by foot outside the city."

"There must be stores of blood. He would know where they are to be found."

"Possibly, but he was executed in the agora along with all the other councilmembers."

In the tales of the gods, Vengeance eats live coals as a treat. My fury feels like that meal, like I have swallowed a burning lump that scalds all the way down my throat and into my belly. "Say nothing," I snap. "I won't hear your reproach!" Mere bites her mouth shut, not realizing that my words were not for her, but Other Nirrim, who is always ready to tell me what I'm doing wrong, in all her simpering goodness.

I don't need a councilman to get what I want, I tell Other Nirrim, and I don't need you.

Sunlight filters whitely through the broken windows. The hall is dark, the tiny mosaic patterns of its tiled floors a shadowed blur. Lanterns have been knocked from their sconces. The air smells of oil and urine. The Elysium squawks and tucks its beak into my braided hair. Annoyed, I shrug the shoulder on which it stands. Even a bird should know that revolution is not pretty.

I quicken my pace as we pass from the corridor of the entrance into an open rotunda. The quiet of the empty hall floats around us. I could call for interrogations of the remaining High Kith in the prisons, and send for my people to ransack the hall and tear it apart to its bones in search of the elixirs, but I have already wasted so much time. Practically my whole life. I cannot wait another moment. I stoop to collect a shard of stained glass, prick the tip of one finger, and lift it to the Elysium's face. It trills, excited by my god-blood. "Find more," I order, and it launches from my shoulder and wings away.

We trace its flight as it dives down a flight of stairs and plows through a series of hallways with barrel-shaped ceilings and locked doors on either side. Fleetingly, I wonder if these were private rooms for the councilmen, but I do not deliberate long, as each hallway is dark and the bird its only brightness. The Elysium seems to have its own glow, like a darting flame. Its song trails behind it, tinkling against the cool floors, which are tiled yet plain terracotta, a strange contrast to the rest of the building's marble and stained-glass splendor. The walls of the hallway are wood, not marble, the doorknobs plain black iron, not gilded as the metalwork on the doors to the library had been when

I entered—a lifetime ago, it seems—and was confronted by the god of thieves.

The Elysium slows at the hallway's end, batting its wings to hover as best it can, like a hawk pausing midflight to sight its prey far below. In a luminous blur, it drops to settle on a doorknob, and sings.

"Open it," I tell Mere, who tries. The door is locked.

My patience for humans wears thin. Divine memory can do nothing to manipulate a locking mechanism, and Mere is useless.

"Find Aden," I instruct the bird. Aden will use his gift to heat the metal lock until it oozes out of the door. "Go with the Elysium," I tell Mere, "so that you may explain the situation to Aden. Do not try to run away, or when you are caught there will be no mercy."

"Why would I run," she says, a slight dryness in her voice, "when I have the rare protection of your friendship?"

When Aden returns with Mere, it does not take long for him to do as I require. The lock and knob flow down the door in black, molten ribbons, and he shoves the door open.

"Light the room," I order. As before, he gives me a quick look of dislike before obeying, but I have taught him well the pointlessness of defying me, and the pain I can cause him. He mounts no arguments nor tries to assert his own views and ways, as he did when I was his lover, before Sid set foot on this island. Aden's skin radiates, and as light cloaks his body, I understand why girls in the Ward found him so handsome, with his long, firm limbs and bright blue eyes. I admire him for a moment, as I would a favored possession, until the light grows enough for me to see the contents of the room. Mere, who has lingered by the door, gasps.

We stand in a storage room with shelves upon shelves of large glass vials stoppered and labeled, filled to the brim with dark liquid. As the light brightens further, I can read a label: *Flight*, it says. Another reads, *Nightmares*. As I walk among the shelves, the Elysium chirping excitedly as it bobs in the air above me, I understand that this room must hold the blood of generations. There are too many vials to have been accumulated in my lifetime. Aden makes a choking sound.

A rustle comes from a far corner of the room. As soon as I turn in its direction, Aden stops me with a firm hand I shake off, at once pleased and annoyed at his instinct to protect me. I do not need his help, and am about to tell him so when I see that Mere has located the source of the sound—a councilman in his robes, an opened vial beside him, cowering behind a shelf. Mere has what looks like a dagger at his throat. I squint further, disbelieving—how did she come upon a weapon?—and see that she must have secretly collected a shard from the broken windows in the entry of the Keepers Hall.

"Did you plan to kill me, Mere?" I ask, amused.

She ignores me, but I do not care, so pleased am I to see her angry at her own kith. "Where does this blood come from?" she hisses at the councilman. "How did you get it?"

He creeps back, knocking over the vial, which spills blood onto the floor and rolls, the label clear: *Nourishment*. His story is evident. He hid himself away from the wrath of my people and drank someone's magic to keep himself alive long enough to wait for an escape. Pleadingly, he says to Mere, "The Half Kith are dangerous." He gestures at Aden and me. "Look at those freakish people. They will destroy us all." Dirty though Mere's dress may be, he is able to tell she is High Kith from the fabric's deep purple color, the depth of an indi flower newly opened, and the frothy trimmings of elaborate lace. "You should not threaten *me*, lady."

"This is *wrong*," Mere says, flinging her free hand at the rows upon rows of bottled blood. "You are a murderer."

"No," the man says desperately, and I notice he is not much older than I am. The fullness of his black beard tells me he has hidden here for what must have been days, since the start of the revolution. "I have killed no one. They are all perfectly safe, I promise."

"*Who* are?" I demand. "Where are they?" But as soon as the question leaves my lips, I know its answer. I draw Aden from the blood-filled chamber, leaving Mere, my new acolyte, to guard the councilman, and we return to the hall of doors. I turn a knob. It rattles in my hand. When I knock at the door, a small cry comes from within the room. "Aden," I say, my pulse mounting in fury, so sure am I of the sin this door hides: the very worst crime the High Kith could commit against us. Aden needs no urging. His hot hands seize the doorknob. He runs his palms flatly along the face of the lock until the metal scallops like whipped cream. The hot iron smells like a coming thunderstorm. Although I see the beginnings of fatigue line his face—his power, though spectacular, is always quick to fade—when the reddened metal slides down wood, he shoulders the door open. Light flows from his skin into the room. We see clearly who made that cry, who must have supplied blood for the Council's collection.

She cowers under a narrow bed, her hair long and unkempt, her hands small yet plump in the way of children who have just begun to walk.

Aden's gaze catches mine. I see my rage mirrored in his eyes as we both realize that the hall with its many doors must hide countless children like her, milked for their magic.

SID

---◈---

I THUMB POMEGRANATE SEEDS INTO a bowl I know my mother likes, a matte white ceramic one that looks like water-polished stone. When I asked her why, she replied that the Valorian dishware she used when she was young was too elaborate, painted with heroes from long-ago wars. Unusually for her, given that she taught me every code she knew and challenged me to invent more, she said that sometimes it was nice for something not to mean anything, for a bowl to be no more than a bowl. A spoon, a spoon. It is as it is, she said, smiling, holding the bowl out for me to admire its simplicity.

I shiver to remember those words. I remember Nirrim reciting them, her tone dull with the habit of acquiescence. It frustrated me at first, because I did not reckon with how necessary it was for Nirrim and everyone of her kith to repeat them, as though they were internal law that the Half Kith imposed on themselves. If she did not pretend the rules of her society were simple, immutable, like this bowl, she would be punished.

My hands falter as they cut bread. Nirrim stopped pretending. I did not fully realize, then, how courageous it is to no longer go along with a lie. I remember her angry tears as she made me swear to help her make the High Kith pay for what they did to her people. I promised, and broke that promise, and left her to the danger of Ethin and her determination to plot against it.

At first, when I explained to Nirrim that my mother was sick, I thought I would return to Herrath as soon as she was well. But that island holds nothing for me now. Nirrim does not love me. I understand. How many times have I tried to explain to a girl that love cannot be forced, that I could not make myself feel what they wanted me to feel? Nirrim had started to say the same words, and I couldn't bear it.

Do you not love me like I love you? I asked. Won't you come with me?

No, she said. I can't come with you.

I stopped her next words. An apology will make it worse, I told her.

I don't want to apologize.

Good. There is no need. I lifted my hand to block the sight of her beauty, her pity, and left immediately, grief and shame rising in my throat like bile.

And yet I cannot leave Nirrim, not entirely, not when I wake up thinking she sleeps beside me, that after I have my fill of looking at her full, gentle mouth and the thick lashes of her closed eyes, I will stir her out of dreams with a light touch. Wake up, I will murmur against her throat.

Mmmph.

Lazybones, I will tease, and touch her in a way that will make her eyes fly open.

Sid!

Yes?

I was sleeping.

You were?

You owe me an apology.

You're right, Nirrim, I do. How shall I make you forgive me?

You know, she will murmur.

I always stretch out on the bed, imagining what I will do, my limbs alight with desire. But then I come fully awake, and of course the bed is empty.

The serving tray is complete. The bread, the bowl of garnet fruit, the cup of warm milk. My hands rest on either side. They are no lady's hands. Usually that makes me feel good. I like my nails cut to the quick, the strong knobs of knuckles, palms calloused from years of weapons training and the skid of a ship's ropes. But today they look useless, help-less, as I think about how a month has passed since I left Ethin. I do not know Nirrim's fate. I will never know. But I cannot imagine that she is safe, not when she was ready to risk everything to save her people, and had no one to protect her.

Yet she would not come with me. I asked. I begged.

Enough. Remembering doesn't help me. It is painful. I grab the tray with such vehemence that a cook, who had been politely giving me a wide berth, shoots me a startled glance. I ignore it, and bear the tray to my mother.

She is awake. She smiles to see me, though I can tell she is too weak to shift herself up against pillows behind her, so I help until she catches my hand in hers and says, "You are a good child."

I could say: Yes, when I do what you want. Or: I am not a child.

I feel hot, my face tight. How often have I wanted to hear her say what she has just said? It comes now, but too late, and not because of who I am but because I am taking care of her. Maybe someone would say that taking care of my mother *is* who I am, that it is what I always want to do for those I love, but I would insult that person, mock them as a fool, even when I know the words to be true.

I do not know what to do with my anger. I do not understand how it constantly feeds itself, how sweet it is, how I need it so badly.

My eyes prickle. I place the tray beside her. "What does that yellow feather mean?"

She glances around her bedchamber, her brow furrowed. "The yellow feather?"

Indeed, it is not here, not now. "The one that is sometimes in your suite, sometimes in Etta's. Small, and speckled. I don't know from which bird."

"A southern bird," she says, her voice tired, dreamy. She has fallen into some memory that has nothing to do with me.

"If I am such a good child, maybe you should give it to me."

She blinks up at me, confused. I have rarely seen her confused. She pushes bright hair off her brow to look at me better. "Why would you want a feather?"

I shrug.

"I found it during the second war," she says, "when I was on a campaign with your father. We were traveling, fresh from a battle, and discovered an ancient temple to the gods. It was overgrown. That temple meant so much to Arin. The Valorians had destroyed most temples during the colonization of Herran. We pulled away the vines and saw mosaics of gods I did not even recognize. He believes in more than just the gods. He believes they will return, though he is too shy to say so." She glances at a window. It is full of pink dawn. The light touches her face softly, and she looks no older than I am. "I saw his wonder. His hope that not everything was lost. Do you understand? And I knew I loved him. I kept the feather as a memory of that day, and gave it to him when he went into battle without me. I told him to return it to me when he had won. I suppose . . ." Her voice trails off, and again I feel that I am not even here, that she is speaking into the past. "I believed it would keep him alive."

I say nothing. Longing fills me. I want the feather even more, now that I understand how impossible it would be for her to give it to me.

"It is yours, Sid, if you would like it."

"It is?"

"You will have to be content with my promise. Arin has it, for now."

"Oh," I say, realizing that the feather is as much his as hers, and maybe he would not like me to have it. I flush. All this over a feather.

She understands my worry in an instant, of course. I believed I had gotten better at not showing my every thought, but she is who she is, like that bowl is a bowl, and there is never any hiding from her. "He would want you to have it, knowing it means something to you."

The cup of milk will grow cold. I lift the porcelain cap, designed to guard warmth, from the cup's brim and offer the milk to her. "Only I will serve your meals."

She drinks. "That is wise."

"It is common sense. I am surprised you did not restrict your meals earlier to the hands of someone you trust."

"I was too tired." She bites her lip. "I wasn't thinking straight. I feel better."

"Not so sick?"

"Not so hopeless," she says, "now that you have returned."

I shift in the seat beside her, my dagger digging into my side. I don't want to feel the softness that steals through me. What can I say? Her words are so tender that they hurt. They are what I want, yet she doesn't even know what it cost me to leave Ethin, how I had to give up my heart to be by her side.

She lets the silence linger, then says, "I wish you had a friend. You never really did."

"I have Roshar. Emmah. Things were always complicated with anyone else."

"You *did* ignore young men. Instead you seduced women whom you befriended, and then abandoned them. Hardly a model for lasting relationships."

The dagger's pommel jabs my ribs. I stand, towering over her. "What would you know about my relationships?"

Quietly, she says, "Only what you tell me."

"Don't act like you were so heartbroken over my departure. You know why I left."

"That night, we barely spoke. You shouted at me. You wouldn't let me get a word in edgewise."

"Because I knew what you would say!"

She sets the empty cup in its saucer. "Let me remind you, Sidarine, that it was *you* who chose to be engaged to Prince Ishar of Dacra. *You* said that you would. *You* said it was what you wanted."

It is true, and I cannot bear it. I storm from the room.

"Oooh, I know that look," Roshar says slyly from the low bench opposite the fountain in the atrium, stopping me as I speed through the house like a shot bullet. If I enjoy the atrium, he does so even more, especially this time of year, when heat drains from the air. So cold, your country, he always says, shivering. Once the leaves change color he returns to Dacra, complaining that the wind bites his bones. The atrium, with its peaked glass roof, traps the heat on a sunny day. White flowers, their petals thick as curls of shaved soap, look up at me from their green beds along the fountain. Roshar lounges on the bench like it is a bed, faceup, head pillowed on arms crossed behind him, one long leg dangling. I recognize the way he looks, because I have tried to appear this way many times—careless, seductive, lazy, clever. I have endeavored so much over the years to imitate Roshar that sometimes when I see him like this I do not know if he is simply being himself or imitating me imitating him. "Why are you even here?" I demand.

"To muse upon the sweet scent of the flowers, Princess."

"Not *here*, the atrium. *Here*, Herran. You did your duty to my parents and dragged me home. Your ship waits in the harbor. The weather grows cold. Why don't you return to Dacra, *Prince?*"

"I am needed where I am."

I renew my suspicion of him. My mother trusts him wholly. He was visiting Herran before he sailed to Ethin to collect me. He could have poisoned her, then been compelled, in order to pretend his continued loyalty, to seek me out at my parents' request. If he claims he is needed here, could it be to finish the assassination he began?

He sits up, the lines of his body loose and lithe, an open reminder of how deadly he is as a fighter. Fearless. Quick to attack. Yet his sleek, black eyes are tender when he says, "Sid, I have stayed for you."

"Me?"

"Who else?"

"Well . . . my parents."

"Not this time."

"But you sailed to Ethin for me, for their sake."

"Yes. But I also did that for *you*."

The fountain whispers. The humid, perfumed air of the atrium feels like a veil over my face. He says, "When I received word that you were in the city of Ethin's prison with an evidently charming local girl, and that you both needed to be released on my royal authority, I did as you asked, and left you alone. Were your parents wrecked with worry, wondering where you were? Yes. Am I their dearest friend? Yes. Did I tell them where you were? No. You are my godchild, and I swore to take care of you as though you were my own. You ran away. You insisted upon your freedom. Who was I to take it? Was it not my role, as your godfather, to give you what you needed?"

I sit beside him on the bench, my anger and suspicion dampened by surprise.

"But when Kestrel fell ill," he says, "I had to come find you."

"To make me come home."

"Sid, no one has made you do anything."

My throat tightens. I stare at the tumbling water.

"I know a little," Roshar says, "about making a mistake, and grieving it. I didn't want that to happen to you. Your mother is dying. I knew that Kestrel held the hand of the goddess, and might walk with her forever. If she died, and you learned of it later, you would never forgive yourself for missing the chance to say good-bye. I came to Ethin to give you a *choice*."

This hadn't occurred to me. When he came to me in my house in Ethin with the news, my need to return home was so strong that it never felt like a choice. And although I asked Nirrim to come with me, I nevertheless chose my family first. It occurs to me how deeply I might have hurt Nirrim, even if she understood my choice, and that when I begged her to be by my side and live with me in my country it was so that I need not feel the pain of choice, and not surrender anything—neither the girl I loved, nor my mother.

"I think it would be easier for you," Roshar says, "to blame me for forcing your return. But it is not the truth."

I sigh. "Doesn't someone miss you in Dacra? Your sister?"

"The queen *hates* me."

"Your tiger?"

"Arin will climb all over me when I return, and lick off what remains of my face. He will consider eating me, but I will remind him that I do not taste good to tigers. He will lean against me, and purr down to his bones. I have that effect on men."

"Surely you have a lover who wants your return."

"*Loads* of lovers."

I look at him sideways.

"Kestrel and Arin have a true love enshrined by the heavens," he says, "but that is not for everybody."

"I know." I can't quite keep the wistfulness out of my voice.

"I mean: not everyone *wants* that. The way I live makes me happy. Why must I be with one person until the day I die? How dull."

"I suppose."

He looks at me narrowly. "Do you not agree? Given your reputation—"

"Yes," I lie. "I agree." I feel too raw to say otherwise, though I now understand that what he has told me about himself I have long already known, and that the way I have—as people like to put it—*run through women* is because I have yearned to resemble Roshar in every way, including the freedom of his heart. I have been afraid of loving someone like my parents love each other. To love like that is to live with the knowledge that the end will come, one way or the other, because we are mortal, and the loss will be incalculable. Better, I always thought, without realizing that I thought it, to love lightly, and never lose too much.

It's hard to want something and deny you want it, to long for the very thing you're afraid of. Anger spouts up again inside me. I am angry at everyone. I am angry at myself.

"I note," he says, "that you were stomping and stalking your way from the east wing."

"My mother is impossible."

"Terrible! Imperious and calculating."

"Exactly."

"And a sore loser!"

"That's *you*, Roshar. You *always* lose when you play her at cards, Borderlands, Bite and Sting—"

"You are an ungrateful child."

"Will you really not leave?" My voice is small. "Even when it grows cold?"

"Even then."

"And when it snows?"

"Snow is nothing to me. I laugh at snow."

My eyes sting. He roughs up my hair as though I were a boy. I lean into his hand, then rest my head on his shoulder, grateful . . . and guilty for ever suspecting him. "She is so sick," I say.

"I know."

"She makes me so angry."

"Fight me, then, and feel better . . . at least until you lose."

I look up at him. It has been a long time since we sparred.

"As your godfather," he says primly, "I retain the right to exploit any vulnerability of yours and trounce you so that you acknowledge I am superior at hand and sword and am generally the best you shall ever know, or have the honor to encounter. This is all for your personal growth, of course. To make you a better warrior, even if you cannot possibly be as good as I am."

"You *do* look out for me."

He smiles. "In my own way."

We walk out into the sunshine, Roshar tipping his face up to it as though he were his tiger, and cross the lawn to the fighting salle my father designed. It is a simple wooden structure about as large as the stables and not very different from them, with sandy rings open to the air, some unroofed, so that he could train me to fight in snow and rain. Other rooms, where I learned how to fight with short knives and defend myself without ever being able to extend my arms fully, are boxed in tight like a horse's stall. Once, when my father and I left the salle, sweaty and tired, he claimed I could wield any weapon with grace, and we had exhausted all that the salle had to offer, had fought in its every corner. My gaze floated to the roof. He noticed, eyes widening. You are just like your mother, he said with a smile. When we returned to the salle with a ladder, he pinned my shoulder in one heavy hand just as I set my foot on the first rung. His expression pretended humorous anxiety, but his voice was serious enough when he said, Don't tell Kestrel.

Then we fought on the roof, and I fell only once.

In the weapons room, Roshar chooses a Dacran blade, long and slim, with a blade that curves slightly to its point. I lift one brow.

"Youngling, do not give me that look," he says. "Find another slip-water blade for yourself and let's begin."

"Are you *that* afraid to lose to me at fighting that you must choose a weapon you've wielded since the time you could toddle?"

"So rude to your elders. You should look upon me with naught but awe. Now, I prefer one of the rings open to the sky. I want to drink in the sunshine while it lasts."

I choose a slipwater blade lighter than his, and longer, to give me greater reach, and unbuckle my dagger so that I may strap this weapon in its place.

"No one beats me," he says, "let alone a little half-grown Herrani."

"No one?"

"Your father is good, I allow, but he *cheats*."

"Cheats how?"

"He is too big."

"That is not cheating."

"Uncannily gifted."

"I do not think you are proving your point."

"He is not natural! His god helps him. How can you best someone blessed by the god of death? *That* is how he cheats."

"You don't believe in our gods. I'm not even sure you believe in your goddess."

We walk into an achingly bright ring. The sand beneath my boots is washed white by the sun, so that it looks like thinly spread cream.

"Faith can be a choice," he says. "I choose to believe in my goddess, because I want to believe in mystery, in another world I cannot see until I die. It makes my life better to feel that something waits beyond it."

"Philosophizing will let you stall only so long, Godfather, before I beat you."

"So cocky! Wager me, then, if you are so sure of yourself."

"What stakes?" My mother warned that I should never ask this question, that I should instead seize the opportunity to set the stakes myself, rather than let an opponent make the first move by setting terms that suit him, but I am tired of listening to my mother, tired of how her voice rings in my mind. Anyway, I disagree. Sometimes there is an advantage to hiding what you want, and making your opponent show his wants first.

"If I win," he says, "I will ask a question, and you will answer."

"Questions and answers are highly irregular stakes."

He laughs. "Not in your family. Now put up your blade, and promise you will answer honestly when you lose. Swear by your gods."

"Roshar, I am always honest."

"You lie all the time. You have lied just now. Now swear by your gods. The full pantheon, please."

"Very well, I swear by the hundred to be honest. But I want something different, when I win."

"*If.*"

"Give me your ship."

Roshar shifts in surprise, and the sun catches his blade and turns it to ice. "My ship cost a fortune. She is the swiftest in the Dacran fleet."

"I know."

"My prized possession. You do realize that it is worth, say, a minor country? Like one of those Caynish islands. Not even the smallest one. A midsized island."

"I could have asked for Arin the tiger."

"Arin is mine." He *tsks.* "Are you planning to leave again so soon? To sail back to your Herrath sweetheart?"

"No," I say, and mean it. I just want a ship that is mine, truly mine. One that I don't have to steal. I am beginning to worry that to find my mother's poisoner, I might need to travel somewhere swiftly. *The answer begins with you,* my grandfather said, and if it is true that my leaving Herran prompted an assassin to attack my mother, it could be for political reasons: because a foreign enemy saw an opportunity to further destabilize the Herrani monarchy, a process I had already begun by vanishing. For now, I must stay close to home. So long as I monitor what my mother eats and drinks, she might recover. Already, this morning, she seemed better. But the assassin might strike again. I wonder, however, whether I will need to sail to Valoria to gather information, or even the

Cayn Saratu, where the band of Valorians unhappy with the dismantling of the Empire lurk, and plot against Verex . . . and possibly against his allies, like my mother.

I want the ship for another reason that cannot linger too far off in my future: my marriage. When I marry Prince Ishar of Dacra, my godfather's nephew, I want to be able to go where I will. I cannot be confined to his castle.

"Fine," says Roshar. "A question for me, or a ship for you. But—"

I strike first, my slipwater sword spinning free from its sheath. Roshar is forced to dance back. He edges to my left, clearly annoyed. His curved weapon darts around me like a dragonfly, never landing a blow, the thrusts too quick for me to parry though I duck easily out of their way. His strategy is bewildering, seemingly aimless until I feel a light nick in my side and realize what he is doing.

My tunic. A brand new one, tailored to my wishes. He is slicing it to shreds. "That is *mean*," I say, and he grins. I catch the next thrust and shove it back at him, making an advance lunge to whack the flat of my blade against his sword hand. It strikes his thick gold ring with a sound like a tiny bell. I feel the force of the blow judder up my arm, but he does not drop his weapon, merely takes the blow and curves around me to push one boot into the back of my knee. I stumble, fall, and roll, but when I am up I see that he has steered me directly into the sun's glare.

Now I understand why the Dacrans call this sword a slipwater: the sun flashes off the blade with such brightness that it leaves an afterimage across my vision even as the sword darts someplace else, so that I see the brightness of the blade moving *and* the bright ghost of where it used to be. Rippling light falls like water over my sight.

After that, it is over fairly quickly. My eyes stream in the sun. I can't tell where his sword actually is, or where it goes. He knocks the blade out of my hands and onto the sand.

I wipe my eyes. I can barely see Roshar gloatingly sheathing his weapon. He shakes out his right hand. "That hurt." He pouts, looking down at his long brown fingers and the glinting ring.

"You must really want that answer." My voice is surly. I sit down in the sand. My tunic is in tatters. Roshar is still complaining about his hand, saying that I am lucky he doesn't bruise easily, or he would kill me for my impudence. I lift my hand into a visor against the sun. Although the loss doesn't make me doubt my skill, I feel ashamed. As I blink my vision back into clarity, I realize that the shame is not because I lost, but because I wanted his ship so much, for what it represented: freedom that was not a gift or an inheritance or a theft but truly mine, honestly earned.

Roshar sits beside me, luxuriating in the sun. I, of course, will burn.

"Well, ask me," I say.

"Why are you angry?"

"I am not angry."

"You swore to be *honest*."

"You beat me fairly. I can't complain."

"I don't mean the fight. I mean your mother. Your father. Even me. Sid, you are a rangy little lion of anger. Always looking for someone to bite. You were like this before you left Herran. Now you're back, and it's worse. Why?"

I drop my face into my hands. The gesture shows too much of what I feel, but letting him see my expression would be worse. I realize he made a decision, from the moment he saw me hurtling through the atrium, to bring me to this point, to force me to answer this very question. Roshar being Roshar, he had to make a pageant of it, from pretending a friendly spar to proposing that absurd bet to making sure I knew he had fully won, in every possible way. "You could have asked me like a normal person."

"Where is the fun in that? Besides, you wouldn't have answered. Now you must. You're sworn to answer."

I breathe out slowly, my hands still pressed against my eyes and cheeks. "I am not like you."

"You must admit that you *are*, in a number of important ways."

"I have been with many women."

"You are a legend," he agrees.

"I didn't mean to be unkind to them. My father thinks I have been. I suppose he is right. There is . . . a hunger in me."

"For what?"

Quietly, I say, "To be wanted."

"Ah, Sid. In this, we are very much alike."

I have not given him a full answer. My vow to the hundred swells in my chest. I should never have made such a promise. Sunshine beats down on my head. I have already shown too much. Maybe I am already the gods' plaything, I cannot tell, but I have foolishly made a bet in their name. If I don't hold true to it, I might as well surrender myself wholly to whatever cruelty they might devise for a vow breaker.

It is easy to believe only halfheartedly in gods until you imagine how they might punish you. Then your faith solidifies very quickly indeed.

"We are different," I tell Roshar, "because I want one person. I want forever. I want what my parents have."

"What Kestrel and Arin have is a rare thing."

"I know."

"I am glad you want it," he says. "It is not for me. But only you can choose what is right for *you*."

"I kept looking."

"Sid, you are so young. You will find someone."

I think of Nirrim, of plucking a white petal from her hair and rubbing it between my finger and thumb, releasing its scent, and how I was able to make her want me but not love me. I shake my head.

Roshar says, "That girl in Ethin? Nirrim?"

"Nirrim didn't feel the same way."

He winces. "Should I feed her to my tiger?"

"It's not her fault. I didn't earn her love."

"That might not be true."

"This is me, being honest, sworn to honesty by the gods."

"I mean that you might not see the whole truth."

"There is more."

"Goddess help us."

"I don't want to be with a man. Ever. I never have. I never will."

"I am hardly surprised, but this is . . . rather inconvenient, considering that you are engaged to my nephew."

I shrug.

"I was given to understand that you *wanted* the engagement." His black eyes are wide, the green paint rimming them bright. "Kestrel said so. Did she lie to me?"

Miserably, I shake my head. Roshar heaves a great breath and flops backward onto the sand. "Of all the self-defeating . . . you are just like Arin. I swear he almost walked himself into an early grave countless times over. *You* are walking *me* into an early grave. And Dacrans don't even have graves!" More seriously, he says, "Sid, did you not know your own desires? I understand that maybe, when you agreed to the engagement, you weren't sure then, and thought you enjoyed men, or you *did* and then you changed your mind—"

"No. I knew."

"Did you want the political power? The royal marriage, to be queen of two countries, and to love whomever you wanted in secret? There's no shame to that. This, too, I would understand."

"No."

"Then why?"

This sun. It will blind me. How can it be this hot so close to autumn? How can summer hold on so hard? I want to plunge into snow. For ice to imprison my face. I want the hands that rest so uselessly on my upturned knees to dissolve into white powder and blow away in the next wind. My vow. The hundred. I say, "I wanted to make my parents happy."

His face fills with love. "Sid, youngling, you *do* make them happy."

I shake my head. "I am angry at my mother because she is glad to marry me to someone for political convenience. I am angry at my father for not seeing any of this. I am angry at you because you should know better than anyone who I am and what I want."

His expression twists.

"Can we be done?" I say. "Is that enough? I have answered you. You asked and I answered."

"It is enough, but—"

"Good." I scramble to my feet, not bothering to shake the sand out of my clothes, and hurry into the salle, plunging into the blessed, cool dark. I hear Roshar behind me. His hand on my shoulder drags me to a halt.

He says, "I think you should talk with Kestrel and Arin."

"No. Herran needs this engagement. We are a small country. Dacra is vast and powerful."

"We are your ally."

"Your sister the queen will eat our country whole the moment it serves her."

"Well, now, that is true."

"I thought, when I sailed away, that I would find something that would help Herran. An asset. Like our guns. A weapon or skill that would help us keep our independence. I thought if I could find it, I wouldn't have to marry."

"Did you?"

Nirrim feels so far away, the magic I tasted at the tips of her fingers a dream. I am no longer sure if what I experienced in that country was magic, or simply the desperation of my hope for a solution. My memory is not perfect, not like Nirrim's, and all I am sure of now is how I needed the feel of her fingertips against my mouth, and the way she knew me. "No."

"I still think—"

"I don't want my parents to know what I have told you. They wouldn't understand. Promise me you won't tell them."

"Sid." He sighs.

"None of this is yours to tell. Promise."

"I promise." He holds out his right hand and I take it. As he looks down at our clasped hands, he frowns. My eyes adjusted to the dark interior, I see that the heavy black stone set in his gold ring is not a gem at all, but glass. It has cracked. Swearing, he tugs the ring off his hand, reaches for the hem of my tattered tunic, and rips a strip from the bottom.

"Roshar!"

"The tunic was ruined anyway." Quickly, he wraps the ring in the cloth. "I am lucky the ring didn't leak."

I am confused. "Why would your ring leak?"

"It is filled with poison."

My heart falters. "Poison?"

"Well, not exactly. A liquid derived from an eastern worm. The ring has a mechanism that allows me to prick someone once, to send them to sleep. A stronger dose could kill someone." He walks outside. I follow, and watch him kneel and begin to chop at the earth with his slipwater sword. "I shouldn't have been wearing it in Herran anyway," he mutters as he digs a hole.

"Why not?"

He drops the cloth bundle into the hole and buries it. "Because of your mother."

He cannot be the poisoner. If he was, he would never speak so frankly about this to me. "What does my mother have to do with your ring?"

He tamps a clod of grass-rooted earth down with his boot. "It's a replica of one I loaned Arin years ago, when Kestrel was imprisoned in the tundra. He said he lost it, but that wasn't true. He threw it away."

"Why?"

"Kestrel wanted it."

"For revenge?" I know so little about my mother's imprisonment in the work camp, only that my grandfather sent her there, and that when my father rescued her, she was near death.

"For herself. In the camp, they gave her a drug that made her work hard, and stole her memory. She came to love the drug. Even when Arin brought her home, she wanted it. I think part of her always will."

"Why did she never tell me this?"

"Why do *you* never tell *her* certain things? Because you find them painful to share, or you consider them yours alone to know . . . or because you are ashamed." He sees my worry and says softly, "This was long ago, before you were born. The worm poison is not the same as the drug used on Kestrel in the work camp, but it reminds her. I was careless to wear the ring, but I'm not afraid that she would try to take it, or use it, only that it might hurt her to remember that time. Kestrel's body needed that drug, and then her mind did, and her heart, but she was stronger than her need. She has been for a very long time."

I realize he is telling me a story of my mother's strength, but also a weakness in her that I have never seen. She has always seemed so invulnerable. The night I fled Herran, she had simply grown quiet and pale as I yelled at her. She stood, posture perfect, braided hair golden over her shoulders, slender eyes as amber as those jewels that hold trapped insects from another time. She did not look human. She looked like an icon, like an image set in mosaics, each chip of ceramic slick and hard. *You are an apple, Sidarine*, was all she said, and then I was gone.

But I wonder if it has been easier for me to think of her as an icon, as a hard, untouchable image. She has always been more than my mother. Kestrel: the impervious queen. As much as that infuriated me, maybe I needed to see her that way, too, because it meant she could always protect me, and I would never lose her. What would it mean for me to see her as Roshar did long ago, when he first knew her: fragile?

The sun has advanced in the sky. I promised to bring my mother each meal. I cannot look like this: sweaty, worried, my tunic in tatters. In Dacra it is customary to thank your opponent for the pleasure of being beaten, so I do, formally—which Roshar adores—and hurry across the lawn.

Emmah awaits me in my breakfast room, though it is long past breakfast, and says nothing about my appearance, so used as she is to seeing me in worse shape, whether from fighting or slipping into my suite with my clothes in wanton disorder, trailing the perfume of lust. She smiles to see me, and despite the wrinkles from the burns on her face she looks young, her teeth even, her dark hair not so silvered as my father's, or Sarsine's, though they must be the same age. Surely Emmah was beautiful once. "I have something for you," she says.

My mind is too disordered; I do not really hear her. "Emmah, you must know Herran's medicinal herbs well." I will not say the word *poison*.

"Of course. Any nurse to the princess needs to know the rudiments of medicine. But you were a healthy child, thank the gods."

I stop myself from saying anything further. Every territory in the world has its own native drugs and poisons, and the secret to my mother's condition might lie not in Herran, but in Dacra, Valoria, or the Cayn Saratu. After I change and visit my mother's suite, I must ride in to pay a call to the redheaded Valorian ambassador whose eye I caught at the state dinner.

"Sid, I said I have something for you. From your father."

I blink myself back into where I am, instead of where I plan to be, and see that Emmah holds out an envelope. What could my father write to me, that he would not say to my face? The envelope is light, as though it contains nothing, not even the paper of a letter. I open it.

Inside is a speckled yellow feather.

I lift it by its milky quill. The vane is the color of honeysuckle, its tip whisper soft when I touch it to my lips. *The answer begins with you*, my grandfather said. I remember what Roshar told me, how my mother had to conquer her need for a drug. I remember my grandfather's prison, and how my mother designed it by thinking with my grandfather's mind. How she would beat me at Bite and Sting, tricking me into believing that four scorpions were enough when she held tigers in her hand. I wanted this feather too much. Can the gift of it, requested of my father by my mother, be only what it appears to be—a gesture of love? Does my mother *ever* say or do anything without meaning something more? An apple! She called me an apple. I think of apples and feathers and poison worms, and wonder if my grandfather was right, if the timing of my mother's poisoning has something to do with me. Was it meant to bring me back to Herran?

Queen Kestrel is capable of anything, they say.

Would she be capable of poisoning herself, if it brought her wayward child home?

THE GOD

———◇———

THE YOUNG WOMAN CARRIED ME gingerly, as though I might
bite her again with my thorns, and although she paused occasionally to
marvel at my slightly shirred petals, the deep red of them, so dark that
my center shadowed black, she conducted her task at the sugarcane
estate, her face serious, concentrated, then returned to the city gate
just before nightfall, when the sky was striped in blue and pink, and
the cooling wind carried the sea's salt. She presented her documents
to the militiamen standing guard, the red of their uniforms an insipid,
thin color compared to mine. She offered her Middling passport and
her High-Kith mistress's written command.

The soldier passed the documents back and was about to wave her
forward, into the city, when he paused. What is that? he asked, pointing
at me.

I found this flower, she said, on the jungle path.

Had she lived during the time of the gods, she would have been warned away from that path—indeed, the path would never have been built, for it cut through land sacred to us. But the god of thieves ruled Herrath, disguised as a mortal, and he despised us for casting him out. He made certain humans showed the pantheon no honor. Although he did not destroy the clearing in the jungle, or raze the temple one could find there, it was only because he had his own schemes, and believed the temple would one day serve *him*, for it was the only way he could ever return home to us.

I'll buy it from you, the soldier said, and I immediately worried, because men who wield weapons are not known for their ready compassion.

It is not for sale, she said.

She carried me through the gate and into the High quarter. Just before she entered the servants' door at the back of an ice-white mansion with gilded balconies, she slipped me inside her pocket. I was glad to be hidden away. The rich rarely pity anyone, because to do so is to question their own right to a position of power, or to envision themselves ejected from it. Neither is a comfortable feeling for those whose every waking hour is designed around comfort. I did not want to belong to the mistress. Should she see me, I would be taken, or become a forced gift. I liked where I was, snug in the girl's pocket, soft against her thigh.

She brought me home: a low, modest house made from sand-pressed brick. A cup was fetched from the cupboard and filled with water. My broken stem slid into the water's coolness and I sighed open, petals perfect, uncrushed. I had high hopes for the girl, whose face was the stuff of stories: plain, even for a human, and easily overlooked, save for her murky green eyes. Yes, I was held in a humble earthenware cup, hardly a fit vessel for a god, and I remained trapped by my bad bet, but the girl looked at me as though I were the whole world, and I thought surely it would not be impossible to do something—though what *can* a rose do?—to snag her tender heart.

"How gorgeous!" exclaimed another black-haired young woman who had appeared at the door. She resembled my girl yet was clearly a little older, more elegant, her manner constrained, her gestures imitative of someone wealthier than her clothes suggested. Her hair was as glossy as lacquer, brushed with five hundred strokes per night and scented with indi oil, her face finely cut. She might have even appealed to a god, were this before the time of our flight from the mortal realm. "Does it have a perfume?" She pressed her nose and mouth into me. "Heavenly!"

"Would you like it?" my girl said, and her older sister's cool eyes glinted even though her mouth flattened into a somber line. "Oh no," the sister said, "I couldn't possibly."

I shrank on my stem. Not *her*, I willed my girl. Give me to a child if you must, or someone lonely, or elderly, not this vivacious, acquisitive human. I yearned to be free, to find my form again, to retake my power and punish the god of games, that troublemaker.

This older sister was someone who would take what she could, and pin it to her forever. She would pity no one.

My girl lifted the earthenware cup. My leaves trembled. She set me in her sister's waiting palms. "It is a gift, Raven," my girl said. "I knew it was meant for you, the moment that I saw it."

NIRRIM

◇

THE HALF-KITH CHILDREN RESCUED from the Keepers Hall
follow behind me, all twenty-two of them, carrying my long train. How
their parents blessed me when I brought them home! They listened,
rapt, as I told them of their children's talents. They will help us remake
the world, I said. Will you help me?

Anything, they said.

I smiled and said humbly, I ask for only two things.

The parents of the lost ones, in answer to my first request, oversaw
the reconstruction of the Keepers Hall. They employed Middlings and
forced the remaining High Kith prisoners to shift rubble out of the way
and restore broken glass to re-create the hall into my palace. A queen
needs more than a small house on a hill. I have been too attached to
Sid's house, too eager to slip into my perfect memory of her, as though
into a warm, scented bath.

And so today, after a month of my subjects' labor, I process through the streets of Ethin, my Elysium soaring overhead, my dress a river of silk as green as the bird's eyes, my starry earrings and mended crescent moon necklace as bright as a galaxy. I love the sumptuous feel of silk on my skin. I never let myself feel this way before. Even when Sid gave me beautiful dresses, I felt like an impostor. Now I want to crow with delight. The whisper of my skirts. The admiration of the crowd. My people throng the streets, and they are my mirror, showing my lovely face, my jewel-green eyes. I am angry that, before, I never believed I was pretty.

I wish Sid could see me now.

She loved you without all these trappings, Other Nirrim says.

Stupid Other Nirrim! Sid would love me *more* like this. In fact, any woman could be mine. Who would not desire me: a divine, ravishing queen?

As soon as the pleasure of this thought fills me—I could snap my fingers and make anyone mine!—the pleasure fades into frustration. I don't want anyone else. I want Sid. I want her hand pinning my wrists above my head against the bed. I want her mouth on me. I want her to see me, and know what she gave up, and regret it. I want her to make it up to me.

Irritated, I sweep past the crowd, their admiration of me now stale.

I see Morah, her face as prim as stitched linen, lean to whisper in Annin's ear. Fools, both! They could glow in the reflection of my glory. They are no godlings, but I would be good to them, as I will be good to all my people, and they would be fine examples of how even ordinary mortals can contribute to our new world. But no, they frown, and judge, and disapprove, as though I am not enchanting. More than enchanting: I am a hero! The Children's Queen, they call me, and my rescued little ones trail behind me: the painfully plain girl who can bestow beauty upon others, the boy who can manipulate water, and more. Then there is the sweaty baby that I carry in my arms, whose gift we cannot yet know. It twists and mewls. I can't wait to thrust it from me, but I smile down upon the infant for the crowd's sake. Mere, my handmaiden, nods from the sidelines. It was her idea for me to carry the baby. Mere has done well, and whether her horror at the discovery in the bowels of the Keepers Hall was real or performed, I care little, so long as she continues to honor me.

A throne stands in front of my new palace, hewn from pink marble plundered from a High-Kith home. Aden, tall and luminous beside it, resplendent in finery stolen from High-Kith wardrobes, offers a hand to help me onto the throne, a planned pageantry that makes the crowd sigh. They expect me to marry him, and no doubt he expects it, too, given the confidence of his smile, but I have no intention of sharing Herrath. Aden is a conveniently handsome ally . . . and boring, his hunger for me and for my power obvious. His hope amuses me, and it is good for him that I am amused, or I would surrender to my anger at how he used to shame me for wanting a woman. He berated me for not wanting to marry him. What do I need, from men? From him? He can offer me nothing. He never could, and I am astonished that he—indeed, the entire Ward—made me believe for *any* length of time that it was expected and right that a girl belonged with a boy. It is nonsense . . . but nonsense that I will use, for now, for a good show. I imagine telling Sid. I imagine lying naked beside her, and laughing.

I pass the baby to Mere and lean to brush a kiss on Aden's cheek. His hand on mine tightens. The crowd loves it. How easily people swallow lies!

As I settle into my throne and the lost children kneel at my feet, I survey my people, wondering again what the god of thieves took from me. Not pride; it burns in my chest. Not longing. I uncap the vial of Sid's perfume every morning, almost shyly, as though she might see me do it, as though she knows the desire that wells up within me. The god of thieves did not steal my ambition, oh no, not when I have plans to solidify and extend my rule. And not resentment, or my throat would not tighten as it does to see that Morah and Annin do not cheer with the rest of the crowd, nor Sirah, that one-eyed crone, wrinkled as a naked mole rat.

"My people," I call. "Look to the sea."

Today the sea is a purple haze, almost as still as the heat-misted sky, like twins clothed in different colors.

"Look to the harbor."

Anchored ships float sleepily in the bay.

It is time to wake them up.

"There is a world beyond this one," I say. "The councilman who held our innocent children captive has revealed that beyond the island of Herrath, there are more countries than we could count. The ships in the harbor were not merely for Middling fishermen, but also for High-Kith merchants who secretly sailed to islands called the Cayn Saratu, trading goods made by our immortal hands, infused with our godly blood. We have overthrown those who would use us and keep us from exercising our gifts. Surely there are other lands where people suffer as we suffered, where the wealthy take their advantage to grind the poor into dust." My heart beats loudly in my chest, my ears. Whatever the god of thieves took, it was not my passion, for I believe wholeheartedly in what I say, and in the dream I am about to share. "Let us strike out across the sea to drag down the mighty, and lift the humble high."

"You want war," someone calls. It is Morah, damn her.

"Liberation," I correct with a smile. "Justice."

"You have no army." Sirah folds her twiggy arms across her chest. "And little in the way of weapons." Annin, like a frightened puppy, looks between the two women. Morah must secretly poke her, because Annin startles, then says, "How would we even go to war? We can't sail the ships in the harbor. None of the Half Kith know how."

She will come nowhere near a ship. *She* will stay safe at home.

The vehemence of that thought surprises me, and as I wonder where it came from—what do I care if Annin places herself in harm's way?—I realize that it is not my thought, but Other Nirrim's. Such a pathetically loyal big sister Nirrim was! Irritated, I say, "We do not need weapons. We are gods." I sweep a hand at the kneeling children, whose skills were inscribed in a ledger I forced the quivering councilman to show me. My second request of the children's parents was that the lost ones offer their powers to my cause. I would never force your choice, I told the parents and children. No one will force you again. What I want, I said sweetly, is your love.

And they, filled with joy and gratitude at their reunion, agreed, even down to the lisping four-year-old who can make a twin of herself—not an obviously useful skill, but I am sure I can think of a way to use her to my advantage. The godling children were taken by the council, clearly, because divinity ran stronger in their blood, their gifts greater than what could be harvested through the imprisonment of older Half Kith. There was a genealogy, the councilman explained, that recorded Half-Kith families going back generations. The Council monitored adults whose blood, obtained through the frequent imprisonments, had promising results. When they were released, and married others like them, the council sometimes stole their children, hoping for undiscovered gifts that ran rich in their veins.

Where is this genealogy? I demanded. The man shook his head, terrified, claiming he did not know. I wondered if he was lying, and whether I could pull a memory from someone's mind and make it mine. I tried to do just that to him, but couldn't. Finally, disgusted, I ordered

Aden to have the man imprisoned, and although I would like to see his head struck from his neck for his crimes, I have insisted he be kept alive, for the information he might give on the inner workings of the Council.

The baby squalls in Mere's arms. So far its only talent seems to be making noise and soiling itself. I suppose I will have to wait a few years to get anything good out of it.

"We do not need to sail when we can control the water." I wave an elegant hand toward the young boy—tall, with a soft face and kind eyes—who possesses that gift. "Who can stand against us? No one else in the world has our magic." So Sid said, and although she was a liar, I believe her in this, since she seemed to need magic so badly, as a way to escape marriage and secure her country's future.

"Then tell us, my queen," says Aden, a halo of light lingering on his skin, his smile dazzling. "Which country will fall to us first?"

Herran looms in my mind as Sid described it: rocky coasts, slender cypress trees, the mountains of the north, the greenery that fills its capital city, the blond lands of its hot south. *If you wish to rule alone*, the tree's fortune said, *you must destroy her.*

"No," I say, and Aden frowns, confused. I want to clap my hand over my mouth. I did not say that. It was Other Nirrim, that meddling memory, seeking to control me as though she were something more than a ghost. She is the past, jealous of my present. I recover quickly. "No one shall know just yet. Plans must be laid." I smile benevolently upon him, and know how we must look: like the sun and the moon, a natural pair. Well, let Aden live in hope, and the crowd along with him. Hope will occupy the people, who always enjoy gossip, and make Aden seek to please me.

Aden turns to the crowd. "For Herrath," he calls, "and the new gods!"

My people—except a silent few—cheer.

"Hey, Nirrim!" someone calls through the dark.

I halt, despite myself, immediately giving myself away, though I have changed my finery for simple Middling clothes and covered my hair with a modest scarf. Although I now have a palace fit for my stature, I could not sleep, and wanted to walk alone, unseen and unbothered.

One last time, I thought. I will visit Sid's house one last time.

Now I am doubly angry: at being so rudely hailed, and thwarted in my wish. A queen can have everything she wants except, it seems, privacy. I turn around to find the culprit.

It is Sid's Middling boy, her young informant, the one who spied for her. "The art of spying requires constant replication," she once explained. "The spymaster has her spies, and those spies have yet more spies. The boy who works for me probably has a little brother working for him." I remember—of course I do—that he kept my secrets, and that he, too, yearned for more than life gave him: the fate to be a soldier, or some High Kith's servant, the only occupations allowed to Middlings. I soften a little as he runs up to me, breathless, but arrange my face into a stern expression. He stops, scanning my eyes, and then says, tentatively, "I mean . . . 'Hey, Queen'?"

"*My queen* will do," I say, very nicely. He tips his head, studying me in a puzzled way, with a half smile, his black hair sticking up all over like spiders' legs, his eyes lively. He will grow into a young man soon, but still has the face of a child. Like Mere, he recognized something valuable in me even when I was Other Nirrim, and for that wisdom he shall be rewarded. "Tell me your name," I say, deciding to forgive him for intruding upon my evening. Queens must inspire awe, but it is good if they are also beloved, the stories of their generosity trickling among the common people so that they hope to one day be blessed by the queen's grace.

He does not, however, look either properly awed or grateful. "Killian," he says, still examining me.

"And who are your parents?" Do all Middlings raise their children to be this unimpressed by authority?

"Who says I have parents?"

I lose my patience with his stare. "What is so interesting?"

"You're just so *different*."

"Thank you," I say, pleased.

"How do you know you're a god?"

"Because I met a god, and he told me I was one." Well, he said that god-blood ran in my veins, which is surely close enough, and I am obviously more powerful than any Half Kith of my acquaintance. "And because of my gift."

"Are you faking it?"

"Would you like me to try it on you, so you may see for yourself?"

"No, thanks!"

"I thought so."

"Did you plot all this—overthrowing the High Kith and becoming queen—with Sid?"

"Killian," I say, making sure my smile is just right—friendly, easy, and not too interested, "I would like for you to pay me a call at the palace tomorrow, and tell me all you know about Sidarine of Herran."

"Uh, you know her better than me."

"I think you must know some items of interest."

"Well, sure." His eyes get sly, which somehow makes him look sweeter. "For a reward."

"Yes, of course. For a reward. Now, my young subject, I have business to attend to."

He lifts his black brows. "Royal business?"

"Yes," I say, pleased that he is catching on quickly, and turn to walk away.

"Hey, Queen?"

I sigh, but his irrepressible impudence is preferable to Morah's disdain and Annin's fear. At least Killian acknowledges my right to rule.

"How do you know you're immortal?" he says. "You've been calling yourself *god* this, *immortal* that. *Immortal* means you can't die, right? How do you *know* you can't die?"

I *don't* know, and have assumed, most of my life, that I would die. I will not say this, of course, but he seems to guess my thoughts anyway. My worry. "Be careful," he says. "People always want to eat the biggest fish, and you've made yourself into a real catch: pretty scales and a long tail and plenty of meat." Then he is off, whistling into the night.

At Sid's house, I stand upon her balcony, a vial of her perfume resting on the table. She prepared breakfast for me on this table, once. The sea is black glass, the moon as bright as the bowl of a spoon. My mother's jewelry glows of its own accord, creating a soft light around me. I want the Council's genealogy. Who was my father, that my power runs so strong, stronger than anyone else's, even Aden's?

I slip my hands into my pockets, where I carry sugar cubes. I enjoy their rigid shapes, the way they crumble slightly along their lines.

Bring me the past, I think, and show me who I am. Bring me the future. I will be a queen such as the world has never seen. Why should Herrath be my only territory? My palace library, which once served the Council, has many maps. Before the procession today, I unfolded several, studying the formidable country of Dacra, Herran's peninsula to the north of us, and the sprinkle of islands to the west: the Cayn Saratu.

Which country will next be blessed by my rule, my mandate to honor the poor and downtrodden? Who is to say that Herran, for example, would not welcome me with open arms? The Herrani king and queen were entirely selfish, putting their political agenda before the happiness of their only child. And Sid hated being a princess anyway—or so she said.

Then again, she was a liar.

Other Nirrim murmurs, She might have told you untruths that she herself believed.

I push that voice away. What would Sid think, if she saw me now?

I must become someone she would never dare abandon.

I remember her hand slipping up my thigh and stopping short. Tell me what you want, she said.

You know, I answered.

I like to hear you say it.

I want you, I whispered, and then she did touch me, and I buried my face in her neck.

The small table rocks beneath my touch, the legs uneven, as I reach for her perfume. I drip some onto my wrists. I rub it against my neck, where my pulse beats. A jacket she loved to wear hangs in her wardrobe. I take it and a pair of trousers to lay on the bed in the shape of a person. My fingers are slow to unbutton my dress, because I pretend that they are Sid's fingers, making me wait for what I want. My skin glows in the moonlight, revealed little by little. The dress drops to the floor. I slide into Sid's clothes, liking the friction of the fabric against my skin, fasten everything, and lie on the bed to wait. When I feel that I have waited enough, too long, that I deserve it now, I begin to undress again. My eyes close. It is not I who reaches to fold the jacket open, but Sid. Not my hands that skim over my flesh, but hers. Not my fingers that undo the trousers and slide inside, but hers.

The memory of her covers my body. My breath catches. She is here, I tell myself.

Here.

I open my eyes to stronger moonlight. I must have fallen asleep. How much time has passed is unclear, but Sid's perfume has faded on my skin. This will be the last time, I promise myself. I cannot come here again, to dwell in the past. To avoid a future. *If you wish to rule alone, you must destroy her.*

I push myself up from the bed. How like a mortal I behave, seeking something in objects, wanting clothes and perfume even when I can conjure a memory of Sid so perfect it burns me.

But I *do* want these things that remain of Sid, that touched her skin. I unstopper the vial of perfume. Its scent is not enough. From the pocket of my dress, where it lies abandoned on the parquet floor, I draw one sugar cube, soak it in perfume, and then, quickly, before it can dissolve, place it upon my tongue. The taste of Sid runs down my throat, sweet and bitter and burning.

Under the black sky with its bone-colored moon, I stand on the balcony and listen to the wide, secret sea, remembering Sid.

How sweetly I tumbled into sleep earlier, thinking of her.

How empty I feel now, in the shell of her clothes, the acrid taste of her perfume on my tongue.

THE GOD

—◆—

RAVEN SETTLED ME ON HER dressing table amid her treasures. Her true name was Raveneh, shortened affectionately by her younger sister, who said she was as clever as a raven, and as fond of collecting things. Oh, let me give you something in return for this flower! Raven said, and hunted among her treasures. A ribbon? Raven stared at it, aloft in her hand: a cyan strip of fabric whose color was beyond her kith. She set it back down. No, she said. You could get in trouble for owning this.

My girl smiled. Sister, you just can't bear to let it go.

But I *also* don't want you to get in trouble! Raven chewed her lower lip, picking up objects and setting them down: a violet shell whose inner curl was a shiny pink, a gold coin, an embroidered cloth doll, and more items, each time finding a reason not to give it to her younger sister. This shell is pretty, Raven said, but not *worth* very much, is it? And where would you spend a gold coin? Who would even have change for such a sum, in the Middling quarter? Now, you are obviously too old for a doll.

Give me nothing, my girl said. I'm glad your collection makes you happy.

Raven's face softened. As handsome as she was, this was the only time she looked truly beautiful. She said, No one understands me like you do, Irenah.

You see my dilemma. The kind sister was my best chance for compassion—and I was truly worthy of it, if only she knew! I had been cheated and entrapped. Irenah, perhaps, would pity me—if any human could pity a rose. But she was too good even to *keep* me, and certainly too good to take me back from her grasping, delighted sister.

Irenah left the room, and Raven fussed over me for a while, positioning me just so in a new cut-glass vase, lifting my leaves and letting them fall as though they were a lace collar in need of straightening. She inhaled my perfume, and I do not care to tell how many times she subjected me to *that*, her face so close. That a mortal would take such privileges with a god, unbidden, was unheard of. Somewhere, the god of games laughed. She has a very particular laugh, that god: like the jingle of tiny bells mixed with the clash of knives.

Then Raven forgot me. She showed me to no one, for fear that I would be stolen. My only view was of her bedroom, her bed made with what were surely the softest sheets in the house, the curtains sewn from the sheerest, prettiest fabric. The window showed me the street, and the wall beyond it. The god of thieves had commanded it be built, many hundreds of human years ago, to imprison the mortal children of the gods. They lived and died. (Nirrim liked to believe herself immortal, but even *she* could die like the others—like you.) They bore children of their own, god-blood watering down through the ages. From Raven's bedroom, the wall rose in a white crest, like a foaming wave, above the houses.

But I was a god, and could see beyond the wall. I saw the jungle, the sea.

The bay of Herran.

A baby's wail split the night. Arin, Death's Child, looked up from where he sat, hollow-eyed, face carved with worry. His infant howled in her crib. His large hands, which knew how to do many things—forge a blade, sew a button, murder an enemy, caress his wife—looked useless to him, clumsy. He had not been able to help Kestrel. He had not known how to stop the bleeding of birth, and the doctor, frantic, had banished him from the room.

He should call the baby's nurse. But the baby screamed, ruddy-faced, her fists the size of pebbles. He reached for her and settled her against his chest, against his loud, nervous heart. He had been a father for barely a few hours, and already he felt he was failing his child. Sidarine, shh.

The baby quieted.

Your mother is strong, he said. Wait for her. She will survive, you will see. But I am here. I am always here. I will care for you. No harm will ever befall you.

I promise.

SID

---◆---

"EMMAH?" I SAY, PULLING ON my softest leather boots, the ones that look ordinary but whose soles are made of padded fabric. All the doors within my suite have been left open, and the breeze blowing through smells like autumn. Outside, the leaves have caught fire. Roshar has stayed, even though my father has warned him that if he wants to escape the cold he had better do so before green storm season. Roshar has refused to give me any more of the Dacran black brew I like so much, the drink that sharpens my mind. Sorry, little lion, he said. I must ration my own supply. Too bad for you.

I smell tea and hear the clink of spoons and porcelain in the breakfast room. Emmah must hear my call, but she ignores me. If you have something to say, say it to my face, she always scolded me when I was young. My parents could have employed any number of women as my nurse, and while I sometimes thought they chose Emmah because they saw their own past in her ruined face, I suspect my mother sensed that

Emmah wouldn't let me get away with anything . . . and that my father, in turn, sensed that Emmah would let me get away with just enough of the right things. I hurriedly pull on clothes—nothing with flair, for once—and follow the scent of tea to Emmah, who is arranging a small bouquet of trillin, a pink, autumnal flower with slender stems, and red-and-yellow leaves. She has poured a cup of tea for herself and sips it as she slips into the vase some sprigs of dried lunaria, which has flat, papery pods of sheer silver. It is the god of the moon's plant. I have thought that the god of the moon might love me because of that god's shifting nature, sometimes female and sometimes male.

"Emmah?"

"Yesss?" She draws out the word, making it clear that she doesn't appreciate being shouted for.

"Emmah, I'm sorry."

"Say it, then, whatever you are so eager to say."

I pour myself tea, which I like without milk: a clear, rich brown. "Would you do me a favor?"

"Sid, I am *paid* to do you favors."

"Oh," I say, uncomfortable at the reminder that although I think of her as a friend, a second mother, a confidante and keeper of my secrets, she is paid to be all those things. I look again at the lunaria, which has other names, too—fittingly enough for the plant of a shifting god—and is sometimes called the money plant, for how its disks look like silver coins.

Gently, Emmah says, "And do you think I couldn't have quit my job, any moment I liked, if you were an unbearable brat?"

I touch one of the lunaria's silver disks. The plant is also called honesty. The disk is slippery beneath my touch, smooth as Nirrim's skin. "Am I?" I clear my throat. "Am I an unbearable brat?"

Emmah sits beside me. "You are very bearable." She smiles. "I missed you."

I smile back tentatively.

"Now," she says, "what is this gods-all important favor?"

"It's about Lyannis."

"The ambassador from Valoria? Sid, not her, too! She is almost twice your age!"

"It's not like that."

"So you always say."

"I just need you to occupy her for a while. This afternoon would be ideal. Couldn't you, oh, say that a merchant ship has just docked at the harbor, laden with Valorian goods? Once the green storms come, such things will be hard to come by. A trip into the city to see what the ship has unloaded would be a welcome suggestion to Lyannis, wouldn't it?"

"It might."

"And she wouldn't think anything of such a suggestion, if it came from a servant, would she?" Ambassadors are really just spies by another name, sent openly to other countries to gather information for their monarchs. My father always said that Verex, Magister of Valoria, can ask us anything he wants to know, but my mother would keep quiet, since she doesn't ask Verex everything *she* needs to know, nor would she do that with Queen Inishanaway of Dacra. Ambassadors are a necessary piece in the game, was all she would say. Indeed, in the game of Borderlands, with its many carved pieces that move intricately in their own patterns, the ambassador plays a key role, usually in the middle of a game in play, and is ideal for nudging the king into a vulnerable position.

"Sid, what are you up to?" Emmah asks.

The white lunaria disks make me think of paper. I will have to bring tishin paper when I search Lyannis's suite. "Nothing. Don't worry, Emmah."

"I only ever want what is best for you."

"I know."

"Sid," she says seriously, "you are not unlovable."

"I said *unbearable*," I say awkwardly, thinking back to earlier.

"Do you think I can't guess what you meant?"

My face prickles. I busy myself with drinking my tea.

"You are the only one I love," she says, "in this whole world. I wish you could see yourself the way I see you."

I set aside my cup and look away, trying to keep my expression even, to not show how sad it makes me that it is easy for her to tell me this. "I need to visit the queen."

Softly, she says, "I know."

I lean to kiss her burned cheek, then startle. "Emmah, you are missing an earring."

She claps a hand to her bare earlobe. "No," she says, "not the earrings you made for me!" She looks stricken as she takes the other tiny hoop from her ear, her eyes welling.

"Don't worry. I will make you another."

"You were so proud. You lisped then. Do you remember? Such a sweet child. So good at loving."

I laugh a little. "You speak as though loving were a talent or skill."

She closes her hand over the small gold hoop. "It is. Never forget it."

"Maybe I inherited it, from my parents."

I can tell that irritates her. Defensive—of *me*—she sniffs. "People always say, 'Sid is just like her father,' or 'Sid is just like her mother,' but to me you have always been just *you*."

This is a kind thing to say, but it makes me sad that everything can be so easy between her and me. That she can lose my gift and I can say,

Don't worry, I will make you another, and the grief is gone and we are both better, when all my parents and I seem to do is wound one another. I am sad that Emmah can praise me not for something that I *do*, like spying or accepting a marriage proposal, but something that I *am*.

You are an apple, Sidarine.

"I love you, too," I tell Emmah, then make sure I have everything I need for the day and hurry from the room, my boots soundless across the wooden floor.

My mother, when I bring her breakfast, is sleeping. She has been improving lately, and has sometimes gathered enough energy to move from room to room within her suite, which makes me sure that someone must have poisoned her food or drink while I was away. There are slow poisons which, administered in small doses, can accrue inside the body, and so gradually weaken a person that she will seem merely sick of some unnamable malady. I let myself hope that the worst is over, and that the assassin, now cut off by me from the easiest route of murdering my mother, can do nothing, and my mother will heal on her own, though she is still too frail. I dread a relapse—or the assassin making another attempt via some means other than food and drink.

I set the tray beside my mother—not wholly quietly. I am not loud about it, but make just enough noise that I won't seem rude if I rouse her. A floral arrangement adorns her bedside table—her servants must have made it for her, just as Emmah made mine for me—and a long, shallow box rests farther off on a larger table with a Borderlands set. The pieces are not in play. Orderly, each on its home square, they wait for a new game. But Bite and Sting tiles lie scattered across the surface, which makes me wonder whether my mother has played against my father. More likely, since the pieces have not been put away, she has been awake, stirring them into different patterns, playing a kind of solitaire. She is, after all, the only opponent worthy of herself.

The box lying next to the games must contain a new dress. I suspect my mother plans to return to an active role as queen. She hates being sidelined.

I can't be seen as weak, she said. It was during that time I visited her after being horribly beaten by Roshar, fighting with slipwaters.

You *are*, I told her, frustrated and worried. Amma, you are sick. You always want to be everything all at once, I know, but not *now*.

She shook her head. Herran can't be left defenseless, she said, then added, to the immediate and horrid leap of my pulse, Sid, I want to talk with you about the night you left.

Well, I don't, I told her. I couldn't bear again the accusation of being an apple: a frivolous dessert, easily cut open, so full of air that it floats on the water. Worse, I am afraid I might tell her the things I confessed to Roshar, that I might spill my embarrassing wishes before my mother out of hope that she understand, when what I know is that she always plays to win, and winning means keeping Herran safe. I am keeping it safe for *you*, she would say. So that *you* are safe.

My engagement to Prince Ishar ensures the safest future for our country. She knows it. I know it. I just didn't—*don't*—want to hear her say it. So that day, when my face was clean and clear, wiped fresh of sweat from my fight with Roshar, I told her, I don't want to talk about the night I left. Ever. I will marry Prince Ishar. If you try to discuss this with me again, I will leave, and this time I won't come back.

She shut her mouth, eyes wounded, too bright.

It is a rare thing to win against my mother. It didn't matter that it felt like I lost. I felt as though I had erected a wooden shell of myself around me, a statue that looked exactly like me. While I didn't want her to see my true self, my roiling insecurity, how desperate I was for her approval, I could not believe that she couldn't see through that fake, wooden version of myself. How could she not, when she always sees everyone's motives and moves so clearly? How could I be so self-sabotaging, to want to hide from her and be found, at the same time? I left her rooms before I could take back everything that I had said. She has not raised the topic of my marriage since.

Now, as I gaze down upon her sleeping face, I wonder if her breath is a little too even, a little too deep. I wonder if she is pretending, in order to avoid me.

Officially, there are two sets of keys that unlock every door in this house. One belongs to my father, made from old iron and passed down through his family for generations. The other set is one he forged for my mother. I am told the gift was a romantic gesture. Not what *I* would choose to impress a girl! When I asked for a set of keys, too, my father examined me suspiciously (so what if he had reason? So what if I was known for sneaking around? My very mother trained me to sneak around!) and said, Of course, Sid. When I go home to my god, my keys will be yours.

So when Roshar came to visit a few years back with a bottle of green Dacran liquor and teased my father into drinking some, I joined them in the study, encouraging them both. It was ridiculously easy. My father has no head for liquor, despite his size. When he wasn't looking, I stole his keys. I put them back, of course—after pressing each one into piles of wet tishin paper (that stuff was made by the gods for spies, I swear). Once the paper hardened, I had the molds I needed. My father never taught me blacksmithing, despite my begging. He was forced to learn as a child, sold after the first Herrani war to a smith. Although he still enjoyed making gifts like my gun and dagger, he couldn't bear to remember learning the skill—and he would be forced to remember, if he taught me. He helped me make Emmah's gold earrings, then refused to do more.

I couldn't forge the keys myself. But there are often many solutions to a problem, and it just so happened that I had been regularly bribing a smith in the city for a year, in anticipation of getting my hands on a set of keys.

So now I have a set of my own. From one of the windows set in an arcade along the house's upper story, I saw Lyannis ride into town. I set the right key into the outermost door of her suite and slip inside, my steps silenced by my soft shoes, just in case she returns or someone else enters.

I search her room, admiring the several sheaths she has for the dagger she wears, as any Valorian does, at her hip. At her dressing table sits a small glass pot of glittering gold cosmetics. She must be engaged to be married—promised Valorian women wear a line of gold across their brows. It's a good thing I am not really Valorian. I dislike cosmetics, though I have been warned I will need to wear eye paint once I marry into the Dacran family. I imagine it will be one of many things Prince Ishar and I fight about, once we see each other again.

I sniff each of the cosmetics at her table, searching for anything that smells odd. There are botanical books in our library—my father was a sickly child, they say, and fond of studying plants while recovering from fevers—and I have done my research on poisons. But nothing among Lyannis's cosmetics looks or smells like the murky brownish poison the Valorians once used to try to eradicate the Lahirrin population, just before the second war with Herran. The Valorians had secretly installed a device in Lahirrin's aqueducts, the poison seeping slowly into the city's water supply. I had thought that maybe the brown poison—called somnum, and used in lesser doses as medicine to calm the nerves and induce sleep—could produce the symptoms my mother had. But nothing in

Lyannis's rooms resembles that—nor simberry, a deadly, tiny fruit that grows near here, nor nightlock, a mountain weed my father used to murder a whole host of Valorian colonists on the night of the First-winter Rebellion, though nightlock likely would have killed my mother instantly, and the death would have been an obvious assassination.

In Lyannis's desk, I find correspondence. I do not think the letters will contain anything interesting—they have been left about too freely. Ignoring them, once a quick glance confirms they are filled with lines of court gossip, written in a messy hand that left several blots of ink, I rummage about some more, looking carefully at her dresses in the wardrobe. Among the many secret codes my mother taught me for communication, using colored threads knotted in a specific way is one, but the embroidery on Lyannis's dresses and gloves tells me nothing. Nor do I find evidence of other forms of secret communication, such as counters, which were used to translate Valorian military instructions, or a Caynish double ring, a device that contains two concentric rings, the outer engraved with a normal alphabet, and the inner ring containing an invented one. No such tools, or anything like it, are to be found, no matter how hard I look—and I did my job thoroughly, even finding the rather boringly expected false bottom in her trunk, which contained nothing but certain spicy drawings of herself, possibly meant for (or drawn by?) her fiancé.

But the very *lack* of anything suspicious makes me especially suspicious, so I return to those boring gossipy letters. And when I do, I notice that every single page contains little ink blots—flicks, here and there, that seem made by a faulty pen. But if the pen was so bad, why didn't the writer exchange it?

I grin, in a good mood for once, and take some tishin paper from my pocket. Laying it over each letter, the tishin so sheer that I can see every written line through it, I painstakingly copy the blots.

Back in my suite, it takes me hours of studying the copies I have spirited away, leaving the originals safely in their place. At first, I see nothing but specks and dribbles of ink.

There is always a pattern, my mother says. A code is never actually secret. It cannot be, not fully, in order to work. It is secret only to those who cannot see the pattern at the heart of every code.

Eventually, the blots begin to make sense, and when they do, I sit back at my desk, my breath coming quickly.

Lyannis has received some news about the Cayn Saratu. They are being invaded by a foreign force no one has heard of. One island has already fallen to the invaders.

The invaders call themselves Herrath. They are led by a cruel, beautiful black-haired queen.

And the weapon they wield is magic.

"Exactly *how* did you come by this information?" my father says when I find him in the library, shut the door behind me, and tell him what I know.

"Etta, you know perfectly well how Amma trained me."

"Against my better judgment. I wanted you to be free of all that: the conflicts, the intrigue——"

"There is no escaping it. I was born into it."

Quietly, dangerously, he says, "Entering the ambassador's suite was a violation of our hospitality to Valoria."

"I didn't violate our hospitality," I say: a lie and not a lie. After all, Lyannis didn't *tell* me I couldn't come into her rooms.

He covers his eyes with one hand. His hands look like a peasant's hands: rough, unlovely, strong. "Of course. She *let* you in," he says wearily, and he is not being sarcastic. At first I don't understand, and then I do. "Etta," I say, just as wearily, "Lyannis and I are not lovers."

"I would like, just once, to trust what you tell me."

"May we please discuss what I discovered and not my methods of discovery?"

He shrugs. "I will raise the issue with Verex and ask if he needs Herran's help. Otherwise, there is nothing for me to do about a Caynish invasion, save to monitor it."

"It's almost as if twenty years of peace has made you lazy."

His eyes glow with sudden, silver fire. "There is nothing about this news that demands Herran's involvement, or even Valoria's. The Cayn Saratu is an independent nation and they are not fond of us. If we involve ourselves, it might look as though we hope to establish ourselves as new imperialists, under the guise of friendly aid. If Verex steps in, it will embolden the Valorian rebels in the Cayn Saratu who are eager to see those islands be once again part of Valoria. This is a mess, and we are well out of it. Verex knows this, or he would have raised the issue with me himself. Herran is in a delicate enough position as it is. My duty is to my country first, always."

"Etta—"

"Sid, you are not Kestrel. You need not try to take her place."

My face burns. "But she is sick, and you are alone, and I want to help."

His expression softens, and I see, suddenly, how he will look ten years from now. His eyes look old—gray as pewter, as deep mist—and sad. "I miss her," he whispers. "Does that make sense, to miss someone who isn't yet gone?"

I remember Nirrim sleeping next to me, her palm on my shoulder, and feel like I have been wading out into the ocean along a sandbar that has dropped away without warning, a cold darkness opening up beneath me, fathoms deep. "I think we can't help what we miss, or how we miss it, and the god of the lost knows it."

He swallows. "I'm not sure you can understand what it means to know you have placed your heart in the most fragile of vessels, which could break at a moment's notice, and destroy you, and *still* you would choose this. You would choose this person, over and over again, for as much time as the gods allow, even if that time is hours and not years."

Shame tightens in my chest, because I *do* understand this, otherwise I wouldn't be so afraid of loving someone so much. Even though I chose to leave Ethin for my mother's sake, even though Nirrim refused to come with me, I could have promised to return. Maybe I would have, if she had allowed me any hope. Do you not love me like I love you? I asked her. Won't you come with me? The pain of her answer drove me out the door and down the street to the wharves, where my docked ship waited.

Not just pain, I realize now. Fear, too.

"Sid," my father says, "do you really want to marry Prince Ishar? You met once on your twelfth nameday. You barely know him."

I shrug. "One man is as good as another."

"But you don't want to be with a man. Do you?"

"Ishar is not just *any* man. He's the crown prince of the world's most powerful country, since the Valorian Empire's fall."

"You have never cared about political power."

"Can we please not pretend that this marriage isn't something you and Amma want?"

My father stands and walks to the bookshelves, his broad back to me as he traces the richly bound books, the leather of the spines darkened with age. His fingers rest atop the spine of a poetry book I have seen him hold many times as though it were as delicate as a soap bubble. Once, alone in the library, I took it from the shelf, to understand its worth to him. When I opened the book, I saw that the flyleaf was inscribed with ink faded by time. *To Arin,* it read in old-fashioned script, *From Amma and Etta, with love.*

His fingers lift and he moves away from the poetry book to pull aside a heavy gold curtain fringed with red. Outside, a green storm is brewing. The sky looks viridian. Wind tears orange leaves from the trees and whirls them over the dry lawn. When he turns to face me again, his expression is hesitant. "I want you to be safe," he said, "and I want you to be happy, but maybe you can't be both. A marriage alliance between Herran and Dacra will make you safe, because it will make our country safe. Will it make you happy?"

"As Amma said, I can always have lovers on the side." She presented the possibility of marriage to me on my twentieth nameday, a few months before I fled Herran. You do not have to do this, she said, but would you want to? You could still take your usual liberties.

I saw myself suddenly as she must, as the entire court did: an inveterate rake. Well, I deserved the reputation. But her question made me heart-sore, because she saw me only as everyone else saw me, and could see nothing more. Feral with vulnerability, too proud to correct her, I said, Yes, why not?

"Doesn't every ruler get a moniker?" I say to my father. "Sidarine the Philandering Queen. Sidarine, Queen of the Hollow Heart. Something like that."

"I think you don't really want this marriage."

"My kind of philandering isn't going to produce bastard children, so the royal line would be secure. Plus, Ishar can have his own dalliances without my interference. The Dacran-Herrani alliance will be cemented. Seems like a good deal for all concerned." The storm darkens in the window behind him. The sky looks as green as a summer forest.

Thunder rumbles. It feels like the storm is inside my chest. I say—my words sudden, accusatory, surprising myself in their directness—"I know you don't like that I want women."

"You misunderstand. I dislike how you treat them."

"Because you are so perfect, and honor Amma with every bone in your body."

"I am not perfect. I haven't always been good to women." He smiles ruefully, to see that he has stunned me. "I misled some of them." My eyes must be as round as the moon. "This was before I knew Kestrel loved me."

"How . . . many?" My voice breaks like a boy's.

"Two. Maybe three."

"What happened?"

"It was so long ago." He spreads his hands helplessly in the Herrani gesture of skepticism, possibly because he cannot believe his memories are real. "I was careless. When I was enslaved, another woman on the general's estate was kind to me. Her name was Lirah. She was pretty, but I didn't even notice her, didn't realize I had let her believe I returned her feelings. And then there was Inisha—"

"Queen Inishanaway?" I feel uncomfortable in an almost itchy way. I don't really enjoy this particular glimpse into my father's past, but I am also fascinated. "You bedded the Dacran queen?"

"No! I kissed her. She wanted me, and I believed your mother didn't, and that I had to try wanting someone else. My love for your mother felt like a sickness I had to cure." He closes his eyes for too long a moment. "I used Inisha. I still regret it."

"It was just a kiss. You are making too much of this."

"You make too little of it."

"You said *three* women. Or: *maybe* three."

"There was a Valorian bookkeeper I made a bargain with. She hoped for more than a business transaction. I let her know I wasn't interested."

"That's it? Your entire list of women you have supposedly mistreated? That's nothing!"

"To you, perhaps." He stands so stiffly, rain streaking the window that frames him, that I can tell he is made uncomfortable by this conversation, too. His shoulders are squared. He stands as if in judgment. He looks as noble as a sculpture in the city square.

I say, "If I felt as guilty as you did about every selfish kiss, every misunderstanding, and every—what exactly *do* you think you did wrong with that bookkeeper?—every time I turned someone down, I would have to lock myself in my rooms and never creep forth, for shame of my sins."

"That is my point, Sid."

"You are saying that your real problem with me is not that I want women, but that I can't stay true to one." A slow irritation grows inside me. "You advise me not to treat women lightly, as playthings, but rather to be faithful, to find a love blessed by the god of souls, to have what you and Amma have." As I speak, my frustration becomes clear, and my father's face changes as he begins to understand why, even before I say it. "But marriage is between men and women, Etta, in every known country in this world, including Herran. What you want for me is impossible. And you, a king, have helped *make* it impossible by your inaction."

He looks stricken. "Sid, I am sorry. This never occurred to me."

"Why not, I wonder? Because you thought I would change? Grow out of it? Or because your love with Amma is so perfect you can't imagine a different way?"

"I will make such marriage into law."

I shake my head. "There is no woman I plan to marry. I am already engaged, and will keep that engagement."

"I will write the law anyway. I should have done it long ago. For everyone, not just you."

Such a law feels too late, too long after my habits and needs formed. Sid the sly, they call me. As bad as a boy. *You are an apple, Sidarine.* Only now do I realize that I might not be this way if it hadn't always been clear that there would be no story for me, no tale wrapped like a present that gets to be opened again and again to reveal the kind of love my parents have, the kind that everyone sighs over, because it is forever. The kind that makes a family. Who would I be, how would I have acted, what might I have said to Nirrim, if I had ever believed that kind of story could be mine?

I cannot know.

"It's a good idea, Etta," I say heavily. "You should write the law." Are you supposed to thank someone for doing the right thing, if it is years too late?

The rain sheets down the window. Ships will stay docked in the bay throughout autumn and winter.

My father comes close. My eyes burn, but I feel myself standing the same way he did a moment ago, like my bones have been replaced with something harder, a pride as strong as steel. "I won't question you again," he says.

Is that what I want? "You said you want me to be safe, and happy. What if I can only be one, and you had to choose?"

He kisses my brow. "I don't know," he whispers into my hair. When his voice falls low like this, I can hear the singer in him.

The sound of the storm is loud, and I still wear my soft boots. When I walk to the door, I am as soundless as a ghost. Just before I reach the door, he speaks again: "I would choose to let you choose."

As I walk through the house to the kitchens, my father's words still ringing in my mind, I realize that we forgot too quickly the news from the Cayn Saratu. We didn't even discuss the fact that the invading force was led by a beautiful queen. Herrath has no queen. The island is ruled by the Lord Protector, a man elected to a lifetime position by the Council, also men. Has the Lord Protector been overthrown? Could the High Kith have chosen someone else to rule in his place?

But the coded report I read also described magic used as a weapon. As far as I know, only people of Nirrim's kith possess magic, and it is harvested by the Council through imprisonments and blood drawn as payment for made-up crimes, like dressing too nicely for one's social status. Could it be that the Half Kith rose up against their oppressors and chose someone to lead them?

I think of Nirrim, but I can't imagine her as this warlike queen. She was determined, yes, to right the wrongs perpetrated on her people. And strong. I do not doubt she could lead an army . . . but not to colonize another country. Not to wield magic as a weapon. Nirrim was too good-hearted for that.

Worry grows within me, as spongy and creeping as moss. This news of a deadly queen unsettles me. I wonder what Nirrim is doing now, if she is at the mercy of this queen. I hope she is safe.

Do you not love me like I love you? I asked her. Won't you come with me?

But her answer was no, and my place is here. Finally, I understand what other women meant when they accused me of breaking their hearts. I can feel the pieces of my love split within me like a glass flower, blooming to pierce me from the inside. It closes only to open again. Sailing to Herrath to investigate the rumors would be stupid. Impossibly painful.

Even if my mother were well, to see Nirrim again would shame me. Who would beg for something that cannot be given?

I put Nirrim from my mind, and go to prepare my mother's meal.

My mother is awake when I bring her dinner. She is even on her feet, neatening her bedchamber, returning Bite and Sting tiles to their velvet bag, pinching dead petals from flower arrangements. The long dress box lies open on the table, its undone ribbon as elegant as a swan's neck. Tishin paper hides the box's contents. My mother wears a simple silk day dress from a few seasons ago, as pink as a blush on fair skin. I think she has chosen it to make herself look healthier. With her neatly braided hair; her small, determined movements; and the soft glow of her dress, she looks like a golden-headed flower, not like someone who has been exchanging whispers with the god of death. I notice the hollows beneath her eyes, and an edge of exhaustion to her burst of energy. Still, I am hopeful, and smile when she notices me.

"I am glad you're here," she says, but doesn't stop her task of making the bed, and fluffing the pillows so they don't show the dents where her head rested.

"Amma, someone else can do that." Although I forbade the servants from bringing her food, they still clean her rooms as usual.

"I want to be myself again," she says. "I *must* be."

"No one expects you to be. You should rest more."

She shakes her head, and I decide definitely *not* to tell her about the news from the Cayn Saratu. It will only give her purpose to get up to her usual tricks, when what she needs is to recover. She asks, "Will you help me into my new dress?"

I pull aside the tishin paper to reveal a brocaded dress, as red as the leaves outside, its fabric rich enough for winter. I am surprised at my mother's eagerness. She cares little for fashion beyond how it serves her purposes. To her, a beautiful dress is merely a tool. "Why did you order a new dress? How can you even have been fitted for it? You are a *convalescent*." I draw out the word, probably annoyingly, to stress my frustration and worry. "You are supposed to rest."

"I have rested enough."

"You didn't answer my questions."

She waves an irritated hand. "The dress is a gift from your father, obviously."

My worry grows. "It is not obvious." He wants her to rest as much as I do. Why would he deliver a dress to make her feel like she needed to rejoin society, and take up her mantle as queen?

"Well, *I* did not order it, and he knows my size perfectly."

"As does every dressmaker in Herran."

"There was a card," she says, but refuses to let me see it, and begins unbuttoning her dress, revealing a sheer chemise beneath.

"You want to believe this. You can't cope with the thought that the kingdom can carry on without you."

"Arin needs me," she says, "more than ever."

The card falls from her hand to the floor as she reaches for the red dress and steps into its heavy circle. I scoop the card from the floor. The handwriting is my father's, but I don't like the words. *For Kestrel*, the card reads. *Something you deserve.*

To me, this sounds like a threat, not a gift.

Samples of my father's handwriting lie all over this house — in his letters, his drafts of laws and the speeches he hates to give.

Anyone could copy it.

"Wait," I say, but she is already pulling the dress up around her.

I snag her wrist, and am glad that I am strong, stronger than my small mother, who protests even as I use my other hand to pull the dress from her grip, and let it fall to her feet. I kneel to examine the dress. I order her to step out of it, and to my surprise, she obeys, her face ashen as she realizes what I suspect—and what she, too, now suspects.

On the outside, the dress is all scarlet beauty, the brocade intricately—innocently—embroidered. But as I bend back the fabric to study the inside of the dress, I see that the fabric is not normal, that it is thick for a reason not apparent to the cursory eye.

Inside, the dress is embedded with tiny barbs, each smaller than a cat's claw. I prick my finger on one of them. Numbness spreads through my skin.

The dress is poisoned.

THE GOD

RAVEN NEGLECTED TO POUR FRESH water into my vase. Still, I bloomed. My petals sealed shut at night and flourished in the day. Raven added to her treasures, and I became invisible among them, an item that had lost its luster of newness.

Until the day she decided to wear me.

She sat before the mirror, applying cosmetics beyond her kith, braiding her hair into an elaborate, black crown suitable only for a lady. Once finished, she stared at her reflection, her admiration dissolving into wistfulness. Like Irenah, I understood: it can twist a human to long for something constantly denied, to see what others have and know it will never be yours. As Raven regarded herself in the mirror, she knew she was as beautiful as any High Kith born, but the thought filled her not with satisfaction, but the desire for revenge. She did not want to be equal to a High Kith. She wanted to be *better*. She wanted something no one else had, not even the most privileged of Ethin.

Her eyes fell upon me.

Yes! she cried, intending to weave me into her braided hair. She pounced upon me, snatching me from my vase.

But she had forgotten my thorns.

They studded into her fingers, my little nails digging deep enough to make her yelp.

Raven? Irenah called from another room. Are you all right?

Damn you, Raven hissed between her teeth, and ripped my petals from their crown. Pain shredded me. I fell apart over her dressing table, throbbing, dizzied. She bent my stem, blood running down her closed fist, and tossed me aside. I lay in so many agonized pieces that I could not think. Raven ran from the room, shoving past her sister, who had come to offer aid.

You call *that* a gift? Raven sneered, and was gone.

Irenah leaned above the dressing table. With one finger, she touched a petal. I wanted to beg her to stop. It was too much. She looked down at the small heap of my petals, soft and ruined, her ordinary face growing horrible in its expression, yet dear to me, even through my pain, because I realized that I had missed her, that the only happiness I had known in many human ages had been to rest between her fingers, to lie hidden in her pocket, to behold the simplicity of her mouth, her eyes as green as a storm. Three tears fell from her eyes upon me: one that slid down the bowl of a petal into the shape of a crescent moon, the other two beading into perfect stars. Although to her I had no feelings, no senses, no soul, she pitied me for no other reason than that it pained her to see something beautiful destroyed.

Her tears hardened into jewels against my skin, and I was free.

Oh, Irenah gasped as I shone forth: whole, myself, a miracle. And in the light of the divinity she returned to me, I saw the fullness of her good heart.

I fell in love.

Which had surely been the god of games's design all along. I heard the god's terrible laugh. Well played, I told that god, full of bitter desire. It is the ultimate suffering to love a mortal, whose life is as fleeting as dew upon a flower.

NIRRIM

◆

I STAND IN THE GREAT dining hall of the orphanage where I
grew up, where Raven abandoned me after the death of my mother,
her sister. Considering how fuzzy memories are for normal humans—
fragmented, half imagined, colored by the emotions of the current
moment—I assume that humans do not experience the vertigo I
sometimes feel when a memory rises within me, sharp and *real*, just as
though it were still happening, and lives alongside the present. Once, I
sat on that wooden stool at that long wooden table—my body small, my
eyes big, my limbs as quiet as possible so that I would not get in trouble.
Once, I reached across that table for my tin bowl full of rice—and, on
special days, fish. A High-Kith girl sits there now, just as quietly as I
did . . . and even more afraid.

Even though all the girls are dressed in the same sand-colored
wincey dresses, it is easy to tell the orphaned High-Kith children from
the orphans who have lived here since being abandoned, as I was

abandoned, in one of the baby boxes outside the orphanage's door. *My children have wise faces. My children look at me with fascination and hope, because they have already heard of my great feats.*

The other children look upon me with dread, because they have heard the same thing. They study me warily. Their gazes dart over Aden and a few godling children I have personally selected for this event. We are stunning: I in my Elysium-colored silks, the bird resting on my shoulder, Aden in cloth-of-gold, and the children in shades of the sea, to represent our triumph over the islands we have conquered to the west of Herrath.

The headmistress claps her hands. "Children, kneel before your benefactor, our savior: Queen Nirrim."

They do, dropping from their stools to kneel upon the gray stone floor.

I walk down the aisle, my silk dress hissing over the stones, Aden beside me, the godling children fanning behind. With pleasure, I note the Half-Kith children who turn worshipful eyes to me. I understand that not all the children gathered here do the same. Some of them stare at the floor. Of course they are ashamed. Their parents were traitors to our divine blood. Their parents were criminals, descendants of the acolytes of the god of thieves, who employed them to build the wall around my people and make them forget their power. These children are lucky they have been spared by my people—more, they are lucky that they have been taken from their old lives, where they would have been ignorant of their own privilege. Now, they have the chance to be part of my new world.

I stop and place a hand on the shoulder of Tarah, the plain girl who can create beauty. Her oval face is serious, her gray eyes so pale they look like water. One might not think she would be useful in our conquest of the first island of an archipelago we learned was called the Cayn Saratu. But when our ships landed on the shore, she painted all of us with awe-inspiring splendor, so that the Caynish soldiers who had come to beat us back faltered, suddenly loath to attack. Those who would easily crush a spider will not kill a butterfly. "Show the children," I say, and her power spins radiantly from her, casting rainbows. She turns tin bowls into gold, transforms the wincey dresses into silks. It is all an illusion, and will fade, but the orphans gasp. Aden casts a shower of light over the hall, golden droplets sprinkling over everyone.

I say, "My children—for you are *all* my children now, no matter how you were born—we have come with a message of hope. Would you like to be able to wield the power we do? My Elysium will discover who among you has been blessed by the gods."

"Oh," a brown-haired girl says, her word a little cry of disappointment. "I wish it could be me!"

"But it *could* be," I say gently.

"I would know if I could do something like *this*." She trails her fingers through a veil of Aden's sunshine.

"I didn't know," Aden says, and although he is playing his role perfectly, his handsome face encouraging, I don't like that he has stepped into a conversation that was mine.

Smoothly, I say, "The ability to use magic seems to rely on you *knowing* that you can."

A small High-Kith girl places a tentative hand over her heart, the gesture all of us in the orphanage were trained to use if we wished to ask a question.

She is not to blame for her parents, Other Nirrim says.

I *know* that.

Be kind to her.

I have already been kind to her.

By having her parents executed?

For crimes they committed against us, I remind Other Nirrim. I tell her, It is a kindness to raise the girl in a new way: with the right guidance, the right ideals.

Other Nirrim says, You sound like Raven.

This makes me so angry that I frighten the girl by the expression that must twist across my face. It is unfair for Other Nirrim to suggest that I am manipulating truths to make everything the way I wish it to be—that I, like Raven, would punish anyone who might interfere with those lies.

Is it unfair?

I wipe my expression clean and smile brightly. "Yes?" I say to the High-Kith girl who wishes to ask a question.

"When can I go home?"

"You *are* home. These are your sisters. Your teachers are your mothers. And I am a very special mother to you, as your queen."

"But I miss my old home," the girl whispers.

"Your new one is better."

Another girl pats her chest, eager to speak. She looks typically High Kith, in that way we call Old Herrath, with thick black hair and silvery eyes. When I call upon her, she says, "Will your Elysium try me? Please? I want to see if I have magic!"

Other girls cry out, eager for the same. I smile indulgently, and begin to speak when Aden says, "Of course, little one." He lifts the Elysium from my shoulder, which, although it squawks, lets him handle it. Maybe the bird is attracted to his god-blood. Maybe the bird cannot help this betrayal of me, but I fume at Aden. He is supposed to be here as my second-in-command, as my loyal officer, not to speak and act as though he were my equal.

As though he were king, Other Nirrim warns.

In the midst of girls crying out to be first, the shy brown-haired girl, still sitting on her stool although others have leapt to their feet, places her hand again over her heart. She says, "Where are my parents?"

I do not know, but before I can speak, Aden says, "You will see them one day."

This is a midnight lie, because even if her parents are dead, the girl will one day see them in the realm of the gods.

Reassured, the girl touches a spoon, her fingers passing through the rainbow puddle that sits in its bowl, and smiles.

I feel a twinge in my chest. The sensation is strange, because I do not think I am affected by a real feeling. Why should I care if Aden lied and the girl believed it, beyond caring that he has overstepped with *me*? No, it feels as though I have a muscle memory of an emotion I would have felt if I were Other Nirrim. The emotion steals over me like a phantom. My memory is so perfect that it seems able to conjure an emotion I *did* feel in the past, and *would* have felt, if I were the person I once was.

There it is again: a squeeze between my ribs.

Guilt.

Abruptly, I leave the dining hall, my godlings stumbling after me as I hurry, surprised. The Elysium bird flies ahead.

I don't *actually* feel guilty. I have been tricked—worse, tricked by *myself*. Why must I be haunted by a shadow emotion, a guilt that isn't even real, but only a memory of insipid Other Nirrim?

Outside, in the courtyard that separates the girls' wing of the orphanage from the boys', I tell my godlings—Aden, too—to leave me alone. But while the gifted children I rescued from the Keepers Hall obey, Aden steps in front of me, his blue eyes bright—probably because he senses he has gained some advantage.

"Stop getting in my way," I tell him.

"We need to go back. We are here to recruit more children to our cause. We have a job to finish."

"You do not command me."

"Because you are *queen?*" He draws the last word out in a sneering tone. His eyes are bright with something else now, something that looks like vengeance. "You are queen only because you say so, and enough people in Ethin agree. But not everyone does. Some people think that we would be better ruled by a king."

I should not have brought him to Cayn Saratu. His ability to create fire from the heat of sunlight was useful in beating back the Caynish defenses, but I am well aware of the whispers that it was *he* who won the battle. I should have guessed that my people, so starved of agency throughout most of their lives, would be drawn to the showy nature of his power. They do not realize how it fades quickly and leaves him exhausted, far more tired than I feel when I use my magic. If anything, I grow less tired the more I practice the skill, building my strength as though it were a muscle. But the Ward adored Aden even before I revealed the city's past. Everyone thought he was special just because of how he looked.

He says, "I did everything you asked, even when you treated me like your servant. I have been patient. I have helped you."

"Because helping me *served* you. Who would you be, without me?"

"A lot happier, probably. Nirrim, you once loved me."

"I assure you I did not."

"We had something special," he says doggedly. "You let yourself be fooled by that foreign girl, but where is she now?"

The memory of sugar and perfume burns my tongue. Sid's skin sliding over mine. The buttons on her jacket, her trousers. My serious little moonbeam, she called me.

"Here I am, right by your side," Aden says. "I have always been here for you."

"Yes, like a barnacle on a boat."

"You should reconsider how cold you are to me. How disdainful. There is something wrong with you, that you would treat me like this. No one else does."

"I am not to blame for the stupidity of others."

"Marry me, Nirrim."

I laugh, the sound sharp, echoing around the stone courtyard.

He says, "I won't ask you again."

"Thank the gods."

He seizes my wrist, his hand hot.

"You asked me before," I say, my voice deliberately bored. "I said no. My answer is still no, and will always be no."

"Because I'm not a woman?"

"That is one of many very good reasons."

"It's not normal."

"Well, it should be."

"It is against the will of the gods."

"The original gods are gone, and you have no idea what the pantheon believed. *I* am a god, and *you* must let me go. Find another girl to love."

"Oh, I don't *love* you. Not anymore. I just think we should give our people what they want. You have even *encouraged* them to want it."

"A pretty tale of the perfect king and queen? That was all for show. Too bad, Aden, that I have no interest in sharing power with you."

His hand grows hotter. Soon, I know, he will burn like a brand. "You have no choice. Marry me, or I will rise up against you."

He thinks he threatens me, but he has forgotten that my skin has a power of its own. I push my magic to where he touches me, and make him remember, as though it were freshly happening, all the times he kissed me and I did not like it, when I went to bed with him out of obligation, when I resented his possessiveness. His expression tightens.

Then, because I feel I have not hurt him enough, I make him remember how his mother abandoned him, how she tried to leave Ethin and was executed for it. I used to console Aden, saying she probably chose not to take him with her out of fear that if she were caught, he would be punished along with her, but now I make him remember that I was not sure this was true, and that I wondered if in fact she sought to escape the burden of him.

"Nirrim," he gasps.

And then, because he has threatened the only thing I care about—my rule, my mission to make the world fair for all—I torment him with a false memory of his skin so hot that it burns like flame. I turn his power against him. He cries out in agony, and drops my hand.

"Only fools warn their enemies they are ready to strike," I tell him, and leave the courtyard, my wide-eyed train of god-blooded children scuttling behind.

"My queen?"

It is Mere, my loyal handmaiden, hands folded neatly as she waits. Other queens might have ordered their handmaidens to wear no finery, but I allow her the dresses I know she enjoys, the styling of her hair in the fashion to which she is accustomed. After all, we are friends.

My Elysium chirps from its perch on a bedpost. This bedchamber used to belong to the god of thieves. I find it fitting to sleep here, in what used to be the Keepers Hall. If this bed was good enough for an old god, it is good enough for a new one.

"Morah wishes to see you," Mere says.

I sigh impatiently. These relics of Other Nirrim's life are bothersome. Still, I have decided—and announced—that even those with no god-blood have an honored place in Ethin. I must, since the ordinary humans outnumber the god-blooded. Morah could be useful, if she decides to show her loyalty to me. I tell Mere to send her in.

When Morah enters, Mere leaves the two of us alone, aside from the Elysium, who trills at her appearance. "Sister," I say, and kiss her cheek. "Have you come to live at the palace with me?"

She pulls away. "No."

"Don't be shy. You are always welcome, you and Annin. The Ward knows that we love one another. Everyone will be happy to see us together again. Our little family."

"Except Raven," Morah says, "whom you murdered."

"*I* did not do that. An angry mob did." The Elysium flies to my shoulder, digging in its little green claws. "Don't forget what she did to you."

"Nirrim, you are not yourself."

"I am *better* than myself."

"Tell me what has made you like this. You are . . . some horrible copy of Nirrim. The Nirrim I know never would have hurt Raven, no matter what Raven had done."

"Is that why you are here? To try to turn me back into a weak girl everyone treated badly?"

"*I* didn't."

The Elysium cocks its head, peering at her.

"I know," I say, "which is why I am ready to give you a place of honor by my side. You and Annin. All you must do is swear your loyalty."

"I *am* being loyal, by telling you that there is something wrong with you. I want to *help* you."

I smirk at the idea that I need help. Then the Elysium launches from my shoulder with such suddenness that I feel its claws slice my skin. The bird flies to Morah's shoulder, singing.

Suddenly, I realize that the Elysium has never been in Morah's close presence before.

I have never tested her with the bird.

The Elysium, who tasted the blood of Discovery, the god who could sense the divine gift lurking in the bodies of the half-gods, sees something immortal in Morah. Her gray eyes widen. "Morah," I say, delighted, heedless of the blood dampening my shoulder and the pain from the bird's talons, "you are one of us!"

She backs away.

"What is your gift?" I ask. "Usually, once the awareness that we are gifted fills us, we know exactly what we can do. Tell me."

She shakes her head, her expression filled with wonder and alarm. She knows. I know she knows. She has felt the knowledge well up inside her.

"Don't be afraid," I say, annoyed now. "You are late to the knowledge, but that is fine. The important thing is that you can truly join our cause now. Just tell me what you can do."

"No."

"This is foolish. Why not?"

"I don't want to be used by you."

Some people cannot seize an opportunity when it is right in front of their faces. I touch her hand. When she doesn't pull away, I slip a little of my power into her. False memories always take more energy, but I strengthen my gift and push it through her mind. "Morah, you wanted to tell me. In fact, you have already told me."

"I did not."

I frown. No one has resisted me before. I must be more tired, my energy lower than I thought. "Morah, you were so excited by the awareness of your god-blooded gift that after you told me, you decided to tell me again, for the sheer joy of it. Go ahead, and tell me again now."

She wrenches away. "No," she says, and runs from the room.

I run after her. We were never wild girls, growing up together. A few years older than me, she always held herself sternly, which made me feel that I had to do the same. We never played games, for fear that Raven would punish us. We never ran, so I do not know who is the swiftest. But as I career down the palace halls, never quite catching up with the flag of her black hair, my jeweled slippers slapping against the marble floor, I push myself to my limit and it is not enough, even though the distance between us narrows.

What is her gift? What could make her impervious to me? How could she resist me?

I must know.

I call to the Middling guards to stop her, but in a fresh burst of speed, she plunges outside. I am ready to follow, satisfied now, because surely she will be stopped on the street.

A heavy hand falls upon my bleeding shoulder. I am spun around as though I were a toy, a little rag doll.

It is Aden. One of his hands still grips me. In the other, he holds a knife. "Only fools don't heed warnings," he says, and brings the knife down.

SID

---◆---

I TAKE THE POISONED DRESS back to my suite and lay it on
the table of my writing room, where I get the best light. The window-
pane exhales a chill. Outside, almost all the leaves have fallen. I see
groundskeepers raking leaves into colorful piles and setting them on
fire. Even without the window open, I smell the sweet, musty smoke.

Slicing open the dress, I examine how cleverly the tiny hooks are
sewn into the fabric. Someone skilled with a needle and thread did this.
While I cannot assume it was a woman who crafted this dress, my mind
leans that way. A man could possess this skill—even my father can sew
simply—or he could have commissioned the dress from someone else,
someone who might not even have known which life it threatened.
Someone who might not even have known the dress could be used as a
murder weapon. A seamstress could have sewn in the tiny barbs while
another brushed poison over them, later.

The finger I pricked remains numb, and the numbness has spread from my fingertip to the heel of my hand. If my mother had pulled the dress on, and been pricked multiple times, her death might very well have been certain, and swift.

I don't need to visit my grandfather to know what he would say: the assassin has lost patience, and whereas once they would have been content with a slow death that looked natural, now little caution is being taken. The assassin no longer cares whether the queen's death is known as murder.

"Sid, what are you doing?"

Startled, I flip the fabric over so that the barbs are hidden, and all that can be seen is the dress's red, embroidered exterior.

Emmah, who has entered my suite without knocking, slips the key she holds into her dress pocket. I don't usually mind that she comes and goes at will to my rooms. It has always been that way, ever since I was a baby. But I flush, torn between disliking the intrusion and welcoming it. My mother wanted me to tell no one, and I have already broken that trust by bringing my worries to my grandfather. I am tempted to break it again. Emmah could provide useful information—as a servant, she knows the world of the people who live and work here in a way I never can. She might have noticed something suspicious that could help me identify who wanted my mother's death, or was hired to accomplish it.

"I know you hate dresses," Emmah says, "but you don't need to *dismember* them."

I decide to risk a subtle question. "What do you think of this embroidery?"

"It is very fine."

"Is whoever did this as good as you at embroidering?"

Emmah runs a light hand over the fabric. "Better, I think," she finally says.

"Do you know who could have made it?" Maybe the workmanship has a signature pattern that could be traced to an individual.

"You don't know yourself? You didn't commission the dress?"

"No. Have I *ever* commissioned a dress?"

Emmah smiles and shakes her head. "I'm afraid I can't help. Sometimes a dressmaker will sew her initials into the inside of a dress's hem."

But I have already examined the hem, and saw nothing like that. I think of the god of sewing, the youngest god, who was born human. She was made immortal by Death, who loved her. We Herrani mark time by the gods, each year belonging to one of them until a hundred years have passed, and the cycle begins again. My father was born in the final year of a century, Death's year, but his mother chose to celebrate his nameday the following year, the first one in the new century: the Seamstress's year. It is not odd to me that Death could love a mortal, or that he would be drawn to an artist whose skill is to create when he brings an end to every creation. But it surprises me that the Seamstress stitches thread that binds, and Death cuts the stitches of life, and yet they can still love each other.

Using my dagger, I slice away a portion of the outer fabric, careful not to take any barbs with it, and tuck the swatch inside my pocket. Then I bundle the dress carefully, place it back inside its box, and reach for my jacket.

"Going somewhere?" Emmah says.

"Into town." I will visit the dressmakers.

"You'll need a thicker jacket," she warns. "It's colder outside than you think."

But I am already halfway out the door.

I don't get very far. I'm striding down a hallway, letting my long legs go as swiftly as they can without running, when I see Ceciliah turn the corner. Her eyes—a gray so pale they look like silver snow—go wide.

Oh no.

I halt abruptly and gird myself for the insults and accusations about to come my way. I wish spurned lovers wouldn't feel so . . . spurned. I never made any promises.

But then my heart clenches, to remember once more Nirrim's rejection of me, and I feel ashamed, and ready for what I deserve.

Ceciliah smiles, her prettily perfect mouth curling with secrecy. "I was looking for you," she says.

"You . . . were?"

"We need to talk."

"Can it be not right now?"

"Do you have somewhere better to be?"

I don't want to tell the truth, and I don't want to be rude. "No, but—"

"Good." She steps close, edging me toward the corridor's wall.

"Cecy," I say, determined to be as gentle—and moral!—as possible, "I am sorry that I hurt you."

"I forgive you."

"You do?" I say, surprised that apologizing is so easy. Then my back touches the wall and her hand is on me and I am surprised again in a totally different way. "Ceciliah, I don't think—"

"You don't have to explain. I have missed you so much. No one makes me feel the way you do."

I catch her hands between mine to put some distance between us, then see from her expression that even this gesture has misled her. Quite possibly, I look like I treasure her hands, and am holding them the way I have seen my father hold my mother's, cradling her small fingers within his larger ones. I drop them as though scalded. Trying again to be gentle—but not *too* gentle this time, I say, "It is over between us."

Her face contorts. "But . . . don't you want me? Aren't you sorry you treated me the way you did?"

"Yes." Then, horrified at her tender look, I scramble to add, "No! I mean, yes, I'm sorry. You deserved better. But no, I can't be with you anymore."

"Why?" she demands.

I am about to answer very, very carefully when my mouth clamps shut. I am assaulted afresh by the memory of my last conversation with Nirrim. Do you not love me like I love you? I asked. Won't you come with me?

No, she said.

But I asked two questions, just as Ceciliah had done with me. What if it was the same between Nirrim and me? What if she only meant to say that no, she could not come with me, and I had taken the answer to one question to stand for both?

"You should at least have the decency to tell me why," Ceciliah says, her eyes welling.

I take her hand again. How hot it feels, and slender, and rigid. She might very well punch me with it. When I speak, I try to be as true as I can. "I want you to be happy, and you can't be happy with me, because I have given my heart to another."

She wrenches away from me. "I always knew you were a liar," she says, and crashes past me to race in the direction from which I came.

I can't blame Ceciliah for disbelieving me. Once someone has a reputation for being a liar, it is difficult to trust when she tells the truth. I feel horribly guilty . . . but in the midst of my regret, I can't help but think of Nirrim, and hope.

"Well, that's a first," says a dry voice.

I turn my gaze from one end of the corridor, where Ceciliah has vanished, to the other end, where I had intended to go. Sarsine stands, arms folded across her chest, her expression interested, as though I am some hitherto unknown scientific fact, suddenly revealed.

"This is a very popular hallway," I say.

"I have never known you to turn a lady down."

"*Too* popular. This can't all be coincidence. Which god have I offended?"

"Sid, are you in love?"

I cover my eyes. Of course she heard everything. "I have an errand to run."

"What is so pressing, may I ask?"

"I need to see a dressmaker."

"You obviously do *not*. You hate dressmakers. Unless . . . the dressmaker is the young woman you mentioned?"

"I don't have to answer your questions."

Her face is amused. "Now, Sidarine—"

"*Sid*. My name is Sid. For the love of the gods, you *know* that."

"Sid," she says, her voice serious now. "I'm sorry. You don't have to tell me anything."

"Wonderful." I begin to maneuver around her when she says, "But I would like to meet her, this girl who has captured your heart."

I stare. "You would?"

"She must be very special."

My serious little moonbeam, I called Nirrim when I saw her in a silver dress, but it wasn't just the dress that made me say it. It was her way of being: her gentleness, her touch as soft as moonlight. But also her intelligence, her unexpected strength. She lit up the night. "You won't meet her."

"Why not?" Sarsine says.

"She's a foreigner. On that island I visited. I asked her to come here, to live with me, and she refused."

"Well, did you try asking her again?"

"I . . . What good would that do?"

"People change their minds." When I stammer—how could Sarsine pretend things are so *simple*?—she says, "I am a practical person. You, on the other hand, are just like Kestrel and Arin. So much drama. Perhaps whatever has gone wrong between you and this girl could be solved with more honesty, and less wounded torment."

"Impossible."

"Why? Kestrel's health has greatly improved. What is to stop you from returning to that island?"

Any *number* of reasons, including the presence of an assassin I'm not supposed to tell Sarsine about. But also: "I am engaged."

"May I suggest"—there is that droll tone again—"that you end your engagement, since you are in love with someone else?"

"It's not so easy. Herran needs this alliance."

"Does it?"

"I must marry him."

"And be unhappy forever? Sid, maybe your marriage is not something you have to do, but something you only *feel* you have to do."

"You would have me invite international chaos, ill will from Dacra, and the disappointment of my parents?"

"If it means your happiness, yes." She must see the surprise on my face, because she adds, "Little one, I was there when you were born. I knew then, as I know now, that we are all held in the hands of the gods. Our lives are so short and fragile. We must waste none of it."

Then she kisses me tenderly on the cheek, and leaves.

It is almost dinnertime when I return from the city. I hasten my horse, whose breath floats in the air like a white flag. Soon, it will be cold enough to snow. My stomach is empty and my mind is full, filled to bursting with the uselessness of my errand (none of the dressmakers recognized the embroidered fabric, though they could have been lying), the lack of any one good suspect in my mother's attempted murder, the possibilities presented to me in that corridor (could Nirrim love me? Could I have misunderstood? What was the very worst that could happen, if I ended a political engagement?), and—most pressing of all—the fact that I am late to serve my mother.

The silver sun is low in the sky, the clouds as thin as tishin paper. I guide my horse across the brown, brittle lawn to the stables, passing the fighting salle, when I yank the reins in surprise. My horse whuffs and stops, stamping.

There, in the ground near the salle, is a hole. It is exactly where Roshar buried his poison ring.

I get down from my horse and come close to the hole. I reach inside, down to its very bottom.

The ring is gone.

I am hasty in the preparation of dinner, stuffing dried apricots into a quail, a fowl small enough to roast quickly, as I mull over the missing ring and its numbing eastern poison, which has the same properties as what tainted the barbed dress sent to my mother.

Emmah enters the kitchen, in her hand a chalky round of aged goat cheese, which she must have taken from the stores. "The other servants said you had returned from your errand into town. You are cooking for the queen?"

Distractedly, I tuck boiled lemons and twigs of rosemary that were grown in the atrium around the quail in its iron roasting pot, shove it into an oven, and add more wood to make the fire burn hotly.

"She is lucky to have such a child, but why do you cook *all* her meals?"

"No reason. I like cooking."

"Yes, but this level of domesticity is unlike you. Usually, you are too busy training in the salle, or attending parties."

Even if I were not preoccupied with the continuing threat on my mother's life, I cannot believe that the usual social events would pique my interest now. Something changed when I saw Nirrim in splendid green, the color of high summer, the glossy fabric sliding down her skin. I didn't care about the party we attended. I didn't care about the dress. In fact, I wanted that dress gone. I wanted to be alone with Nirrim, to hear only her low voice. I cared only for her company.

"Eat with me," Emmah says, "while your quail cooks." She sets the goat cheese, which she knows is my favorite kind, on a cutting board. The fragrance of hot rosemary rises in the air. "You look starved," she adds, and she is right, so I cut into the cheese with my dagger—never mind how outraged my Valorian ancestors would be—and offer her a piece. We both eat. The tangy cheese crumbles in my mouth. "Did you find what you were looking for in town?" Emmah asks.

I shake my head, mouth full.

"Why did you go?" she says. "Was it about that dress?"

"Mmm-hmm."

"I might be able to help you find who embroidered it."

"Emmah, would you know if someone in the house has been watching me? A servant? Or even a lady, like Ceciliah, or Lyannis, the Valorian ambassador."

"A jilted lover, you mean."

"Must everyone always cast aspersions on my reputation?"

"You earned it, you must admit. Why are you asking about someone watching you?"

When investigating, my mother always said, let the people you question know only what they need to know. I decide against explaining my suspicion—that either Roshar retrieved the ring and used it to poison my mother's dress, which I cannot imagine him doing, or someone surveilled us and dug up the ring after we left. I must hesitate too long to reply, because Emmah waves away her own question and says, "Forget the reason. I know of no one who would follow you, save the lovelorn, but I will play your spy." She helps herself to another wedge of cheese. The quail sizzles in its pot. "I will pester the other servants for some answers."

"You are wonderful, Emmah."

"I know. Mind that quail. Small as it is, it will be done for dinner sooner than you think. Wipe that worry from your face. If you are being watched, I will soon find out by whom."

When I enter my mother's suite, it is empty. In her quiet bedchamber, the bed is perfectly made. The dining room is silent in its simple intimacy, the curtains plush yet not overly elegant, the wood of the furniture a light, sanded ash. I set down her dinner. I listen to the suite's silence, and worry returns as my boots tread the sapphire patterned carpet. By the time I enter the sunroom, my worry has turned into fear and self-blame. I should have told my father about the assassin. There should have been guards placed around my mother at all times. Why did I not do this, how could I be so arrogant as to think I could solve the problem all by myself?

Could my mother have been abducted?

Will I find her lifeless body?

Then I hear, though the windows, footsteps across gravel. It's the sound of someone small, and I recognize the short, quick paces of my mother in a rush.

Of course. The garden.

My mother's rooftop garden has a door that allows her to pass into my father's rooftop garden, which lies just on the other side of the garden wall. The garden is a way for my parents to enter each other's suites without the entire household talking about it.

I step out onto the garden. The sky has darkened to iron, the air bites, and the potted trees have lost their leaves, but the walls of the garden are afire with an ivy that changes to red in the cold, and the low, bushy damselthorn will keep its color throughout the winter, its broad leaves a glossy green traced by a red-pink pattern. My mother halts at the sight of me, her heels grinding into the gravel. She blushes. She is dressed impeccably, and I have an image of my father tenderly buttoning each button up the back of her dress, buckling her dagger belt into place, and sliding a wisp of dark gold hair back into its braid. "I'm late for our dinner," she says ruefully.

Now I flush, because I feel stupid for believing that she needs me to serve her. How many times has she slipped away to my father's room and snuck back just in time for me to bring her a meal? When did she get well enough to walk?

Then I feel terrible for being jealous of my father and wishing that my mother had stayed ill a little longer—not *very* ill, but just enough for me to remain important to her. "We have no appointment to keep," I say. "You can go back to Etta."

"And miss the meal you made? And your company?" She crosses the crunching gravel to me and reaches up to tuck a short lock of hair behind my ear. "You are so tall."

"Too tall for a girl, you mean."

"I mean that I can't believe how you've grown, when you were once so small, and all mine." Her fingers are icy. "I have been lucky, to have you three times a day. Even before you left Herran, you would avoid me." My mother's hands are cold when she is afraid. I realize that she is afraid of me.

It makes me sad. I don't want her to be afraid that she has offended me just by visiting my father. I don't want to feel possessive of her, or greedy for her attention. I want to feel normal. I want to be Kestrel's normal daughter, the kind she raised me to be. "Come inside, Amma. I want to talk with you."

"Yes?" she says eagerly. When I say, "About the assassin," her face falls, and I wonder what she hoped for.

Inside, I undo the holster and place the gun with a clunk on a petite, decorative table near the door of the dining room and then join my mother at the dining table. I keep, of course, my dagger at my waist, as does my mother. A Valorian always wears her dagger. I light lamps. The room glows as if it has been made suddenly happy. As I carve the quail, which vents its steam, I tell my mother about fighting in the salle with Roshar, about his broken ring and how he buried it, and about discovering the ring was gone.

"Roshar would never hurt me," she says.

"I agree."

"If he were the assassin, why would he mention to you that he wore a poison ring? It makes no sense for him to make such a song and dance about a broken ring and then later return to dig it up."

"Well, this *is* Roshar. He makes a song and dance about everything." When she begins to protest, I interrupt. "I don't suspect him. But it is interesting that the barbs on your dress had the same numbing effect as the poison from the eastern worm. I think before, when I was gone, someone was contaminating your food regularly, possibly with the same Valorian drug poured into the aqueducts decades ago. Your symptoms match those of that drug: you grew fatigued, and it seemed like you had a wasting illness." I set the carving knife aside, and we sit. The tablecloth reaches all the way to the floor. It is made of a heavy gray fabric with embroidered blue kestrels, its hem fringed with thread-of-gold. A gift, probably, from a visiting dignitary. Some of them aren't very imaginative, and often give her something with her namesake on it instead of something she would actually enjoy.

"The assassin grows bolder," she says, "to take advantage of the opportunity to use a new poison—which, with the right dose, would kill instantly."

"Yes, but that's not what troubles me." Neither of us can eat what is on our plates. "It's that the person must have been spying on Roshar and me. It's someone who must have easy access to you, the house, and the grounds. A servant? A guest?" Many Valorians resent my mother for bringing an end to the Empire. Is Ambassador Lyannis one of them?

"The assassin must have been very close," my mother says, "in order to overhear Roshar describe the properties of his ring to you." Her expression tightens with anxiety. "I don't like the thought of this man following you."

"I'm not so sure the assassin is a man," I say, though I am not surprised my mother thinks so, when so much danger in her past came from men like the emperor, or even her father. I think of Ceciliah, haunting the hallway, looking for me.

"True: the dress," my mother says. "It was made by an expert hand. Likely a woman's, though not necessarily." She toys with her fork, amber eyes narrowed, and I wonder if part of her has liked, even if only a little, being threatened, for the challenge of trying to name the culprit. I confess that although I wanted to bring the name of the guilty person to her, to do the job she had assigned to me, with none of her help, I like better working on a puzzle with her, even if it is a grim one. It reminds me of when things were good between us. When I was small, and we would play round after round of Bite and Sting, sometimes I would beat her, and she would be thrilled. Do it again, she would say, and then we would play, and I would lose, and so we would have to play yet again, and so on until I fell asleep at the gaming table. Time for bed, she would murmur, and I would pretend to keep sleeping so she would carry me to her bed. In the morning, she would wake up next to me, soft and warm, and say, I kept you up too late.

No, you didn't. I want to be good like you.

You *are* good like me.

Amma, I said, filled with sudden, childish guilt. I confessed, I was faking to be still asleep. So you would carry me.

She smiled. Do you not think I knew that? Do you not think I love to carry my one, my only tadpole?

A stone rests in my throat. I think of Sarsine, and how she said she wanted me to be happy. I think of my father, who said he wanted me to choose whether to be safe or happy. Most of all, I remember Nirrim. She was abandoned as a baby, left in a metal box outside the Ethin orphanage, and raised by a woman who used her and made her blind to her own worth. Nirrim was imprisoned. She could not even wear certain colors, or taste certain fruits. And yet, in spite of all this, she was brave. She was ready to risk her life to change her country. The way she kissed me was brave, the way she brought me to bed. She would have been punished for it, if caught. For her kith, it was forbidden for a woman to be with a woman. How could she be so brave, when every pleasure and freedom was denied her?

How could I be such a coward, that I cannot bear to tell my mother the truth?

Finally, I feel the full force of how much I miss Nirrim. I wish she were here. I wish I were like her. "Amma," I say, "I don't want to marry Prince Ishar. Please don't make me do it."

Her expression rumples. I must have horribly disappointed her. I grow rigid, hands stiff on the table, and await her anger. She will try to persuade me. Already, it hurts. Already, I feel outcast. She will banish me from her heart. Yet what can I do, save this? I cannot continue to lie to her. Even if Nirrim is lost to me, I can't forget the lesson of how brave she was, and how much I wanted to live up to her example. The god of games does not love me . . . or loves me too much, and gave me the gift of playing a part too well. I pretended too convincingly to be the person my mother wanted me to be, until I became a coward hiding in the shadow of my phantom self.

My mother says, "I know you don't want to. I would never make you do that."

"But . . . you wept when you caught me with Ivaline." I remember my mother's stricken face. "Because you knew then, for certain, that I liked women, and could not want Ishar."

"I did *not* know then that you didn't want him. Some people do not want only women." She traces a blue kestrel on the tablecloth. "I cried because you didn't trust me enough to tell me about Ivaline. What we had when you were little was gone, when you would bring every beautiful thing you found to show to me: every pretty stone, every irrielle's egg. A leaf. A horse nail. You were grown, and would one day fall in love, if you weren't in love already, and you didn't want to discuss any of it with me. Instead, you said you wanted to marry Ishar, yet grew angry whenever I raised the topic."

"Because I knew you wanted the marriage!"

"For the good of Herran, maybe, but not for *you*." She spreads her hands helplessly. "There have been times when I planned to write to Queen Inishanaway to end the betrothal, but then I thought it would make you only angrier at me for taking the choice out of your hands, for acting so imperious, as you have called me. So *all-knowing*."

"Amma—"

"You are right. I *do* act that way." Her eyes are golden with tears. "But I don't know *you*. I haven't known you for a long time. I only know what you let me know, and I have missed you so much."

I drop my gaze to the golden fringe of the tablecloth, which blurs in my vision. "You called me an apple." I can't keep the accusation from my voice.

"What?"

"The night we fought. When I left. You said, You are an apple, Sidarine."

She places a small, cold hand on mine, where it rests on the table. "Because I thought of that day on the pier. Of the apple and the stone."

"I *know* you did. You called me that because you disapproved of how I was with women, how much I loved pleasure, how I wanted my life to be as sweet as a dessert—"

"No. It was because I knew you would leave me."

As my eyes fill, I remember the apple, floating away from the pier, bobbing on the waves, floating out past the ships, until it was lost in the great bay.

"I am sorry I left," I whisper.

My mother touches three fingers to the back of my hand: the Herrani gesture to seek forgiveness, or to give it. "I am glad you did, if it means you were able to return, and let me tell you how much I love you."

Outside the window, tiny snowflakes drift down against the purple sky. Soon it will be too dark to see them. I hold my mother's hand and feel warm inside. Soft, the way I was when she carried me to her bed. I think of Sarsine's advice, and of Nirrim, and say, "What if I must leave again?"

"Tadpole, all children leave their mothers, in one way or another. But we always wait for our children, and are so happy when they come home." She smiles, and my eyes clear. I understand that although I have tried for years to be like my mother, she is telling me she knows I need to be myself.

The snow falls more thickly. The quail has grown cold. I shift in my seat to reach for knife and fork, eager to be busy with my hands, and when I do, the sole of my boot comes down on something small and hard, just beneath the edge of the tablecloth.

I lean back and look down to see what the object is. Something golden twinkles up at me from the carpet. I might have noticed it earlier, perhaps, had it not blended in with the tablecloth's fringe.

"What is it?" my mother says.

I bend down to retrieve the object.

It is a small gold earring.

"Amma." My voice sounds very far away. I look again at the tablecloth, whose embroidery is so intricate. "Where did you get this tablecloth?"

"Your nurse made it for me." Her face pales as she realizes why I am asking. In a hushed voice, she adds, "Emmah is so gifted with needle and thread."

I remember Emmah coming to me late at night to light candles to the gods, her thimble glinting on her thumb. Some new project, I thought. She was always working on some piece of embroidery. I remember her stricken face when she realized she had lost an earring I had made for her, an earring exactly like the one gleaming on my palm. I remember asking for her opinion on the fabric of the poisoned red dress, and how she had hesitated, and asked me if I knew who had sewn it.

No, I said.

But I know now.

NIRRIM

I LEAP AWAY FROM ADEN'S knife. I am not a fighter, but I thank the god of thieves for taking my heart. Other Nirrim would have been frightened. While she recoils within me at the thought of fighting Aden, I welcome this moment. Other Nirrim saw Aden as a wounded man abandoned by his mother, smart and talented yet too under society's thumb to live his full potential. So what? I sneer at Other Nirrim as I dodge Aden's next wild lunge. *Everyone* in the Ward was wounded. *No one* was allowed to be special.

Several of my Half-Kith guards cry out. They rush to save me, but others, traitors that they are, hang back to see which of us will win. "No," I call to the guards. "Leave him to me."

"Even now," Aden says, "when you have no weapon, you think you're better than me."

All true . . . except for the idea that I have no weapon. "You dropped your knife," I start to say, gathering my power to push a false memory into him. He falters, almost releases the blade, and then his eyes harden. With his free hand, he hits my mouth.

My mouth blooms with pain. I taste blood.

"Try that again," he says, "and I will hit you harder."

It hurts so much that I can't speak, which is exactly how he hopes to prevent sly words that will twist his mind. Yet his hand was loose, not quite a fist; he could have hurt me worse. He may want to murder me, but he is not as fully ruthless as he could be. Although he slashes at me with the knife, the cold, clear vision granted to me when the god of thieves stole my heart tells me Aden is not fully committed to the action. He cannot quite bear the thought of stabbing me.

In short: he is weak.

"Aden, I am sorry."

"You're lying."

"Be king by my side."

He pauses, the hand with the knife lowering a little. "You say that only because I'll kill you. Later you'll take it back. You'll use your power to make me remember falsely."

"But I'm not using my power now." I lower my voice so that the guards don't hear. "You were right, Aden. Our marriage is the perfect way to give our people what they want. It doesn't matter that I don't love you. Go ahead, kiss me in front of everyone watching. Let's make a good show of it, now and forever."

"You are horrible," he whispers, and kisses me, knife at my throat.

I spit blood into his mouth.

Surprised, he pulls back, coughing, but some of it must have gone down his throat.

As any councilman knew, and as I learned the day Sid drank a drop of my blood, the easiest way to borrow my power is to drink it. Sid went rigid with memory. The High-Kith man in the market, so long ago, when

I left the Ward for the first time, made me give him my blood and the same thing happened to him: he became a sculpture of himself as his mind plunged into the past.

Aden stiffens. "What did you do to me?" His memory, whatever it is, creeps through him and locks his limbs. He drops the knife. It clatters against the tiles, and he cannot see me as I retrieve it. He sees nothing but the past. Briefly, I wonder what he sees. What will be the last image in his mind?

It doesn't matter. I will never know.

A tear runs down his cheek.

No, says Other Nirrim. Don't.

He would have killed you, I tell her. He would have forced you to be his. He tried to make you regret who you are and whom you love. He will continue to challenge our right to rule.

You can't.

I do this for both of us, I say, and drive the knife into his chest.

SID

I DROP THE GOLD EARRING to the table in shock. "Emmah has been in your room," I say to my mother. "She poisoned your food. She embroidered and delivered the red dress." The memory of the goat cheese, eaten so peacefully with her in the kitchen as the quail roasted, floats over my tongue. Could I have been poisoned, too? But no— Emmah shared the savory treat with me, and I feel fine, if queasy from my sudden knowledge. Reassured, my mind moves to exonerate her, to blame myself for my unfounded suspicion, but the earring winks up at me and I remember how easily Emmah knew where I had been, how swiftly she had always been able to find me. Her reaction to the embroidered dress, now that I reconsider them, could have been the words of someone who sought, without betraying herself, to learn exactly how much I suspected. "But why?" *The answer begins with you*, my grandfather said. "Emmah loves me. How could she poison you, Amma? How could she do that to me?"

Behind me, I hear the small, metallic sound of someone cocking the firing mechanism of a gun.

My gun.

My mother's eyes, lifted to look over my shoulder, widen.

Emmah says, "Sid, I would do anything for you."

I spring from my chair, drawing my dagger, placing my body between the gun and my mother. Emmah stands by the door near the table where I left the gun, her hand steady, the gun aimed right at my chest, her green eyes bright and cold in the lamplight. She must have followed me from the kitchens and waited in the recesses of my mother's suite, listening to our conversation. "Sid, get out of the way."

My hand tightens around the dagger's hilt, but what could I do with it? I cannot hurt Emmah, my second mother, the one who always comforted me when I worried I wasn't good enough for Queen Kestrel.

You are the best child, Emmah always said. If the queen doesn't know that, then she is a fool. Now, is your mother a fool?

No, I whispered, and Emmah smiled.

Slowly, so I don't startle her, I set my dagger on the dining table and silently beg my mother to do nothing, say nothing. I have no idea what skill Emmah might possess with a gun, but at such a close range, skill doesn't matter. All she needs to do is fire. The bullet will blast its way so deep into flesh that the god of death must be here even now, hovering invisibly, waiting to see if he will be needed. "Emmah, please don't do this. I can't believe you would hurt me."

"I am doing this *for* you."

"That makes no sense." Fear swirls in my belly. "If you hurt my mother, you will hurt me." Something flickers in her expression, but she doesn't change her stance.

Emmah says, "She has tricked you into believing she loves you, like she tricks everybody. I heard what she said to you. Pretty lies. They say the god of lies loves Kestrel, but I know the truth."

I remember how my grandfather received a poisoned book with a coded message similar to the card that came with my mother's dress. He told me that, long ago, when Herran was newly independent, there had been assassination attempts against my mother. They stopped with your birth, he said.

"Kestrel thinks she is so smart," Emmah says, "but she doesn't see everything. She has no idea what's right beneath her nose."

Behind me, my mother makes a small noise but instantly stifles it. Quickly, to control the conversation and make certain my mother remains out of it, I say, "Is it because she is Valorian?" Emmah's free hand lifts briefly, as if to touch her burned face, but then shifts to join the hand that holds the gun, and steady its aim. "Herran suffered because of General Trajan," I say, "but it wasn't Kestrel's doing. She's not to blame."

"She is. Your heart is too good to see the truth. Arin's, too."

"She saved Herran."

"No one asked her to! Countless people died because of her! And why? So she could marry Arin. Don't you see how selfish that is, to cause a war in order to *be* with someone?"

"That's not why. That's not the whole story."

"*Damn* their story." Emmah's hands tremble.

I worry the gun might accidentally fire. "Set down the gun, then, and tell me what she did."

"She took everything from me!" Emmah doesn't relinquish the weapon. "If she had only left Arin alone, no one would have suffered. He would have fallen in love with someone else."

"Who?" my mother says quietly.

"Shut *up*!" Emmah shouts. "*You* caused the Firstwinter Rebellion."

No. My father did. He poisoned aristocratic Valorians on the same night that other Herrani rebels coordinated an attack on the armory. Rebels burned Valorian ships in the bay. My mother knew of none of it. She would have stopped him, at the time, had she known.

Emmah's green eyes are wild, her wrinkled cheeks flushed with hectic anger. I know I cannot argue with her, that she will see nothing but her own version of history, but I don't understand why she blames my mother. "Kestrel has never been anything but kind to you."

"Oh, yes," Emmah says mockingly. "Such a kind mistress. She bought your father, Sid. She *owned* Arin. And now she pretends to love him? Impossible. She loves no one but herself. After the Firstwinter Rebellion, *she* escaped from Herran. *She* warned the Empire. *She* brought the Valorian fleet right to our doorstep. They attacked us. Fires burned in our city."

I suddenly understand not all of Emmah's rage, but at least part of it. Carefully, gently, I say, "This was how your face was burned, wasn't it? I'm so sorry, but—"

"I know you now." My mother's voice comes low. I hear her rise to her feet. "Your name is not Emmah."

"I am glad I was burned!" Emmah says. "Glad it disguised me, glad I, finally, could have my chance for revenge. I never mattered. No one paid attention to me. Not Arin. Not Kestrel. Not the gods. She is queen, and I am nothing. Kestrel ruined my life, yet no one cares how I suffered."

"I care," I say, but she doesn't listen.

"So many songs," she says. "So many stories about Kestrel and Arin. But none for me."

"Lirah?" my mother says, and for a moment I cannot place the name until I remember my father confessing that a Herrani girl named Lirah had fallen in love with him. She was pretty, he said, but I didn't even notice her, didn't realize I had let her believe I returned her feelings.

A small cry escapes Emmah—Lirah. In the instant I realize she will shoot I know I am already too late. I reach anyway, the horror within me as sheer as ice.

A blur hurtles past my vision. The gun cracks. Something shatters. Lirah screams, clutching one empty hand with the other. A cold wind blows into the room.

The gun lies smoking on the floor. My mother's thrown dagger lies next to it.

Snow swirls into the room. How can it be snowing in my mother's room?

"Sid!" my mother shouts.

Her voice slaps me out of my shock. I kick the weapons far out of Lirah's reach and grab her hands. It feels like a violation to be rough with her. How can I hurt her? How can I capture her? She tended to every childhood wound. Sometimes, she felt like my only friend.

"She might hurt herself," my mother warns, so I listen, and yank my dagger belt from my waist to bind Emmah's—Lirah's—hands fast.

Faraway doors within the suite bang open. The room is freezing with wind. Some of the wind comes, I understand now, from the window Lirah shattered with her wide shot. But a thick tunnel of cold drives into a room from another source. Someone has entered the suite from the garden door. Someone is battering through door after door.

"Kestrel!" my father shouts from another room. I hear fear in his voice but also something I have never heard before, something that makes me understand why people call him Death's Child.

It is a brutal threat.

A promise.

Meet me, it says, and meet my god.

"Sid," Lirah whispers. Her burned face is wet, her eyes emerald. "Before you were born, I planned to murder you. That would be my revenge. Then I saw you, on the festival to honor your nameday. Arin's baby. So small. Innocent. The only pure thing in my world. How could I hurt you? Even in that moment, from where I stood in the crowd, I loved you."

My eyes, too, are wet.

"What, though, was a baby, in the face of so many ruined lives? The god of vengeance had chosen me. The proof? Arin selected me, of all the possible nurses, to care for you. He did not recognize me. He placed you in my arms. You were golden. Valorian. Look at the infant, I told myself. See how she resembles your old masters. Kestrel's child. Yet you curled your tiny hand around my finger. Such blind trust. I will wait, I thought. Let the baby grow. Kestrel's suffering will be all the greater to lose a toddler. But then you were a toddler, and I could not bear the thought. When Sidarine is a child, a girl grown, I decided. Yes, then. That will destroy the impostor queen."

My father shouts my mother's name again.

"But I could not do it," Emmah—Lirah—says. "No year was a good year. From the beginning, I loved you too much. And once I loved you, I hesitated to kill Kestrel. I thought maybe I could forgive her for your sake, because how could such a tender child survive the death of her mother? But of course Kestrel ruined everything, as always. She chased you away. She didn't accept you, not like I did. She was given such a gift as you, and what did she do but disdain it?"

"It's not like that. I returned. I'm here."

Lirah doesn't seem to hear. "You are better off without her."

My father slams into the room, battle sword unsheathed, eyes as bright as murderous stars. His gaze sweeps the scene before him. I see him decide, instantly, that even if he doesn't understand everything, he understands enough. He hurtles toward us through the snowy cold. His broadsword is ice.

"Arin, no!" my mother shouts. "Don't!"

His expression shows that he hears her, but his sword can't stop its swing toward Lirah.

Please, I think, and it is not a good prayer, but it must have been heard, because some force, as invisible as the cold wind, seems to wrench the blade from my father's hand.

The sword drops with a thud to the floor.

"What will happen to Emmah?" I can't speak her real name. *Lirah* feels like a disguise, an invention. I am in the library with my father, who asked to speak with me in private after he summoned guards to bring Emmah to her room and keep watch over her there.

My father sighs. "Nothing."

I am stunned. I was ready to beg on her behalf, and had never expected my father to so easily overlook the attempted murder of his wife. The lines of his body, as he stands before his desk, leaning back against it, still look taut, murderous, and I can imagine what he must have felt when he heard a gunshot come from the east wing.

He sees my surprise, and his body sags into weary lines. "Kestrel told me what Lirah said to you. In some ways, Lirah is right. Kestrel and I did terrible things during the Firstwinter Rebellion and the war that followed. My hands are not clean. Neither are hers. We did what we did because, in each circumstance, we felt left with little choice, or only bad ones. I know you have said you want your own story, Sid, but let it not be like mine. Kestrel and I aren't heroes. What good we did was bought with the blood of others."

"You are too hard on yourself."

He smiles a little, his face handsome, wistful. My mouth, they say, is like his. "You say so only because you are kind."

A tender hope rises in my throat. "Me, kind?" I disguise the sudden shyness I feel with a light tone. "Not a reprobate? Not a breaker of hearts?"

"Yes, kind. Why do you think people love you so easily?"

"Not everyone does," I say, thinking of Nirrim.

"I have to forgive Lirah," my father says, "because I understand her, and her anger did not come from nothing. But most of all, I must forgive her for how tenderly she always took care of you. How she loves you. She could have smothered you in your crib. She could have pushed you as a toddler out the window, and claimed it was an accident. I am haunted by all the ways you could have died. Instead, Lirah protected you from harm . . . including from herself. And I must forgive her because I know the damage it would do to you if I did not."

Outside, the snow comes down thickly. I see it form swirling halos around the tall lamps that light the gravel path to the house, set against the black night.

"Kestrel tells me you have chosen to break your engagement to Prince Ishar," he says.

I hold my breath.

He says, "Will you tell me why?"

I think of the speckled yellow feather passed between my parents. I imagine my mother telling my father that I wanted it. Had it been easy to give up?

What if there was something I wanted that he could not give?

"I love someone else," I confess.

The edge of his mouth curls in a surprised smile. "Well. That is a good reason."

"I know the engagement is good for Herran. I know that breaking it will cause problems."

"Kestrel and I have faced worse."

"Maybe ending the engagement will be for nothing. Things probably wouldn't work between Nirrim and me anyway."

"Ah. The Herrath girl." He pushes away from the desk and comes to sit beside me on the long sofa made for reading, with a tufted headrest at one end. "Why wouldn't it work?"

"She doesn't love me back."

His expression is amused now, which is annoying, though comforting. He rubs the scar that cuts down through one brow and into his cheekbone. "Are you sure?"

Do you not love me as I love you? Won't you come with me? After she answered no, and I turned away, she called to me.

An apology would make it worse, I said.

I don't want to apologize, she replied.

Did she simply want to explain? Did Nirrim see that I had understood her *no* to be her answer to both questions? It is possible to love someone and not be willing to follow that person to a strange land.

"I am not sure," I admit to my father. "But there are other reasons why it wouldn't work."

"Since you are so determined to argue against yourself, give me the reasons."

"She knows nothing of the world outside her island. She comes from another culture than ours."

He lifts his brows. "You mean like how the Valorian culture is different from the Herrani one?"

Point taken. But I add, "Nirrim and I barely know each other. I knew her for not even a month before I left Ethin."

"It is possible to fall in love in even less time."

I am surprised. My father is so serious that I thought he would immediately agree that love is impossible in such brief circumstances.

"You can fall in love the very first time you meet someone," my father adds.

"Is that how it was between you and Amma?"

He laughs. "Not at all."

"Then how do you know?"

"Because it happened to me," he says, "the first time I saw you." He touches my cheek lightly, then lets his hand fall. Even as my eyes sting, I am hungry for more—some recognition of who I am, some proof that he means what he says, that it is more than words. I place my hand on his cheek, half of the gesture Herrani men show each other when they are family. He startles, confused.

I don't know why I want the gesture, but I do. Maybe *because* it is a strange thing to want, and I simply want him to give it to me even though it is strange, even if he doesn't understand it.

He lifts his hand again to my face and places his palm, warm and sure, against my cheek. He says, "If you love her, fight for her."

"Where are you going, little lion?"

The snow covers the ground evenly in a fine layer. Roshar stands idly on the path blocking my way to the stables—*just* managing not to shiver, though his face is screwed up in a scowl at the white flakes sifting down. "Going to saddle a horse, are you, and ride down to the harbor?"

"I am sailing to Herrath."

"I am so surprised."

"Why are you stalking me?"

"There has been a lot of commotion in the house. I hear talk of gunfire, poison, assassination attempts . . . I am feeling a little hurt. I am feeling like I have been left out of things. Are you sure that now is the best time to leave—*especially* without explaining everything in detail to your dear godfather?"

"Yes."

"It's a wicked night to set sail. The seas will be rough."

"So?"

"Sooo," he drawls, "how about you take my ship?"

THE GOD

—◇—

I SAW SID OF THE Herrani sail through sleety wind, ice glazing the ropes and stiffening the sails. I heard her nervous heart. What would Nirrim say, when Sid returned? What if each word Sid gathered inside her, arranging and rearranging, tumbled out in the wrong order . . . or the right one, so that Sid said, I will never leave you again, and Nirrim did not care? Sid might look upon Nirrim's face again only to see it averted—in pity, perhaps, or kind regret. Yes, even in rejection, Nirrim would be kind. She had never been cruel.

Or so Sid believed.

NIRRIM

THE COUNCILMAN WHO HID HIMSELF away with the godling children during the revolution has confessed the location of the Half-Kith genealogy in exchange for his freedom. I do not mind granting it so long as he swears a public oath to me in the agora. "It is not to me only that you must swear," I tell him as I stand outside his prison cell, my gold silks glowing in the lamp-lit darkness. "You must swear to serve New Herrath, our gods, and our dream of equality. No longer will any class rule over another."

"Of course, my queen," he says hastily.

Later, as Mere accompanies me on my walk from the prison to my palace, a set of guards in a phalanx before and behind us, my hand-maiden says, "True equality, Queen Nirrim?"

"Yes."

"I suppose Aden didn't have a mind as noble as yours," Mere says, and while I wonder why she speaks so dryly, I am pleased that she has understood why his death was necessary. "Exactly," I say. "He sought to seize a position of power. This will no longer be tolerated in Herrath." Her mouth twitches in what could be humor or dislike. "You think my actions were not justified."

"You had no choice. Aden would have killed you."

My pace quickens with irritation, which I try to control. Mere is my loyal friend, after all, and as a mortal she perhaps cannot expect to understand what I have done, and why I had to do it, beyond the simple fact of self-defense. "He did not share my vision, and could not learn to do so. You, on the other hand, are apt. You see, don't you, that Old Herrath was corrupt, that thousands of people fed upon the lives of others? New Herrath must wash away the sins of the past."

"I am confused, my queen, about one thing."

"Simply tell me, and I will make it clear." If only Morah had been so willing, so open-minded!

"If you seek true equality, how can Herrath have a queen to rule over all?"

I halt, loose sand grinding beneath my sandal. Mere stops, too, and my soldiers. In the quiet, my Elysium chirrups on my shoulder. I don't like the storm of unease that brews inside me at Mere's words. How dare she question my rule? My methods? My right? Maybe she is not so loyal after all. Maybe she, like Morah, will betray me, and treat me as though I were a villain, when all I want is what I always wanted, what Other Nirrim wanted: a better world, a pure one.

Mere lays a gentle hand on my shoulder, and I allow it, because I see that her face is full of worry, even fear. She must have misspoken, and is afraid that she has offended me—which she has, yet a good ruler will overlook the clumsiness of a well-intentioned servant. A friend will not let a friend agonize over careless words. "We need you," she says, "to show us the way. We will never achieve true equality unless our queen teaches us, and we cannot bring our message to the rest of the world without your power."

"And love," I add. A queen should love her subjects. Even Other Nirrim would say so. Although the word *love* stirs no feeling within me, I remember its shapeshifting sensation: its ache, its weight, the gliding silk of it. How tremulous it could be, floating in my chest like a restless dragonfly near the rim of a deep well.

"Thank you," Mere says, "for explaining to me."

Mollified, I resume my pace, but I cannot rest entirely easy. I never will, until Morah is found, and I discover what her power is. How could it counter mine? "Any news," I ask, though I have already asked several times today, "on the whereabouts of my sister?"

"None." Mere pauses, and then adds, reluctantly, a new opinion. "We must assume she has left the city, and is somewhere in the country-side of our island."

"Impossible. My soldiers stood watch at every gate." How could Morah have slipped the grasp of the palace guards and snuck out of the city?

And yet, no one can find her.

"When we return to the palace," I say, "bring the genealogy to me, and have Annin fetched from the tavern. Tell her she may pack whatever she wishes, but that I will see to it that she has all the finery she needs. One sister yet remains true to her. Unlike Morah, I will never abandon Annin. I will be her sister forever."

Everyone is ordered out of the library. The tome rests before me on the table, as heavy as a large child, its pages brittle. It smells of age. Alone, by lamplight, I open the genealogy and page through it slowly enough that the pages do not crumble at my touch, but swiftly enough that I can commit each page to memory without wasting time. I do not need to *read* each page. The book's contents will all remain perfectly in my mind for me to consult at my leisure. The first pages take my breath away, to see the names of the first gods and their demigod children: the most powerful Half Kith, the ones whose blood was not diluted by time, after the gods left and Half Kith bore the children of other Half Kith, and grew further away from the grace of the immortals. As I trace their children through generations all the way to our present, I learn the origins of some of our powers. Sithin, the boy who can riddle someone's body with holes, is the descendent of Death. This is not surprising, but other revelations are: for example, that the painfully plain girl who can bestow beauty on others is the many-great-grandchild of the god of treachery. Aden, I see, was related to the god of love . . . for the all the good that heritage gave him. The blood that watered the fortune-telling tree was drained from a Half-Kith child descended from the god of foresight. She died a century ago. I feel helpless reading the bare notes of her story. I wish she had been born in my time. If only she had someone like me to fight for her. I wish my power could unfold into the past and save every Half Kith like her. The pages turn in my hands. So many lives.

But where is Morah?

Where am I?

It seems we are not listed in the genealogy, as is true of many other god-bloods that I know, and as I page to the end of the book, I must resign myself to the possibility that the Council did not discover all of us.

Then, finally, I find my name in fresh ink, a notation beside it with the dates of my imprisonment and my gift, which is no news to me. *To be collected,* the page says, *upon the departure of Princess Sidarine of Herran, who requested the Half Kith's release from prison, invoking the name of Prince Roshar of Dacra.*

So, the Council knew Sid's rank, and as for *collected*, this note can mean nothing other than that the Council planned to arrest me the moment Sid left Ethin and sap me of my blood at their leisure. Likely the only thing that kept me safe during Sid's time on the island was the Council's desire to keep the source of their magic a secret from the rest of the world. Had I not taken matters into my own hands, and first sought answers from the Lord Protector, I could have been captured the moment Sid left. This interests me less, however, than what is written about my parents. *Mother: Irenah (Middling, deceased), sister to Ravenah, called Raven (Middling, resident of the Ward).* The genealogy lists their parents, and their parents' parents, and more, all going back to the beginning of the book, but none with any known powers. On the line, however, where the genealogy would list the other side of my family, it says only, *Father: Unknown.* I travel to the end of the book, committing each written page to memory, until I find only blank pages meant for a future that will never come, at least not in the way the Council intended.

That future is mine.

"Nirrim?" Annin stands at the library's door, hands bound, palace guards behind her.

"Why did you bind her?" I demand.

"She didn't wish to come," says a guard.

"Nonsense," I say, and tell him to leave us alone. Her soft, round face looks hesitantly into mine, her blue eyes anxious as I jerk at the tight knots around her wrists and her body sways in response, like a tree in the wind. When the rope falls to the floor I see that her wrists have been grazed raw. "That guard will be punished," I promise.

"Don't blame him, please."

"You have always been too nice for your own good."

"May I go home now?"

"Annin, you *are* home. I accepted, earlier, that you and Morah wanted your independence. You felt too humble to be associated with a queen. Isn't that right?"

"We were useless to you. That's why you left us alone."

It is true, but her accuracy hurts, and I am angry that she wouldn't see my behavior in the most generous light, that she wouldn't invent a lie that protects her image of me, and therefore, her love of me. Didn't I do that with Raven?

Yes, Other Nirrim whispers. You have become like Raven.

Liar! Raven only ever acted in her self-interest.

"I am trying to end suffering." I hear my voice tremble with fervency. Annin must believe me. She must see that everything I do, even what she would consider bad, is for the good. It is for *her*. It is for everyone. "All over this world are countries where the rich live at the expense of the poor, just as the High Kith used us. Yes, I need help. But you are not *useless*, Annin. I am sure Morah has made you feel that way, since she so easily abandoned you." Annin's blue eyes blink back tears. "You are my little sister. Join me. Maybe the god of thieves will return, and he will make you as strong as I am. Wouldn't you like that?"

"What do you mean?"

"He took away my heart." I hasten to explain that I meant that the god took an *emotion* from me. "It is so freeing. Remember how Raven used to strike me?" I trace the burn on my cheek, left from when Raven smashed an oil lamp against my face. "And then she would apologize and act so sorry that I felt that I was to blame for being hurt? I would never react like that now. I am better. Stronger. I made sure that Raven would never hurt me again, or you, or anyone. And now Morah has treated me—and you—like we don't matter to her anymore. I know it must make you sad, but you don't *have* to feel sad. You could decide to free yourself, even without the god's help. Annin, just decide you don't care about Morah. And why should you? What has she done for you but abandon you?"

She shrinks from me. "I don't know where Morah is."

Maybe later Annin will see the purity of my vision, and understand that no beautiful thing is crafted without labor. Some of us must work, must dirty our hands for that beauty. Yet she sees me as a mere murderer. She sees my power as not possibility, but danger. I have no time to persuade her. Cleverly, putting magic into my words, I say, "Annin, you already told me where she is. And since you have already told me, you should repeat it, because you were anxious that I might not have heard every detail."

"I don't *know*," she says again, like she is made of wood, and I want to shake her. Even though I have used my power on her, I don't fully believe her. Her eyes have a skittish look about them. Is it possible that Morah did something to Annin to make her impervious to my will?

Whether Annin truly doesn't know or is somehow able to hide the knowledge from me, my usual trick does not work.

Still . . . maybe Morah will return for Annin. Perhaps all I need is to keep my little sister by my side. And why wouldn't Annin want to remain with me? I am all the family she has left. "You can help Herrath, too, just by being loyal to me. I have missed you, Annin. I want to take care of you, to make certain that you are surrounded by comfort and beauty. I know how you like pretty things."

Annin withdraws a red feather from her pocket. "Like this?" It is the Elysium feather I gave her in what seems like another lifetime ago. "I don't want it anymore."

My heart beats painfully, rapping at the great, empty feeling inside me, as though somewhere in my chest is a glass vessel with nothing inside, and Annin's words ring against it. How can she hurt me, if I have no heart? Who am I, to be wounded because a lowly mortal flings my gift back in my face? Who is she, to affect me in any way?

What did I give to the god of thieves, if I can feel this pain? This shame?

"You will tell me," I say between my teeth, "where Morah has gone, or you will find that my kindness has its limits."

"I don't know," she says yet again, and in that moment I truly understand how Raven lost her temper with me. Violence thickens my blood. "Shall I drag the memory from your mind?" I say, though I have never done this, and am not sure I could.

A knock comes at the library door. It is Mere.

"Go away," I say.

Mere glances at Annin and says, "It's important."

"As important as betrayal? As the sin of one sister turning her back on another?"

"I am not betraying you," Annin says.

"My queen," Mere says smoothly, "why don't you let me take Annin to her new rooms, and explain how she can best serve you? She is young, and I'm sure that once she fully comprehends her current situation, her gratitude to you will know no bounds. She will do anything for you, as I would."

"I am asking for the simplest thing! Where is Morah? You *must* know. She wouldn't run away without telling you somehow. Don't look at me like that, Annin! Don't shy away from me! You act as though I am *threatening* you, as though I would torture the answer from you. If you love me, you will tell me."

"May I suggest," Mere says, "that you set aside the question of Morah's whereabouts? There is something more pressing."

"Nothing is more pressing!"

"A ship has arrived in the harbor," Mere says. "A ship with green flags. It docked, and the crew remained on board, but their captain disembarked, rowing a launch to the pier. Lady Sidarine has returned to Ethin. She wants to see you."

SID

---◈---

THE WAY WAS ROUGH. The ropes were encased in ice. Sails had to be stowed for every storm, for fear the wind would rip them, and my crew cursed me night and day. Sailing in winter was a reckless idea, but I am *full* of reckless ideas. There have been enough signs from the gods lately to suggest that I lie to myself a little less, and be the person I am, so I didn't mind the waves slopping over the deck, because Roshar trusted me not to sink this ship. I didn't mind the fear that squiggled up my spine, because it made me forget my fear of what would happen when I faced Nirrim.

Eventually, we slid out of the wintry seas and into the balmy waters near Herrath. It was strange, even stranger than the first time I sailed here, because the contrast in climate was so extreme. It was as though a velvet cloak fell down on all our shoulders. The night sky cleared, the stars like specks of shattered glass. When day came, the sun rose as juicy as a yellow plum. My crew didn't hate me *quite* so much anymore, at least until they wearied of the heat.

Then the horizon shifted, its indigo line revealing Herrath and its shallow violet waters. We anchored in the bay. I stowed my gun in the captain's quarters and dressed in my finest, changing one sleeveless jacket for the next, tugging on linen trousers and then deciding they were too loose, too informal, so I put on a different, tightly woven pair that I thought gave me more swagger, never mind the heat. I wanted to look sharp: crisp and new, like fresh paper. My fingers trembled as they fumbled with buttons. So what if it was too hot for boots? I liked that they gave me yet more height, and that when I walked, everyone could hear me coming. I yanked them on and belted my dagger at my hip. Would Nirrim like the way I looked? My hair was shorter than ever. In a fit of impatience during the journey, I had cut it into a more severe style. I wasn't sure why, except that Nirrim had often accused me of being serious about nothing, and I wanted to show her I was serious about her. There was no logic to that. If anything, I was acting out of fitful anxiety. Afterward, though, I could see in the mirror how clean my face looked, how the bones of it were more prominent, and grew calmer to see reflected a face that matched the one in my mind. It was a comfort to know that I looked on the outside exactly how I saw myself on the inside.

I took one last look in the mirror before I left the ship. What kind of face was this? A boylike girl with dark eyes. Tight expression. Anticipatory. I felt my father's hand on my cheek. It is a brave face, he said, and it didn't matter that those words weren't real, that I was imagining them, because I knew that what I imagined *was* real. What I imagined was exactly what he would say.

◈

"Oh, it's *you*," says the boy on the pier. My apprentice spy, Killian, has grown at least an inch since I left. "From the green flags on that odd, narrow ship, I thought that scary friend of yours had returned."

"Roshar is not scary." I climb out of the launch I rowed from where the ship lies anchored in deeper waters.

"He looks like he'd gut you with a sword if you insulted him."

"Now, that is true." I have slipped easily into Killian's language, and it is nice to speak it again, to feel its quick pace, how the *m*'s are shorter, so that *Amma*, in my language, becomes *Ama* in Herrath. I hand Killian a gold coin. It is stamped with the sign of the god of death, but it never mattered that Herrani currency isn't the same as the local one. Gold is gold, and mine was always welcome here. Killian once readily accepted my coins, but now he hesitates, and when I say, "Any news from my young spy?" he hands the gold coin back and says, "I don't think I should tell you."

I straighten my collar, fidgeting in surprise. "Why not?" Sudden worry rushes into me. "Did something happen to Nirrim?"

"Um . . ."

"Tell me."

"I might get in trouble."

"Why?" My pulse riots in my throat. Nirrim wanted to stage a revolution against Herrath's ruling class. I didn't consider that she might have actually *tried*, that revolution could come so quickly—which was stupid of me, given my own background. The revolution might not have been of Nirrim's doing. Maybe the rumors of the cruel black-haired queen are true, and Nirrim has fallen victim to her. Has she been imprisoned? Hurt? My mind swallows the next question, refusing to let me even consider it.

No, not dead. Nirrim cannot be dead.

"You must tell me," I say. "Is Nirrim all right?"

"I guess?"

Somewhat reassured, I say, "Take me to my house. You can explain along the way."

His gray eyes widen. "Oh no. I'm trying to escape her notice. She said she wanted me to visit and tell her all about you. No, thank you. I am hoping she has forgotten about me. Has bigger fish to fry, and all that. She likes your house. She goes there sometimes. I say we avoid it, because the gods only know what she thinks about *you* right now. Maybe you want to get back on that ship of yours. This city has changed a lot."

"*Whose* notice? Who are we talking about?"

"Nirrim. Uh, *Queen* Nirrim."

"Queen?"

He winces, his mouth somewhere between a grimace and a smile as he peers up at me. "Yes?"

"Why are you making your answers into questions? Either she is all right, or she isn't. Either she is queen, or she is not." I now wholly doubt the accuracy of the gossip I read in the Valorian ambassador's secret letter about the black-haired Herrath queen who invaded the Cayn Saratu. If that was Nirrim—though how *can* it be? How could she have become queen?—she would never do such a thing. I am very confused.

Killian holds up his hands in mock surrender. "I don't want to make anyone mad. I'm just trying to avoid a short trip to the red agora." This makes no sense at all to me. I think maybe he has used an idiom in his language that I haven't yet learned. "If you want to see her, go to what used to be the Keepers Hall. It's her palace now. But I don't think that's so smart. No, I don't want your gold. And no, I'm not going to explain anything else. Let Nirrim do the talking."

I suspect that Killian must be playing a prank on me. He was a wonderful, natural-born spy, but sometimes he passed me information that was pure invention, just to fool me and laugh when I found out the truth. He is a boy after my own heart. I can't imagine that Nirrim is *queen*, but I also believe he would tell me if she was in danger. It occurs to me that maybe Nirrim has told him to warn me away from her if I returned. I feel myself deflate, my posture sag. "She is probably angry with me. I left suddenly. She expected I would stay longer."

Killian makes that grimace again. "She's mad? Sid, remember when I said you should get back on your boat? Remember how recognizable you are? No one here looks like you. The moment you step into the city, everybody is going to gossip, and then *she* will find out, and——"

"Thanks, Killian," I call over my shoulder, already walking toward the city. Of course Nirrim is angry with me. She should be. But maybe I can make things right.

What Killian said is true.

At least, it seems to be true.

Ethin has changed. In the distance, where the wall should be, there is nothing. Several High-Kith mansions lie in ruins. People notice me as my pace quickens through the High quarter. Whispers carry on the warm breeze. I hasten to the Keepers Hall, and when I arrive outside its doors I am stopped by guards—not Council guards, but men dressed in new livery, in red with a green chevron on each shoulder. Above the hall, a white flag snaps, an Elysium bird emblazoned on its standard.

"Princess Sidarine of Herran?" the guard asks.

"I'm here to see Nirrim. Is she here?"

"The queen said to bring you straight to her."

I still can't quite believe that Nirrim would be *queen*. It is not that I doubt Nirrim's ability to foment the revolution she wanted, or to gain power if she wished it, but . . . she was not power hungry. She was ambitious on behalf of her people, not *herself*. Such ambition would not be wrong, necessarily, and I could see why someone who had grown up without power would want it. Nirrim would rule wisely, gently. But I am surprised, even wary. Questing to govern wasn't in Nirrim's character. Did someone force her into this position? Who attacked the Cayn Saratu?

I am led into a reception chamber where, at the end of a long, shining, echoing floor that seems covered invisibly with my shock, as though by a cloak of cold water, is Nirrim. She sits on a pink marble throne, her dress a torrent of green silk, her hair braided into a black crown. She wears jewelry: diamonds earrings and a matching crescent necklace, though at second glance I wonder if the jewels are indeed diamonds. They seem to have a slight glow, the way a full moon has a hazy halo. Her manner is one of ease, even amusement. She looks perfectly at home on her throne. "Leave us," she says, and the guards disappear, shutting the tall double doors behind them. We are alone, and everything Killian said is true.

"Nirrim?" My voice is incredulous. I am far away, but I think I see her full mouth twitch in a smile. "Only you may call me that," she says. "I have always loved the sound of my name on your lips. Did you know I was named after a rose-colored cloud, the kind that brings good fortune? My good fortune has come to pass."

Encouraged, I draw closer. She doesn't seem angry, and I am so relieved that she is whole and unharmed, even smiling. "Are you truly a queen? How?" I stand right before her now, but she does not stir from her throne.

"My people needed me. They wanted me."

"You were—" I don't know the Herrath word for *elected*, the way Valorians choose their magister. "Chosen?"

"Yes." She has always been luminous, but now her beauty radiates from her. I can tell she is no longer shy about it, that she knows now exactly how she can enchant someone. *Me*. And I am happy for her, even as fear grows within me that maybe I was right all along, that I was not enough. Look at her. She is how I've always imagined the gods.

Her jade-colored eyes narrow. "You left me."

"I'm sorry. I had to. But I came back. I'm here."

"To be with me?"

"Yes, Nirrim, if you will let me."

"You said you loved me, that final night."

"I meant it. I *mean* it." I bite my lip so hard I taste blood. I am ready to beg, I want so badly to hear her say that she feels the same way, but she lifts her palm, silk sleeve cascading down to her elbow. The words catch in my throat. She rises and leaves her throne to stand before me. Relief flows into my bones, because her eyes hold something I recognize well: desire.

"Do you want me?" she says.

"Yes," I whisper.

"Will you take me?"

I reach for her, my fingers spanning her soft face, thumb pressed against her mouth. "I will do anything for you."

Her mouth parts beneath my thumb, and she leans into me. "Will you give yourself to me?" she murmurs into my ear. "Are you mine?"

"Yes," I say, and she kisses me, fingers skidding down my back, pressing me down, eager.

The marble floor is cold beneath me. It rings, the whole room echoing, as she kisses me again, and I cry out at the pleasure she gives me.

Afterward, when I lift the puddle of green silk from the glossy white floor, to help Nirrim into her dress, something crackles within the fabric. Having already witnessed a dangerous surprise hidden in one dress,

I carefully reach into the folds until I find the source of the sound: a folded sheet of paper. From the floor, Nirrim watches me, eyes heavy-lidded. "You are taking liberties," she says, but in a throaty way, a mock warning that really means, I think, that I have made her happy, that she is luxuriating in what has just happened, and is proposing a kind of game. I don't unfold the paper, but lean down to kiss her neck. "Should I make it up to you?" I murmur against her throat.

"Yes."

I continue to kiss her. "How?"

She grasps the collar of my undone tunic. "Never leave me." Her voice has gone suddenly clear and hard. I pull away to study her. "I won't," I say gently. "I'm sorry I did. I had to see my mother, but I should have promised to return."

"Yes, we need to talk about your mother."

I frown, surprised at her brusque tone. Perhaps she just wants to make certain my mother is well. I am about to reply when she takes the dress from my hand and the fabric knocks the folded page from my loose grasp onto the floor. I stoop for it, and see that it bears my handwriting in Herrani. "It's the letter I wrote to you, long ago." I am touched that she has kept it, even though, with her perfect memory, she would have been able to see the page in her mind's eye, despite not being able to understand a language she had never learned. "Would you like me to translate it for you?"

"No, that's not necessary." She has pulled on the dress. "Fasten the buttons in the back."

I do as she asks, a little hurt that she isn't interested in the letter's contents. I would have liked to read it to her, to let her know how tormented I was by my desire for her, and the certainty that she didn't return it. It would have been nice to relish, with her, how different things are now. "Why did you keep the letter?" I neaten my clothes, too, pulling on my trousers, tucking in my tunic.

She considers the question briefly, her expression uncertain, then shrugs. "Habit, I suppose."

"Nirrim, are you still angry with me?"

"No. You have proven yourself worthy of me."

I think she must be making an odd sort of joke, and decide to go along. "I am relieved."

"You should be." She settles back on her throne.

"You know, there isn't actually a place for me to sit."

"Well, you can't sit beside me. The tree said that I must rule alone." She pauses after this strange statement, anxiety flickering across her face. "Maybe the tree is wrong. You may sit on the floor, across from me, while we talk."

I ignore this—another joke?—and remain standing, belting on my dagger. Apprehension rustles through me, and I'm glad for the heavy, reassuring weight of my dagger at my hip. I feel at sea, unable to understand Nirrim's mood, her words. "Tree?"

"Now: your parents." Her left palm folds around her right fist. "I have decided to avenge you."

"For . . . what?"

"For how your parents treated you." The fingertips of her left hand ripple along the knuckles of her other hand. The hazy delight from a few moments ago has vanished from her face, which seems tighter, full of tense, hard lines. Her eyes are livid jewels. "You told me exactly how it was. They wanted to force you to marry a man, simply for their own benefit. I assume it was a political decision. Well, we don't need kings and queens like *that* in this world."

"That's not actually how it was," I hastily say, unsettled by the word *avenge.* "I misunderstood them. And I . . . made them misunderstand *me*. I claimed to want the engagement. I lied."

"That makes no sense."

"I was afraid."

"You are never afraid."

"Nirrim, I am."

"Of what?"

"Of you. That you will turn from me."

She smiles. "That, I understand."

"Are you still angry with me?"

"You have never earned my anger."

Reassured, I say, "I was afraid that my parents wouldn't love me as I am."

"Yet you defend them?"

"It was *my* fear. *I* created it."

"Impossible. This was their doing."

I struggle to explain. Nirrim's fierce protectiveness feels good, but I can't seem to make her see that it is unnecessary. "What they did, they did not mean."

"How convenient. You sound like Other Nirrim."

"Other Nirrim?"

"Who I was when you met me. The way I used to explain away what Raven did to me."

"She abused you. This is different."

"I understand. You want too badly to excuse them. Let me help you, Sid. They can never be forgiven for how they made you feel. And if they treat you, their only child, this way, how must they be to their subjects? Tyrants, I am sure."

While in more resentful moments I have blamed my parents for becoming the monarchs my country wanted them to be, they have always ruled wisely and well. "Herran loves them."

She cocks her head, looking strangely disappointed. "Are you sure?"

"Yes." There is an oddness to Nirrim, something hard and locked in tight, like a dog's jaws around someone's hand. Before, she was not so quick to leap to judgment or condemnation. I try to be as clear as I can. "Nirrim, the engagement is over. My parents want my happiness. It is all they have ever wanted."

"Oh."

"They wish to meet you."

"Of course. But will *I* wish to meet with *them*? A king and queen they may be, but they are still mere mortals. Sid, you must tell me all you know about Herran: its agriculture, its exports, the fortifications of its city."

My building unease suddenly solidifies into a cold stone in my belly. I don't understand what is wrong with Nirrim, but *something* is. I recognize full well that she seeks the information someone would use to mount an invasion. I glance around the sleek throne room, looking for an exit, but the doors are closed, and it feels like I am trapped inside a white egg. A sickening dread unspools inside me. I remember Killian's warning to return to my ship. There was no mistake in the Valorian ambassador's letter about the Cayn Saratu. The confusion I experienced earlier falls away, showing that I was confused only because I had not wanted to understand. The cruel black-haired queen who had captured the islands was Nirrim, and no one else.

"I could *make* you remember," Nirrim says.

My hand wants to close around the hilt of my dagger, but I know a little about Nirrim's magic. She could manipulate my memories so that I would believe that I had dropped my weapon, and then would drop it.

She can present a liar's version of the past, and make people believe it so securely that it becomes the present.

Even if she couldn't, how could I ever use my dagger against her? Carefully, I say, "May I tell you later? My journey was hard."

"I could taste the salt of the sea on you," she acknowledges, and the memory of what we did moments ago feels so far away, so disjointed from my vision of her now, that it hurts. There she is, high up on her throne, eyes as green as snakeskin. Again choosing my words as though handling blackpowder near fire, I say, "I need to rest. My mind isn't clear. I will tell you all you want to know after I sleep. Even if you, ah, helped me remember, I am so weary that I don't think the information I could share would be accurate."

Her hands shift to rest upon the arms of her pink throne. "I hadn't considered that."

"I will sleep on my ship, and then return to discuss everything with you."

"No, you will sleep here, in my royal suite."

"I need to fetch things from my ship. Gold, my clothes—"

"Gold? Clothes?" She laughs. "I will give you gold. I will give you clothes. My handmaiden will personally see to your wardrobe. Never worry, Sid. You shall want for nothing as my consort."

"All right," I say, because at least this buys me time to discover what has happened to Nirrim—and what kind of danger faces me. Nirrim runs her fingertips along the arms of her throne, stroking it as if it were a cat. She so clearly enjoys being seen as regal, so demanding of honor and attention, that I decide it is best to give her what she wants. I make my voice as humble as possible. "May I crave a favor?"

She likes this. "You may."

"I ask that you not use your magic on me."

She purses her lips. "I might have to. For your own good, you understand."

"Let me prove myself to you. If you force me to do your will, how can I show you my true devotion?"

"If you don't do what I want, I can make you."

This threat is just another method of force, but I let that slide. "Will you promise not to manipulate my memory?"

Nirrim's hand lifts to caress my cheek. It is hard not to flinch, to fight my rising nausea, to see all of my hopes twisted beyond recognition. "I promise," she says. "I remember how generous you were to me. How lucky I felt. You understand me like no one else does." Wistfulness lingers in her voice. "I won't alter your mind, so long as you remain loyal to me. Only you really know who I am."

But I don't, not anymore, not at all.

Guards show me to what must be Nirrim's suite, which houses an assemblage of High-Kith furniture from different eras and styles. The furniture has been flung into an arrangement that is sumptuous but makes no aesthetic sense. I am locked inside by the guards. My first move is toward the windows, which are high enough off the ground that I would break my legs if I shattered the glass and jumped.

I wish I hadn't left my gun on the ship. Using it to threaten my way free might work, though then this martial technology would be known in the city, and I *really* didn't like that gleam in Nirrim's eye when she asked about Herran.

I wish I had Roshar's ring. But then I imagine pricking Nirrim with it, and making her sleep. I almost feel her slump in my arms, and shudder. How can I use *anything* against her? Even as I recoil from the idea,

I'm not sure what haunts me more: the thought of treating her like an enemy, or that I might *need* to do so. Guilt wells up inside me. Was what I did, in leaving, so wrong as to wound her beyond repair, to twist her so fully against me?

No. The manner in which I left wasn't perfect, and I could have done more not to be ruled by my hurt then, which led to misunderstandings. I won't let that happen again. This time, I need to *know* what is truly happening.

The door opens, and my hand goes to my dagger, but it is not a guard. It is not Nirrim. It is Madame Mere, the dressmaker, and behind her, Annin, dressed in shimmering pink silk, ribbons in her reddish hair.

"Thank the gods you're here." Madame Mere shuts the door behind her.

"Nirrim needs your help," Annin says.

"We *all* do," Mere says. "Nirrim might be treating Annin as her favorite doll for now, dressing her in fine things and calling her a little princess, but that's only because she is determined to drag information from her—or hopes that Morah will return for Annin."

"But Nirrim also wants me by her side," Annin says. "She still needs people's company, even if she doesn't understand them."

"It is a fine thing she does not," Mere says, "or my blood would paint the agora."

I remember Killian referring, with a shudder of dread, to the red agora. I saw that meeting place, in the center of the Ward, when I first came to Ethin. The agora was paved with black-and-white marble. I was born of revolution, which never comes without a price. Now I understand what Killian meant, and what Mere means: execution. "What has Nirrim done?"

They tell me, pouring out tales of more blood than I know how to swallow: the murder of hundreds of High Kith, of Raven and Aden, of Caynish trying to defend their shores. Bile rises in my throat.

"You have to help Nirrim," Annin says again.

"No," I say, revolted. "I will never be party to what she has done. If I need to lead a rebellion against her, that is what I will do. I have a ship and I have a crew." I also have thirty-pound cannons aboard that ship, hidden behind closed portholes, but Annin and Mere don't need to know that. "Get me out of here, and I will see what I can do."

Annin catches my hand. "It's not her fault. Not exactly. She is not herself. A god stole her compassion."

This sounds like a children's tale. "There are no gods. At least not here, in this realm."

"It was the god of thieves," Mere says. "He lived here for centuries, posing as the Lord Protector. He ruled Ethin, pretending to be human, and every time he pretended to die, he would steal the city's memory from itself, and be elected again by the Council, who believed he was an entirely different person."

"How do you know this?"

"Some of it, Nirrim told me herself," Annin says, "and I told Mere. But it was Morah who explained to me exactly what the god took. Nirrim's magic doesn't affect Morah, because Morah's gift is truth. She is descended from the god of foresight, so Morah simply *knows* things. You cannot lie to her. She said she had a vision of how to help Nirrim, and left the city in search of it."

"Where?"

Annin wrings her hands. "I don't know. Morah told me I couldn't know, or Nirrim would force the information from me. But she said if I could find someone I trusted enough to overthrow Nirrim *because* that person loved her, and didn't want to destroy her, I should say what I *do* know: Morah left a map that will lead you to where she is now. The map is hidden in the kitchen of the tavern, below a tile painted with the god of hospitality. Will you find Morah? Will you save Nirrim?"

How can I do that, when Nirrim's hands drip with blood? She is not the person I once knew, once loved.

Mere says, "I saw Nirrim, after you left Ethin. She came to me."

What does that matter, a visit, when weighed against so much wrong, such violence, such revenge? Why does Mere speak of it?

"Sid, you broke her heart."

"Nirrim told me," Annin says quietly, "that she felt better without her heart. She let the god of thieves take what he wanted for the sake of Ethin, because he promised to return the city's stolen memory to it in exchange. So that we would never say *It is as it is* anymore, but would know *why* our world looks the way it does, what our history is, and how the Half Kith were treated badly for so long. She wanted to give us that knowledge."

"The price the god demanded must have seemed, to her, easy to pay after you left," Mere says. "What good is a heart when it hurts so much?"

I remember the letter in Nirrim's dress pocket, how she kept it. How she wanted me, in her throne room, and tugged me to her. One never bargains with a god—any Herrani child knows that. We have all been told the stories. To win against a god is always also to lose. Whatever price a god demands will be more than you can pay.

Yet I can understand why Nirrim would have felt desperate, ready to agree to anything. Didn't my father feel that way, when he poisoned the Valorian nobility during the Firstwinter Rebellion? Didn't my mother, when she told the Valorian emperor she would marry his son if he lifted his siege against Herran's city? Roshar, when he was enslaved by the Empire, tried to run away even when he knew the punishment, and suffered it, his face mutilated by his captor. What of my nurse, who made a bargain within herself to devote her life to ruining Kestrel's?

I was desperate, too. I made a bad bargain. Desperate to secure my parents' love, afraid that if they really knew me, they would no longer like me, I agreed to a betrothal that would be a loveless lie. I was ready to betray myself.

Nirrim willingly surrendered a part of herself to a god—an extraordinary mistake. But while the circumstances were unusual, maybe what Nirrim did was, in a way, perfectly ordinary.

It was what we are all tempted to do: trade something precious for any chance to claw our way out of despair.

Is it possible that Nirrim could be made whole again?

I remember my father's palm against my cheek. If you love her, he said, fight for her.

I remember how bloody his hands were, and my mother's. I remember how Emmah let herself be twisted by a thirst for revenge, yet had always cherished me. I think of my monstrous grandfather, locked in his prison, searching my face to find traces of his daughter. I think about the wrong that people do for the sake of love, and how it is possible to love a villain. I wonder what my father would do, or my mother, or Roshar.

Oh, you're asking *me*? my godfather whispers in my mind. Little lion, you know full well what to do.

And what is that?

Be the damn hero.

"All right," I say. "I'll try. But I have no idea what I'm doing."

That much is obvious, Roshar says.

"For starters," I say, "can you get me out of here?"

Annin takes a red feather from her pocket. "Maybe you can use this."

THE GOD

IN HERRAN, OUR FAITHFUL CELEBRATE Ninarrith, a day when they pray for our return.

We left for *your* sake, I would tell them. When did a god ever do a human good? What did my love bring Irenah except brief joy and the baby that came of it? Irenah lived long enough after the birth to love the child, and then she was gone. Gods are not all-powerful, not even Death, and had I gone to him and betrayed my sin of visiting the mortal world, and beseeched him, he would not have intervened. I might have accused him. The Seamstress was once mortal, I could have said. You made her one of us. The pantheon is incomplete, after our loss of the god of discovery. Make Irenah a new god, to complete the hundred.

And what of your child? he would ask sadly. Death is stern but the kindest, perhaps, of us all. He would say, What will you do when her time comes, and that of her child, and of that child's child? They will all die. To love a mortal is to know loss. It is the nature of mortality: to know that nothing beloved will be yours forever. Every relationship you cherish ends in death.

Irenah slipped away from me. Death claimed her. He took her to his lands, the shadowy realm beyond where we gods live. As I cannot die, so can I never follow her.

After Irenah's death, I returned home and hid my grief, even from myself. Ethin held nothing for me but suffering. Yet I could not help but watch.

I watched the dark-eyed Sid of the Herrani, released from her prison by Nirrim's friends, present a red feather to the guards.

The queen has granted me passage from the city, Sid said. You know I am her favorite subject. Look, here is a sign of her favor, the sigil she gave to me to prove her orders: a feather from her Elysium bird.

Perhaps I did a little more than watch that moment. Perhaps I also gave Sid's lie an extra aura of believability. Sid walked free, and retrieved the map from its hiding place. She took the path from the city that delved into the jungle. In the heat, which made the thick greenery almost slippery with humidity, she passed where I once grew, my roots curling into the ground, my blossom heavy and soft in the sun. Consulting the map, she stepped off the path, using her dagger to hack her way through vines. Boots muddied, skin traced with thin bloody lines acquired by pushing through bushes with sharp-edged leaves, she stumbled into the clearing made thousands of human years ago.

You came, said Morah, whose blood flowed with just enough of a gift inherited from her long-ago ancestor, the god of foresight.

What is this place? Sid, sweaty and bedraggled, stared at the mysterious objects marking the clearing.

It is the way to the realm of the gods, Morah said. Will you go?

Overwhelmed with exhaustion, with the improbability of it all, Sid sank to sit in the mud. Me?

You.

How?

I don't know, Morah said.

If you don't know, how would *I* know? Sid said, desperate, despairing. I'm not god-touched, not like my father. Even if I could—I can't believe I'm saying this—*go to the realm of the gods,* they probably would be none too happy to see me. I don't light candles in their temples as often as I should, my mother is a complete infidel—

Try, Morah said.

Sid covered her eyes and sighed into her palms.

I love Nirrim, too, Morah said. Find the god of thieves. Ask for Nirrim's heart. Steal it if you must.

Steal from the *god of thieves?*

Try, Morah said again, and Sid remembered telling her father it was cold in her parents' shadow, that she longed for a story of her own. Sid looked out at the clearing, its borders hedged by walls of greenery, the sky above a brutal blue. She took the speckled yellow feather that had belonged to her parents from her pocket, and matched it against the red Elysium one. The humble yellow feather's vane was slender. Sid wondered where the bird that had dropped this feather was now—if it was even alive. This feather was older than she was. The Elysium feather's opalescent quill shone in the light, its pink afterfeather a soft down. Sid thought—as I have often thought—about how humans invest objects with such meaning.

I think it is because mortals always miss what is not there. They long for what is gone—a moment, a home, a person. In this, mortals and gods are alike.

I miss Nirrim, Sid thought.

In the clearing, one hundred slender silver poles stood tall, each at a distance from the other. How could *poles* become a path to an immortal realm? she wondered, when a red blur soared out of the jungle and perched on top of one of the poles. It was an Elysium, though not Nirrim's—this one had strong streaks of green down its back. It opened its mouth to sing, and vanished. It was as if it had evaporated upon the point of that tall, shining pole, like a colorful cloud melted away instantly by the sun.

At that moment, in Ethin, Nirrim's bird sang, too, distracting Nirrim from her search in the Council library. She was looking for information on Herran. It was a beautiful country, Sid had told her once long ago, its crops abundant. From the city, one could see the northern mountains. They looked like smoky blue glass. People rode horses. What is a horse? Nirrim had asked, and when Sid described them, the animal sounded like a mythical creature.

Such a country, Nirrim thought, would benefit from my rule. It did not matter that Sid had claimed that her parents loved her, and stood by her choices. Sid belonged to Nirrim, not to the king and queen of Herran.

Sid must have been lying to herself, Nirrim decided, just as *she* once had, inventing a way for a cruel parent to seem less cruel. Yes, it would be for Sid's own good if Nirrim harnessed the power of her people's magic and seized Herran. It would be for the good of all Herrani. Her fingers paused on the spine of a book and pulled it from the shelf. In the careful hand of a councilmember was drawn a map of the seas around Herrath, and the lands beyond. The map was accompanied by a few pages of history—too little for Nirrim's liking, but enough to tell her the brief story of Queen Kestrel and King Arin. It was a tale of hatred, sacrifice. Devotion. It was the kind of mortal tale the gods love.

Nirrim skimmed through the pages, impatient with the details of their relationship, eager for practical information, such as ordnance, defenses, and the number of the standing army. She found notes on the Herrani language, with pages of vocabulary.

She was barely reading, just committing each page to memory, when her Elysium called again and floated out the door.

It was hunting for something.

Nirrim, my daughter, born of mortal blood and divine grace—the only one of her kind, a true demigod—shoved the book under her arm and left the library to follow the god of discovery's bird. As she quickened her pace through the palace halls, terror and rage churned in her chest. She had already guessed where the bird was going, and dreaded that she might know the reason.

Nirrim followed the bird's elegant swoop toward her rooms, and flung open the doors.

Her lover was gone.

NIRRIM

HOW COULD SID LEAVE? WHY?

The hollow space inside my chest no longer feels like freedom: a light, floating emptiness that gives me a sense of calm and purpose. Instead, it trembles like glass about to shatter. I don't understand. Sid returned to Ethin. She said she couldn't bear to be away from me. That selfish mother of hers lured her away. That father made her feel unworthy, like she could never measure up to his history. But Sid fought her way free of her parents' lies, hadn't she, and came home to me, penitent and loving? She saw me arrayed in glory. My beauty. My strength. How my people adore me.

I shout for my guards. Someone must know where Sid had gone. She could not simply *vanish*. And when I find her, I will make her pay for this insult, for this loneliness washing through me, this hurt to be abandoned twice by the same person.

I slam the book from the library flat open on the floor and whistle for my bird. "Find *them*," I tell the Elysium, pointing at the drawn portraits of the king and queen of Herran. Then I reach for pen and paper. Using my new knowledge of the Herrani language, I write a message—no matter if it is in disordered grammar, my word choice limited to the small number of Herrani words I found in the book. The message I write will be clear enough. I roll the scrap of paper tight and tie it to the bird's leg.

If the king and queen of Herran do not surrender their kingdom to me, I will send them the dismembered head and hands of their only child.

SID

MORAH RETREATS INTO THE SHADE of a small stone temple nearly lost in the twisting vines of the jungle. Dragonflies, their tight, focused bodies a shiny black, their wings like glass, dart among the one hundred poles. Frogs sing in the trees, more melodious than the sizzling sound of cicadas, yet resembling the insects' constancy, their crescendo and fall.

I wander among the silver poles, which shine bright in the sun, each a tall sliver of light. But there is no path to anywhere. As much as I walk among them, I see nothing but more poles and the surrounding trees. I place a palm against one of them, watching my hand cast a narrow shadow on the silver until it disappears beneath my palm. The silver is warm to the touch, but it is an ordinary warmth, one caused by the heat of the day—of the sun and my flesh. I do not vanish as the bird did. I go nowhere. I am simply here.

A dragonfly lands on a pole, wings trembling. It, too, does not vanish.

Perhaps only *one* pole would give me access to the gods. Perhaps the way to the realm is to choose the right pole, and I have been lucky to have the Elysium show me which one.

But when I approach that very pole and touch it, nothing happens. I circle it, searching the silver for some mark or clue—writing, or a seam I can split open. Could a doorway to the gods be compressed inside of a pole? It seems impossible . . . but this whole endeavor seems impossible.

It occurs to me that if the gods are real, then it is no mere story that my father is touched by Death. That god haunted Arin, guided his life. Yet does Death cherish him, as my father believes? Or has that god bided his time, waiting to give Arin the Plain King one final twist of the knife by stealing his only child? Although the weather is hot, the pole I touch feels suddenly cold. I shiver, afraid.

The pole, however, reveals no hidden seam, no clue to how to make myself vanish as the Elysium vanished. I am relieved.

And disappointed. I think of Nirrim, of who she used to be, so ready to see how my arrogance was really self-doubt. She was so true to herself. Brave and honest, while I hid behind jokes and slippery double-meaning words. I think of her surrendering that part of herself for the sake of revealing this country's truth to its people.

I think of myself, yearning to live up to my parents' example.

I want my own story.

I want to save, and be saved.

The pole I touch is identical to every other pole of the hundred. This one, like the others, reflects my face. It reflects the sky. The green of the trees. The frogs' song annoys me now. It makes me feel stupid. My mother would know what to do, if she were here. There is no code Queen Kestrel cannot crack, no riddle she cannot solve.

I sit in the mud, surrounded by one hundred towering needles. I flop onto my back and fling my arm over my eyes against the sun, trying to blot out the sounds of frogs and birds. Perhaps the way to understand the poles is not to look at them, but to *listen*.

Yet I hear nothing but the jungle. If the poles make any noise, or speak in some language, it is inaudible to me.

My frustration grows. It feels like pressure set against a locked door, leaning and shoving, ready to burst through.

But I am my mother's child. I can lie as well as she, and win as well as she. I was born in the year of the god of games. What is this, but a game I need to play?

I enjoy quick moves in a game, the sequence of play where one move provokes a chain reaction, until I sweep what everyone has wagered to me, mine by right, by skill. But I know that not all games have such a rhythm, or don't until the very end. Borderlands, for example, and Bite and Sting build slowly. They involve setting a trap and waiting to see if it will be sprung.

Maybe what this situation requires is patience.

I sit up, eyes open, and wait. I watch the poles as though they are not inanimate objects but living things, and the more I stare, the more they *do* look alive. As the sun moves in the sky, the light changes the poles' appearance. Some of them cease to look bright, but instead pale and dull, as though carved from birch. As the sun goes down, some poles darken until they look like lead, and then vanish, disappearing into the poles lined up behind them. But when I spring to my feet, spurred by hope, and rush to where those poles were, I find that what I have witnessed is only an optical illusion. The vanished poles are in fact there, and have always been there. A mere trick of the light made them seem gone. I shift position in the clearing, turning in a circle. Some poles, depending on how the light hits them and where I stand, appear or disappear, and seem darker or brighter.

Just before sunset, Morah comes bearing a gourd of water and perrins, a deep purple fruit Nirrim loves. They must grow wild here. Morah leaves me again, and I am not hungry but I eat, thinking of Nirrim. It is hard to love someone who is gone. It is a cruel twist of fate that I love the memory of someone whose power is memory. I wonder if what I am doing makes any sense, if I have come to this island, this clearing, only to witness my failure.

Go to the realm of the gods?

Negotiate with one of them?

Retrieve a woman's heart?

Impossible.

Well, I *did* tell you to be a hero, Roshar says. I imagine his signature smirk, and exactly what he would say if he saw me now: Heroes are born to do the impossible. I do the impossible all the time! Lazy little lion. You are being asked to do only *three* impossible things.

The sun goes down into the trees. The tips of each pole light up like stars.

No, like candles.

The hundred poles burn like candles, like the kind we light for the gods on Ninarrith, each pole a taper with a flamelike light at its point. They burn, and I hold my breath, stunned by their beauty. I move to stand in the center of the clearing, surrounded by the candles, one for each god in the pantheon, and think, Now.

I feel like I have waited all my life for *my* moment: the hour when I stop being Kestrel and Arin's child, and become myself.

But the moment, if it was one, is over quickly. The trees swallow the sun. Frogsong swells in happiness. The lights on the poles go out. The clearing is dark now, and will only get darker.

I sit heavily back on the ground, feeling foolish. I feel unchosen. I felt, for one minute, so sure that I was special, that I would be lifted from this earth not for anything that I did but for who I *am*, that all I had to do was wish for something, and ask, and wait, and it would be given. Isn't that what gods do—give mortals undeserved gifts? Don't all gods have their favorites?

It is embarrassing to hope to be a favorite. It is a good thing that no one, not even Morah, is around to witness it.

Except me, Roshar says. I saw everything.

But Roshar's words are a figment of my imagination. He is just a part of me I have loaned his voice to.

I stretch out on the ground, weary from my journey—did I really anchor my ship in Ethin's harbor this morning? Did I really gasp beneath the weight of Nirrim's body, sure I could be loved, not seeing that she had changed, that the way she kissed me was different?

I am weary of myself. Maybe I can't go to the realm of the gods, but at least I can sleep, so I do.

The silence of the frogs wakes me up. The cool air and gray sky tell me that it is near dawn. My clothes are surely muddy by now. The stains will never come out.

My ears ache from the silence. The frogs were so loud they woke me several times in the night, and I'd open my eyes in the blackness and hope that I had somehow found a way beyond this world, but no. I was in a jungle, tormented by noisy amphibians, questing after my villainous lover's missing heart. Wonderful. I went back to sleep. Now it's as if the frogs sang so hard they actually *died*. Maybe *they* went to the realm of the gods. I hate everyone.

My belly is pinched in hunger. Fruit and water is poor food for a hero. I could forage, I suppose, which is what Morah must have done, but stubbornness keeps me rooted to the ground. The poles are dark. But dawn is coming.

What kind of player does not see her game to the end? What coward steps away from the gaming table?

This is a new game, but I will learn it. Maybe the sun will show me how.

Dawn comes pink over the trees. The poles glow with rosy light. Maybe they are the color of the kind of cloud Nirrim was named after. The sun rises, and again the poles become candles, light dancing on their needle points. Frogs sing again, as though they were waiting just for this.

And as I listen, I wonder if they are waiting for me. But to do what? Again, like last night, I feel as though the world is holding its breath, as though I am a child and someone is waiting for me to figure out something obvious.

It occurs to me that this is a game not to play, but to *understand*.

What is my purpose here?

I have come here to disappear.

But how can I disappear? I can never escape myself. Even when I sleep, I dream—or wake up and hate frogs.

I stand, an idea growing at the back of my mind, one that I can't even articulate to myself yet. All I know is a searching urge.

How can I lose myself?

I remember reaching to touch one of the poles and seeing my shadow reflected thinly there, until my hand closed around the metal, eating its own shadow. I approach a pole, and there, skinnily reflected, is the long shadow I throw. *I* look like a pole. I look like a black version of one of these silver poles. I get closer, ignoring the sky, the trees, the sun, the dammed frogs, focusing only on myself, growing longer and thicker until the blackness I cast seems to fill the pole entirely.

I can disappear, I think, if I *become* the shadow.

I focus entirely on my shadow, continually stepping ever closer, thinking that surely I will touch the silver surface.

But I don't.

I step into the blackness I have become, and then the blackness becomes all I can see.

THE GOD

NIRRIM'S ELYSIUM FLEW OVER THE sea, its wings the color of
sunrise. When it grew tired, it rested on the rocky beaches of what the
Herrani call the Empty Islands. It daintily ate shellfish, and tucked its
beak under its wing, against its green breast, to sleep. The weather grew
cold but it did not snow, and the bird, whose ancestor drank the god
of discovery's blood, followed its mistress's command north through
clear skies.

As I watched it fly, a tremor echoed along the edges of the immortal
realm. Even those of the pantheon who paid little attention to human
affairs noticed that someone was trying to blunder into our home . . .
that someone, indeed, had succeeded. The footsteps were blatantly
human: a weighted stride, a balance of uncertainty and purpose.

No one has entered our realm for eons. What was left of the

hundred—save the pariah god of thieves and his dead brother, the god of discovery—gathered to watch Sid of the Herrani come.

In Ethin, my daughter confronted the obvious culprit. Tell me where Sid went, Nirrim demanded.

I don't know, Annin said.

I don't believe you! The guards said Sid showed them an Elysium feather. If you did not help her escape, show me the red feather that I gave to you. Show it to me now.

But Annin could not.

Traitor, Nirrim said, and grabbed Annin's arm hard. I treated you like a princess. I gave you a palace for a home. This is how you repay me?

Though Annin was short, she made herself stand as tall as she could. She tipped up her chin, her soft cheeks flaming with courage. What will you do to me? Annin asked. Will you punish me? Hurt me?

And Nirrim, who remembered how much she had once loved Annin, slackened her grip. Tell me, Nirrim said, power gathering thick in her throat, all that you remember about Sid's escape.

I don't know where she is, Annin said, which was true. But since Nirrim's question had been broad enough, Annin was forced to share her memory of Morah's secret map—which was, of course, no longer in the tavern for Nirrim to find. All Annin could tell her was that Morah had gone into the jungle beyond the city wall, and that Sid had left to find her.

The tremor rippled more strongly. The surface of our realm shivered like a soap bubble does, right before it bursts.

I was the first to see Sid of the Herrani enter, and her eyes widened with terror as she beheld me. Few humans can look upon the gods and not shrink, especially when they are met, as I met her, with anger at her audacity. What gave her such boldness? Who was she, to think she might enter our world and live?

I admit a begrudging admiration. I acknowledge a sense of my misdeeds returning to haunt me, and an awareness that my anger at her was also at myself, for breaking my vow to the pantheon, for costing Irenah her life by giving her a child. Sid was the shape of my guilt. My grief. I can lie to others, but never to myself. I knew that Sid's presence here was the result of many human years—of generations—and that she was here in part because of me.

And I was curious, too, about Sid's purpose here—even how she saw me, and our world. My brethren appeared before her. A human cannot see us as we are. It would shatter her mind. Instead, she absorbed her knowledge of us and our world in the only way her mind could: by translating our infinity, our wholly alien natures, into something that looked almost human.

Sid said, I am here to speak with the god of thieves.

Death peered at her and said, I know you. Death noticed the dagger at her hip and how its hilt bore his sigil, the sign of the Herrani royal family. He was pleased to be remembered—mortals do not usually honor the god of death—and to the boiling cauldron of emotions in me was added something new: fear. I cursed this troublemaking human. No good could come of this, certainly not for me, and my secret sin.

The Seamstress, Death's consort, said to Sid gently, The god of thieves is not here. He has been banished from this realm.

You have no business here, mortal, warned the god of vengeance.

She *might*, drawled the god of games. Anyway, I am bored. Are you not bored? I think the god of hospitality would agree that we should help the little human. Come, it will be fun.

Indeed, Hospitality said, it is already too late to turn her away.

Child, said Death to Sid of the Herrani. You have come here for nothing.

I disagree, said the god of thieves, and we all turned, and saw that he had been among us all along. He must have entered our realm some time ago, and stolen our knowledge of his presence.

You see! the god of games crowed. I told you this would be amusing.

The rest of us swelled in rage, ignoring the mortal in our shock that the god of thieves would dare return. His expression forbidding, Death said to the god of thieves, You have not served your punishment.

The punishment was unfair, Thievery said. You blamed me for Discovery's death, yet who among you is pure of guilt? You, too, have toyed with the mortal world. You have made favorites. You gave them children. The god-blooded of Herrath are your doing as much as mine.

Sid diminished in our consideration. We nearly forgot her.

But in Herrath, Nirrim's people searched far and wide for Sid. They sent Rinah, with her gift of manipulating plants, into the jungle to examine the trees, the leaves, the roots, the vines. She listened to them, wandering until she found a swathe of destruction, a way cut through the vegetation. It was fresh. It had wounded the jungle, and the jungle was eager for Rinah to find out who had done this.

Sid's body was discovered in the clearing—alive, yet trapped in a kind of sleep that could not be broken. Her muddied skin was warm to the touch. Her chest rose and fell with her breath. Nothing, however, could rouse her.

Morah was taken from the temple. Guards came to place Sid's body on a bier, and bring her to the queen.

◆

Death, said the god of thieves, if I can prove the unfairness of your punishment, will I be welcomed home?

Death inclined his smoky head.

I dared not disagree. I did not want Death's attention to fall upon me.

Go ahead, mortal, the god of thieves said to Sid. A smile grew across his face. Dread grew within me. Thievery said, What would you have of me?

Nirrim's heart, said Sid.

Oh, this? Thievery lifted his palm. We could all see the rosy beauty of compassion glowing upon it.

What do you want in exchange? Sid said. Ask, and I will give it to you.

The pantheon went terribly silent. Even the god of thieves, I think, was stunned. Desperate mortals always offer too much. They never see the trap that has been set for them. You do not bargain with the gods, let alone in their realm, let alone with all of us looking on, our attention focused upon you. There is no game you can play with us and hope to win.

Sid of the Herrani, although she did not know it yet, had already lost.

SID

IT IS HARD TO SEE. My eyes water as though in direct sunlight, but the realm of the gods is not necessarily bright, only *too much*: prismatic, shifting in colors I have never seen and could not name, the air so intense on my skin that it reminds me of how water can sometimes be so cold that it burns. There is no ground beneath me. I have no sense of direction, only of dizziness, but when the god of thieves reveals himself, I wrestle down my nausea and think *grass*.

Grass unfurls beneath my feet. I had, I think, forgotten I even *had* feet, forgotten how to stand, but now I see my boots and the grass beneath them, though it is so thick and soft it feels pillowy, and the green is iridescent.

The gods surround me. Many have human features, even if their bodies trail surprisingly into ribbons, or wings, or smoke, or water. One looks made entirely of ivory, pink eyes unblinking, legs changing into tree roots that plunge into the grass. A god whose body is as sheer as blue glass bares icicle teeth at me in a cruel smile.

The god of thieves, however, looks like an ordinary man—so ordinary, in fact, that my mind slides away from him, and I cannot hold on to a single image of any one of his features. It is as if the moment I see him, I also unsee him. He lifts his palm to show me Nirrim's heart, and I see nothing, but hear several of the gods sigh, as though surprised by the sudden presence of beauty.

"What do you want in exchange?" I say to him. "Ask, and I will give it to you."

"So brave," says the god. "What shall I take from you? Your ability to sleep? You shall go mad, you know, without it. Your sense of taste, so that everything you eat is ash in your mouth? Perhaps I should demand your firstborn."

"My ways do not lead to children."

"I was joking," he says. "It is too late for you anyway, no matter what your ways may be."

I don't understand that, but an energy ripples through the gods: a resonant rumble like the growl of a piano's lowest notes. They get the joke, even if I do not. "Wait," I say. "Do you swear that what you hold and what you will give to me is truly Nirrim's heart? Do you swear upon the pantheon?"

He smiles approvingly. "Cautious mortal. Yes, I swear upon the pantheon that I hold Nirrim's gift for compassion."

The sky above the gods is a livid pink streaked with black, as though the dawn was ripped with claws to show the starry night behind it. The stars chime.

"I do not want this anymore." The god seems to toss the emptiness on his palm up and down, as though he holds a ball. I still see nothing, but for an instant I think something rose-colored twists above his palm.

"Are you aware, Sid of the Herrani, that your lover possesses more power than a Half Kith should, for one born so late after the pantheon left your world? We gods left Herrath hundreds of human years ago. What gift of ours that runs in the blood of mortals should have diminished by now. Do you know why Nirrim is different?"

"No," I say, but the hazy god of death seems to know or guess. His cloudy form sharpens into bladelike lines and his underfed face whitens to the color of bone. His eyes burn blue with fury, and all the gods save the human-looking woman at his side cringe away from him. I cannot move from where I stand. Vines as thin and gray as spider legs have crept up my boots and sting against my ankles. I have been afraid ever since I saw the first god, who looked ready to scoop the brain from my skull, but now I am terrified.

The god of thieves continues, "Your Nirrim has so much power because she is not the distant descendant of a god, her lineage mixed with mortality for generations. Oh no. She is pure demigod. One of us broke the pantheon's oath. One of us visited the mortal realm twenty years ago and loved a human. That human bore a child exactly like the ones who murdered Discovery. I declare that one of us is a hypocrite. I shall prove it, and the pantheon shall welcome me home. The god of luck must love you, Sid of the Herrani, for I am feeling generous. I shall give Nirrim's heart to you freely, with no price exacted from you, so long as someone steps forward to claim responsibility for Nirrim."

Now I see what is on his palm: a rose-colored mist, dense at its center, like a peony. The metallic spider-leg vines creep farther up. They wrap around my waist.

"But if that god does not come forward now," says Thievery, "I shall destroy this demigod's heart. I shall swallow it whole. It is mine to do with as I will, given in fair trade by Nirrim. Well?" His coy voice ripples like water. "Who is it? Or would you like to see the most precious part of your mortal child destroyed?"

A red-haired god who looks almost human, save that one hand has far too many fingers, says, in a chiding tone, "Thievery, that will hardly flush out the guilty party, given Sid of the Herrani's predicament."

The cold vines are at my throat. I can barely speak. "You promised you would give it to me."

"I will," Thievery says soothingly. "And if for some reason you are not able to *keep* it, you may bequeath it to someone else."

I struggle against the vines.

"Poor earnest mortal," says the red-haired woman. "It is a fine thing to enter the realm of the gods, but how do you propose to return? There is no way home for you, not anymore. You left behind your body by our Herrath temple, but that body has been taken. Were you to return the same way you came, your spirit would last for mere seconds in the mortal realm, like a fish in air, desperate to rejoin your body. In the space of a few human breaths, your spirit would vanish. Child, you asked merely for Nirrim's heart, when you should have asked as well for the ability to return home with it."

"She made her choice." The god of thieves lifts his hand to his mouth. He touches his tongue to the pink mist. I see it shudder, and the shudder echoes through me. I try to cry out, to protest that this is unjust, but the vines have knitted into a metal gag in my mouth. "Well?" says the god of thieves. "Who is it? Make yourself known, oath-breaker. Claim your mortal child."

A god steps forward. It is the first god I saw once I entered this realm, the one with long hair like silver water, like mercury.

The god of thieves grins. "I should have known it was you," he says to the god. "Well, well. Thank you for being honest just this once, my dear god of lies."

THE GOD

---◇---

"KEEP YOUR PROMISE, THIEVERY," I say to the god. "Give this meddling mortal Nirrim's heart so that she may give it to me, and then wander with the human dead." I see that Sid silently struggles, as if trying to free herself, though there is nothing but what she imagines. Since whatever traps her is a lie she believes, I can undo it easily. I touch her shoulder. She screams as if burned, but whatever she believed bound her falls away. She claps a hand to her shoulder and stares at me.

In Nirrim's palace, where Sid's body lies in the queen's bed, freshly bathed and dressed in clothes fit for a king, her dagger belted at her hip, the cloth at her shoulder smokes and forms a hole, revealing a welt. Nirrim, her expression uncertain, touches the burn, but Sid's body sleeps on, undisturbed. Her eyelashes do not even flicker.

In my realm, from which I may very well soon be banished, Sid cannot look away from me. "You are Nirrim's parent?" she says.

"Yes."

"But you can't be."

"Why?"

"You are a woman."

Members of the pantheon laugh. Wearily, I say, "I am a god. What you understand of men or women and children or no children has nothing to do with me."

Thievery pours the rosy smoke into Sid's uplifted palm. "Well?" he asks Death. "Is my punishment ended? May I reclaim my home? Have I proven the truth?"

"Yes," Death says, and then everyone's gaze falls upon me.

In Herran, Death's godchild, Arin the Plain King, looks up from his lawn in surprise. It has begun to snow, after a week of clear cold, but that is not what surprises him. It is a crimson bird, diving toward him with urgency. It lands before him on the sparse snow and sings.

"This is very sad," the god of games says. "Very grim. Were I a human, I might cry. The last time we invested ourselves in the mortal world, there was blood and suffering and I, personally, could use a little more variety this time."

Arin reaches for the roll of paper tied to the Elysium bird's leg. As he unrolls it, snow flickers down upon his bowed head, disappearing into the silver of his hair. As he reads the badly phrased threat, he remembers what his daughter told him of the island, how she had marked its location on the map, how she had warned him to pay attention to the invasion in the Cayn Saratu.

"I propose some amusement," the god of games says. "Sid of the Herrani was born in my year, and has been touched by the god of lies. Her family honors Death. She is no ordinary mortal. She has found her way to us with barely any assistance. She has risked everything for her lover. Is her story to end now? So unsatisfying. Let us see if she can find her way home. I wager that she can, and if I win, I shall decide the punishment for the god of lies."

All attention falls on me and Death. "No," I say. I know too well the god of games's cruelty. Better that Death decide my fate.

"Yes," Death says. "Should the mortal fail, and I claim her, and send her to the mortal shadow realm, then you, god of games, will cease to gamble and play for an entire human century."

The pantheon murmurs its approval. Even I am not displeased with the stakes. The god of games has wrought untold havoc. She loves to disrupt the pantheon with her giddy wiles. I am not her only victim. The god of night still has not forgiven her for winning his favorite cat.

"You are a bore," says the god of games, "but I agree."

Arin crumples the letter in his fist.

Surrender his country? No one will threaten his child and live. He heads to the stables to saddle his horse, then rides to the harbor, where he tells his harbormaster to alert his vessels and make certain they are loaded with cannon, for he is going to war.

SID

THE GOD OF GAMES STEPS close to me, her long red hair slipping over her shoulder in waves, her narrow black eyes gleaming like the shell of a beetle. Her eyes resemble those of the people of the tundra to the north of Herran. At her throat glows an emerald on a chain, but aside from this jewel she is dressed simply, in trousers and boots.

I glance behind me, in the direction I came, but there is nothing but a void into which I could fall.

The god pats my cheek. I think from her smile that she means to be gentle—or gentle enough—but my skin stings as if slapped. "Make me proud," she says. "Go home, little one."

"I don't know how," I say helplessly.

"Forget *how*. Remember *why*."

I am about to explode in frustration—what nonsense advice is this?—when I check myself by recalling that one does not yell at a god, let alone this god, who is *my* god, if any of them are. And as I pause for a moment, I think of how my mother sometimes, when I was little, waved her hand impatiently when I pestered her about why she had been able to beat me so easily at Bite and Sting. What was her strategy? How had she done it?

Tadpole, she said, sometimes the best way to win is not to think too hard about *how* you will do it, but *why*. What is the outcome you wish to see? Which tiles do you want to hold in your hand at the end of the game? Why do you want *those* tiles? If you know why, you will know how.

I hear again my grandfather, giving me much the same advice when I confronted him about Kestrel's assassin, and he warned me not to think of *who* could do this, but *why*.

He said, The answer begins with you.

And in my mind, now, he says, The god gives you good advice.

"Thank you," I tell her.

She grins broadly, black eyes sparkling. Her laughter is terrifying. "See how quickly you learn!" Then she closes my left palm around the rosy smoke that is Nirrim's heart, claps her many-fingered hand on the shoulder the god of lies did not burn, spins me around one, twice, three times, and pushes me into the void.

NIRRIM

I CAN'T BE PARTED FROM Sid. I don't want to leave her side. It doesn't matter how much I beg her, or shake her, or even howl. She does not wake up. She has slept for nearly a month.

The eeriness unsettles everyone in the palace. My counselors, like Rinah, tell me that Sid is as good as dead, that I need to mourn and forget her. Sid breathes shallowly, but her limbs are as rigid as wood, and her mouth cannot be pried open to accept food or water. No one understands how her skin maintains the glow of life. Her eyelids do not flicker, like those who dream. She is lost to this world, lost to me, and it feels brutally unfair, because surely I should not feel the torment of her loss. The god of thieves took my heart, and yet I am still filled with longing, still aching with grief.

I have imprisoned Mere, Annin, and Morah. I wanted to murder them, to rend them to pieces, but Other Nirrim could not stop staring at Sid, and then finally I could not either, and somehow I lost my anger.

Sid would not want you to punish them, Other Nirrim murmured.

I touched Sid's cheek, the freckle beneath her eye. The three women who had been my friends watched me do it.

"She left me again," I said, my throat tight. For the first time since I had traded away my heart, tears slid hot down my face. "I thought she had come back forever, but then she saw me, and could not bear to stay."

"She left *for* you," Morah said. "Sid is like this *because* of you."

I ordered the guards to take her and the two other women from my sight.

Maybe this was what the tree meant, when it told my fortune. *If you wish to rule alone, you must destroy her.* Maybe, unwittingly, I already caused Sid's destruction, and now all that is left for me is loneliness.

I hear a far-off bursting rumble. The ground trembles. The windows of my bedchamber shatter. Through the shards of glass, I see fires burning in my city, and then I see a hurtling black ball plummet from the sky and slam into a building.

I have never seen a weapon like this.

I rush through the palace, shouting for my guards to follow, and step out into the street. Above the sound of chaos and destruction, I hear a musical warble.

It is my Elysium, diving toward me. A message is tied to its leg. Fingers trembling, I unroll it. I do not understand every word, but its meaning is absolutely clear.

THE GOD

―――◇―――

I SEE THE TINY NOTE, written in sharp lines, the handwriting deliberate and firm.

> *Return my daughter to me whole and unharmed,*
> *or I will burn your city to the ground.*
>
> *―Arin*

Nirrim witnessed how Herran's fleet, anchored in her bay, had sent thousands of soldiers into my city, armed with weapons that tear through Ethin's defenses. Nirrim sends her god-blooded Half Kith to counter them, but once they unleash magic on the Herrani forces, Arin's sharpshooters target them with rifles. Nirrim watches as guns fire and pierce Half-Kith bodies with bloody holes. She has never seen a weapon like this. Nirrim's forces fall.

The pantheon watches Sid tumble into her own mind. She is gone from my sight, my daughter's heart with her, and I am torn: Sid's success means I will be the god of games's plaything again, but if Sid fails, my mortal child will remain damaged and not understand her own damage, so that she damages herself further, and then does not understand why she suffers.

What mortals call pity or compassion they also call mercy.

You might well ask why I withdrew from the world after Irenah's death—why, ruined with grief, I allowed my child to be abandoned in an orphanage by Irenah's bitter sister. Why I let Nirrim grow without love, which to any mortal infant is the most brutal kind of deprivation. It is a wound that does not heal.

I could say: It was for her own good.

I could say: See how powerful she became in my absence.

I could say many things, but this time I obligate myself not to lie.

The truth is that I, like you, know what it is to lose someone to death. To search always for that person. To look up because I expected to see her there, and feel the loss again when I am reminded she is not. I had lost Irenah, and were I to claim our infant, to raise Nirrim and make her mine, for how long would I be allowed to have her? Not even a full cycle of the pantheon. No mortal lives long.

The truth is that I could not bear it. I gave Nirrim up before I could love her, and watch her grow, and dwindle, and die.

Even gods have their limits.

NIRRIM

SECURE THE CHILDREN, OTHER NIRRIM says, and for once I listen. I order that all of the city's children, whether they possess magic or not, be protected within the stone walls of the orphanage. Later, when I withdraw into my palace, and wait for the Herrani army to come and kill me, I tell myself that my decision regarding the children was strategic, the goal of a ruler who has made mistakes but will not let the next generation of her people die.

But the true reason is simple. Frightened and alone, I must turn for advice to the only person left: my old, banished self.

I bar myself within in my bedchamber. I look at Sid lying on the bed: her long body, the arms that once held me, the legs that tangled between mine, her soft face and golden hair. It is cut so close to the head that when I touch it, my fingers skim through it in an instant, and I am left touching nothing. *Whole and unharmed*, the message said.

I could surrender Sid's body to the Herrani and my city might be spared. Sid's cheek is faintly red, as though it was slapped, a mysterious burn blisters her shoulder, and she is unconscious, yet giving her to Arin might be enough to satisfy him.

But I cannot give her up.

She will be mine, or no one's.

The battle is not over. I hear it rage outside my palace. We might yet win. And if I give Sid to her father, who never deserved her, no matter what Sid claimed, how will any threat I make be believed by a future enemy? A ruler should keep her word, or promises and threats mean nothing, and can go ignored.

If you wish to rule alone, you must destroy her, the tree's fortune said.

Did the tree predict this? Is this moment a test of my right to rule?

If I kill the person who means the most to me, will I win this war, and establish myself as the true queen not only of Ethin, but of the rest of this world?

I slide Sid's dagger from its sheath.

SID

I AM IN MY MOTHER'S bedchamber. Her bed is neatly made, the counterpane a quilted blue, thick with down. The gray curtains glow in the dying light. The sunset cannot be seen from this suite, only the sunrise, but I know the sun is slipping down the other side of the world. A light dusting of snow swirls against the windows. My mother does not wear perfume, but I can smell the familiar scent of her skin: the soap she uses, the cream she rubs into her hands. The muffled sound of her piano floats up from downstairs. She is playing a nocturne, something watery and slow. It is beautiful and difficult, which is exactly how my mother likes it. The Senest Nocturne, I think. Sleepily, I think there must be some mistake—either I have dreamed of going to the realm of the gods, or I have lost my way, since if the gods were correct I was not meant to come home, but rather to Ethin, where my body is kept. Yet now that I am here, I do not want to leave. I want to lie down. I want to close my eyes, and listen to the pure notes of my mother's music, and the wind trying to get inside.

"Sid," my mother says, and I turn to see her lying in the bed I just saw empty and perfectly made. Her hair, unbound, is a river of silver. I have never seen her like this. She is frail. Old. My mother reminds me of dandelions when they have turned into a ghost of their golden selves, and are ready to be blown away at a puff of wind.

This may be my home, but it is not my time.

I stare, uncertain, grief tearing at my heart simply to see her like this. She cannot recover from what ails her now, for it is obvious that nothing more ails her than a long life coming to its end. The notes of the nocturne continue to float up from below. There are so many questions I could ask, but the first one that springs from my lips is: "Who is playing?"

"I am playing."

"But you are *here*, not downstairs in the music room."

"Yes. But when I am gone, you will remember the sound of me playing. You will remember this moment, and you will not wonder how it is possible to see me lying here, hands still, and hear the nocturne's melody. Memories of the dead come on their own time, in their own patterns."

"Amma." Anything else I would say is caught in my throat. I kneel beside her bed as I once saw my father do, as I swore then I would not do. I feel her hand on my hair. This is the future, I realize.

"Yes," my mother says. "Even if it will not happen exactly like this, it will happen. Do you remember when I was sick? When I had been poisoned, and you worked so hard to save me?" She speaks as though this were decades ago. I nod, unable to speak. "You were so angry."

"I'm sorry."

"Don't be sorry. It wasn't just because of the misunderstandings between us, or because I had made the mistake of not saying the right things that would let you know that, more than anyone, you matter most to me. You were also angry because you were afraid I would die."

Like a child, I press my face against the blanket, and nod.

"You were angry," my mother says, "because I am your mother, and I am always supposed to be here for you, and one day I won't be."

She is right. I am angry even now, and guilty for blaming her for her own death. I cannot look at her.

"Don't feel guilty," my mother says. "I would be angry, too, that I have to leave you, if I were not grateful to have had a daughter like you. My tadpole, you have made me so happy."

I remember the speckled yellow feather in my pocket. I take it out. It blurs before my eyes. My mother wipes my cheek. The piano music comes more slowly—a silver trickle of sound. Her face is changed, but her eyes are the same color they have always been: a brown so light it looks like honey. The feather is bedraggled and no longer looks beautiful. But it is beautiful to me, its quill unbroken.

"You have kept it all this time," she says.

I place it in her hand, and for a moment I think she will refuse it, but then she seems to understand that I need to give it to her, for precisely the same reason she gave it to me. "It is precious to me," I say, "simply because it was yours."

"I know," she says, and smiles, fingers closing around the feather. Her eyes slide shut.

There are a few final notes, then silence fills the room.

I walk down the steps of my home, searching for the piano, thinking that maybe I will find my mother seated, shuffling through sheet music, looking for something new to play, but the bench is empty.

Still, I hear a voice singing softly—a child's voice—and when I turn, I see a skinny, brown-haired boy. He has a serious face, his eyes an ordinary gray—yet pure, even beautiful amid his features, which seem too large for such a small child.

"Will you forgive me?" he says.

"I have done nothing to you. I don't even know you."

"Of course you do."

"Oh," I say.

"Oh," my father agrees.

"I don't understand any of this. I don't like it."

"Come home, Sid."

"I'm trying. But you don't know how this feels. To see Amma as she will be. You as you were."

He looks at his hands. They, too, are too large for his body, and I can see, in this scrawny boy, his future self—so large that when I was a child I felt he could protect me from anything. I wonder if this is why he asked my forgiveness—because he can't protect me.

"No," he says. "I want you to forgive me for being so afraid of you."

"Of *me?*"

"Of what it would mean to lose you." The boy looks around the music room, and I notice that it is not decorated, not quite, in the way I recognize. The curtains are an old-fashioned color, and I do not know the furniture. The piano, I realize, is gone. "It meant so much to me to have a family. Kestrel. You. We were enough, the three of us. All I could want. At the same time, I was terrified. You were so small. Fragile. The slightest thing could kill a baby. And then you lived and grew and were strong. Bold . . . yet boldness could kill a child. I sought ways to check you, to keep you in line as you grew, out of fear that one day something horrible would befall you that I could not prevent."

The boy looks so worried.

"Arin!" a woman calls from a faraway room. "Where are you?"

"Do you forgive me?" he asks.

I say, "Isn't what you've described the way all parents feel?"

Tentatively, he smiles. "One day you will know," he says, then laughs at my expression.

"Is this for you?" I offer him the Elysium feather, but he shakes his head. "You don't need to give that to me," he says, "any more than you needed to give the yellow feather to Kestrel. She accepted it for your sake, not her own. She accepted it because you felt you needed to give it. But you don't need to pay a fee to come home. Home is always free."

"Arin?" the woman calls again.

"Is that your mother?"

He nods. "She promised to tell me a story."

My heart wells with pity. I cannot bring myself to tell him that his mother will be murdered when he is nine years old. Then I look into his gray eyes, and see that he already knows. I place my palm against his cheek. He startles and looks like he will object, but when he does, I am surprised that the reason has nothing to do with me, or with me being a woman. "I am too young for that," he says. "I am not a man yet."

"Does it matter?"

"No," he says softly, and places his palm against my cheek.

"If you won't take the feather, I have nothing else to give you."

"Sid," my father says, "you are yourself a gift."

NIRRIM

---◆---

THE SOUND OF WARFARE DIMS. The loud, explosive weapons
stop shuddering. I look at the dagger in my hand. Has the war paused
because this is the answer—to plunge the dagger into Sid's heart?

The dagger is finely made. I know nothing of weapons but I know
this. I can tell by how perfectly balanced the blade is, and how the edge
is so sharp it looks like you might not feel, at first, any pain. I have held
this dagger only once before, when I used it to prick my finger, and did
not look closely at it then, but I see it better now: the slightly blue tint
to its hammered steel, and the sigil on the hilt of two eyes lightly closed.
It is the sign of Sid's family, the family she loved so much that she left
me for them.

But now she is mine.

She sleeps, her mouth the perfect shape for mine, her hands long
and a little large, folded over her heart. I shift them aside, and although

before her body had been stiff, as though dead already, now her hands slide away easily at the slightest pressure. I see where I must stab.

Do you not love me like I love you? I remember her saying. Will you come with me?

I remember the force of my love. The memory fills me so strongly that the difference between past and present feels like a lie.

I can do nothing to hurt her, because I realize that to hurt her would be to hurt myself.

I drop the dagger to the floor.

SID

I STAND IN NIRRIM'S ROOM in the palace, in that place of hasty finery, as though flung together by someone who had little idea of what it meant to be rich and powerful, and put together a few expensive items to ensure that everyone would think that she *did* know.

Nirrim is there, at a distance from me, looking down at someone stretched out on her bed. I see her shift, lifting a dagger high, and when she moves, I see that the person lying there is me.

That is my dagger. It is poised to stab into my heart.

But Nirrim's hand unclenches. The dagger falls with such a clatter that I can't help but wince. She might have damaged the blade's edge. I am about to stride over and snatch the dagger from the ground to inspect it thoroughly, when someone behind me says, amused, "Only you would be more worried about your dagger than the fact that I was about to *kill* you, Sid."

I turn, startled, to see Nirrim, dressed as she was the first time I saw her, in an uncomfortable-looking, horribly unbecoming beige dress. She smiles. Yet when I glance over at the bed, Nirrim is also there, dressed in finery, staring down at my sleeping form, her expression twisted in grief.

The Nirrim in the beige dress says, "She doesn't understand what she has lost. She only knows that she *is* lost."

I am very confused. "Are you . . . ?"

"I am Other Nirrim. I am her memory."

"Thank the gods." I lift my left hand, the one that holds her heart, and say, "This is for you."

She smiles again, a little sadly this time. "Not for me. For her. I don't actually exist anymore."

I trace the shape of her mouth. "You do for me."

"Sid," she says, her voice full of wonder, "you went to the realm of the gods for me."

"And came back."

"Not yet. Not quite. Sid, you are going to have to let me go."

"No," I say sharply. "I have been letting everyone go. *Find your way home*, the god said. It has been a journey of loss."

"And gifts. And forgiveness. You know this. I, too, must ask you to forgive me for not being here if you return to the mortal realm. Even if you give me my heart, I will never be the same person."

"Who will you be?"

She looks over my shoulder, and I see that the Nirrim with starlike earrings, as bright as tears, weeps over my sleeping body. Other Nirrim says, "I will be the woman who, even with no mercy in her heart, could not bear to destroy the person she loves most. Will you go to her?"

NIRRIM

---◇---

IF YOU WISH TO RULE *alone, you must destroy her.*

Maybe, however, the tree's fortune was intended to show that I was not meant to rule alone, but beside someone.

Or that I am not meant to rule at all.

The silence rings like that after a thunderclap. I look down at Sid as she sleeps, and I miss her. I miss who I was with her. I retrieve the dagger from the floor and place it beside her, near her right hand. Straightening, I brush my hands over my hair, to smooth it, and wipe my wet cheeks. I am not strong enough to carry her to the Herrani, but I am strong enough to surrender.

Many of my people are dead. I have driven away my friends. The person dearest to me is lost. My message to the world does not matter anymore, or at least I no longer believe I am fit to carry it.

Let the Herrani do with me what they will. I have done much to deserve it, and although I know that compassion exists, that mercy is real, I cannot imagine anyone would feel that for me.

For the last time, I touch Sid's hand. I do it in the way she told me her people do, with three fingers on the back of someone's hand, as a way to ask forgiveness.

Sid's eyes open. They are entirely black, as black as a void, the blackness spread fully across what would be the whites of her eyes. My breath snags in my throat, and I don't know if I should be elated or afraid, if she has been cured of her sleep or if this is a worsening of her condition, if she has returned to me cursed to be my enemy. Then she blinks. The blackness shrinks to the center of her eyes. She sees me and smiles, cozying into the bed as though roused from a blissful nap. "You know," she says, "I thought being a hero meant I would be rewarded with a kiss."

Stunned, I repeat, "A hero?"

"Frankly, I think I am owed much more, but I will settle for a kiss for now."

"Oh?" I say caustically, suspecting some trick or game. Sid is full of them. "Is sleeping for a month newly recognized as an act of heroism?"

She yawns. "This bed is cold. Come lie down next to me."

"There is a war outside!"

"Sounds quiet enough for now. We will go settle everything in just a minute. I don't suppose you have any of that nice, hot Dacran drink I left behind in the house on the hill?"

Even without my heart, I'm infuriated by her. Even without my heart, I love her. "I nearly killed you!"

She lifts her hand to brush hair from my face. "But you didn't," she says gently.

I step away so her hand falls. "I have done terrible things," I choke out. "I cannot forgive myself."

Serious now, Sid tips her chin in acknowledgment. She opens her left hand, and although I see nothing there, the energy in the air changes, and I feel as if *I* am held in her hand. "This is yours," she says. "I won it from the god of thieves. I think it is not something you can be forced to take, but I brought it back for you to have if you want it."

"Are you saying you have my heart?"

"Yes," she says, a little smugly. "I am."

"How?"

"I went to the realm of the gods and made them give it to me."

"We agreed. We agreed about the bragging."

With her right hand, Sid lifts one finger, tocking it back and forth in a kind of scold. "It is not bragging if it is true."

I stare at her left palm, and although there is nothing there, I believe her. I want my heart back . . . yet I do not. I am afraid of what I will feel. Afraid of who I will be. I have gotten used to the hollowness inside me. But as Sid looks up at me, expression somber now, I know that she does not deserve to be with someone less than whole. "You saved me."

"And I would do it again. Be with me, and let me do it forever."

I touch her left palm and seem to see a flutter of pink smoke.

"Will you accept my gift?" Sid says.

I kiss her, sinking down beside her, mouth hungry for something only she can give.

"Is that a yes?"

"Yes."

THE GOD

$\diamond$

"NOW," SAYS THE GOD OF games, "there is the small matter of your punishment."

It is only us. The pantheon has dissipated. "Mete it out. Decide, and let us be done."

If she were a human in the mortal realm, the god of games would have stretched out, as satisfied as a cat on a comfortable chair. As it is, her smirk is all too human. Sometimes I forget she used to be human, before she gambled for immortality and won.

"You must tell me a story," she says. "That is your punishment."

I search her expression, looking for the trick, the sting in the scorpion's tail.

"There is no trick," she says. "It is what I want. Your story is what all this has been for: the winding path that led my godchild, that sly Herrani gamester, to your mortal-born Nirrim. Really, I *chose* you. Aren't you flattered? We are family now! Go on, tell me everything that happened from the time I changed you into a rose. Tell me about Nirrim and Sid, and what they will do in their world. Tell me what they are doing right now. Make it good, Liar, or you shall suffer my displeasure."

And so I tell her about Irenah. I tell her about my grief. I describe the prison where Sid and Nirrim met. I describe how Sid and Nirrim pick their way through a damaged city to meet Arin, who pulls his daughter into his arms. I paint the colors of the Elysium bird diving down from the sky to Nirrim's shoulder, and of the crimson feather Nirrim offers yet again to her sister, Annin, who accepts it. I explain how Morah, whose gift is knowing the truth, recognizes from Nirrim's expression that she cannot yet forgive herself, even if Annin forgives her. Morah thinks about how the path home is not always easy. Then when she glances into the crowd, she immediately forgets her thoughts, because she sees someone she knows: the boy Killian, Sid's young spy. Killian is hers. She sees it in his face. He is the baby who was taken from her, grown into a boy of nearly twelve years. She dives through the crowd to reach him. And although Nirrim will live always with the damage she has done, she will take consolation in this one pure thing: that a mother found her child, and that it would never have happened without her reckless bargain with the god of thieves. She had given her people the truth—of their gifts, their history. The truth is not nothing. Sometimes, it can be everything.

I should know.

"And you?" the god of games says. "Will you see your child one day?"

"No," I lie, for that is my nature. In the mortal world, night falls. It is Ninarrith, when the Herrani light candles in the hope that we gods will return. Their wish, I feel, is already coming true. A new era is upon us. Gods will mingle among mortals again. We cannot resist one another.

"Start again," my sister says. "From the beginning."

I tell her everything. I tell it to her as I have told it to you, omitting nothing. She listens, waiting for more, and I give it to her, for the god of lies is also the god of stories.

ACKNOWLEDGMENTS

I'm so grateful for my sons, Eliot and Téo, whose love shapes everything I do and write. Many thanks as well to my partner, Eve Gleichman, who somehow sees right through me in the most tender way. I'm glad I get to quarantine with the three of you. And the cats, too, I guess.

My fellow writer friends—what would I do without you? Thanks for all your help, whether it was reading drafts, giving good advice, having writing Zoom dates with me, being the world's best host, or badgering me to just finish the book already: Marianna Baer, Holly Black, Kristin Cashore, Cassandra Clare, Zoraida Córdova, Adam and Sabina Deaton, Morgan Fahey, Donna Freitas, Anna Godberson, Daphne Grab, Anne Heltzel, Josh Lewis, Sarah Mesle, Jill Santopolo, Eliot Schrefer, and Ashley Woodfolk.

My agent, Alexandra Machinist, and everyone at ICM, including Lindsey Sanderson, as well as Felicity Blunt, Roxane Edouard, and the Curtis Brown team on the other side of the Atlantic, are stars. Thank you as well to my editors, Trisha de Guzman and Joy Peskin, who always believed in *The Forgotten Gods* duology, and everyone at Macmillan, including Jen Besser, Beth Clark, Molly Brouillete Ellis, Teresa Ferraiolo, Kathryn Little, Kelsey Marrujo, Mary Van Akin, and Allison Verost. Ruben Ireland, what a stunning cover you gave me! Thank you as well to everyone at Hodder UK, especially Molly Powell.

Sabina Deaton, Laura Fields, and Anna Tabachnik, I always appreciate your art and design feedback. A special thanks to Laura Fields for introducing me to the Lightning Fields, an art installation by Walter de Maria that inspired the field of ethereal and earthly poles in this book.

Finally, thank you to all of the booksellers, librarians, and readers. When writers talk about world-building, we mean an invented world's habits, cultures, maps, and landscape. But you are the true builders of worlds, for nothing in these pages would exist without you.